MW01287095

Musky Run won gold in the
Great Lakes Best Regional Fiction
category of the 2023 Independent
Publisher Book Awards.

MUSKY RUN

A NORTHERN LAKES MYSTERY

Award-winning Series
NORTHERN LAKES MYSTERIES

FIGURE EIGHT
SPIDER LAKE
BOUGH CUTTER
MUSKY RUN

Visit www.feetwetwriting.com to sign-up for
email updates and read more from Jeff Nania.

 @jeffnaniaauthor   @jeffnania

JEFF NANIA
MUSKY
RUN

A NORTHERN
LAKES MYSTERY

Feet Wet
Writing

Feet Wet Writing
Portage, Wisconsin 53901
www.feetwetwriting.com

Book Design: Fine Print Design
Cover Design: Chris Nania

Second Printing, June 2023
Printed in the United States of America

For more information or to contact the author visit www.feetwetwriting.com.

Library of Congress Control Number: 2023903039

ISBN: 978-1-960681-00-3 (Paperback)
ISBN: 978-1-960681-01-0 (Hardcover)
ISBN: 978-1-960681-02-7 (Ebook)
ISBN: 978-1-960681-03-4 (Audio)

For Richie Ford—
Forever the Spider Lake Musky King

ACKNOWLEDGMENTS

I hope you enjoy reading *Musky Run* as much as I did writing the fourth book in the Northern Lakes Mystery series. Words alone cannot express my gratitude for each person that turns a page in one of my books.

We work very hard to ensure that the technical details in the story are correct. Any mistakes are mine and mine alone. Our list of technical advisors grows with each book, and they are instrumental in bringing reality to our stories. Thank you to Sheriff's Captain Tanya Molony, Sheriff's Lieutenant JJ Molony, ME and FBI Special Agent Kent Miller, K-9 Deputy Miles Enger, Michael Cooper DVM, and Jim Nania MD. Writing about the Great Wilderness Race would not have been possible without our athletic team: Ironman Myrna Hooper, Ironman and coach Joe Pease, wilderness racer Kelcy Boettcher, and World Champion Lumberjack Kate Witkowski.

When I finish the early drafts of a book, I rely on a small group of dedicated friends that don't run when I say, "Would you mind reading this?" Their honest assessment is essential to each story, and their suggestions are often part of the finished project. Buddy and Marcy Huffaker, Marilyn Davis, Karin O'Malley, and Julie Barnaby have been there since the beginning.

All of the ideas would be a pile of notes and scribbles without Terry Rydberg at Fine Print Design, editor Shannon Booth, my son Chris who again brilliantly blended the mystery into the cover, Miller Law Office, and Kristin Mitchell at Little Creek Press.

Thank you to my wife, Victoria. Without her patience and unwavering dedication, this would never get done. Finally, thank you to my entire family: Jim, Rebecca, Michael, Camille, Chris, Jared, and Jay, and all the extended Nania family for your support.

What I really need to say you've heard before but bears repeating. You, my friends and family, have made me rich in every way that matters. Each word and page we share takes us on another journey, maybe to places we remember or would love to visit.

One last thing. Thanks again to Tommye Heinemann for keeping the tradition of Spider Lake alive so we can pass it on to the next generation. ∎

pred • a • tor | an animal that preys on others

Every second of every day, something is the predator, something else the prey.

To be successful, a predator must have skills either learned or as part of their genetic makeup.

The least weasel roams meadows of the north country. Its fur in the summer is dark brown with a cream-colored belly; in winter, it's white. These little weasels are reclusive but will occasionally be spotted by people entering their domain. Those observers often describe its quick movements as comical, entertaining, cute. There is, however, another side to this animal.

Least weasels are the smallest living true carnivores on earth, about six inches long, with sleek athletic bodies. They are both quick and fast, able to run fifteen miles per hour. This animal has an incredible sense of smell and vision and is believed to have the most powerful bite of any predator in North America. Many believe that the least weasel is the perfect predator—a bold hunter out of proportion to its size.

These animals burn a lot of calories requiring them to hunt often, searching grasses, hollow logs, and just about anywhere they can find something to eat.

The stealthy weasel comes upon one of its favorite foods, an unsuspecting meadow vole who senses the attack too late. As the weasel hops away to a small hollow in a log with dinner in its jaws, it briefly notes a shadow overhead. As quick as it is, it is not quick enough to avoid the owl's talons.

The predator has become the prey. ▪

CHAPTER 1

Change is an interesting thing. When I was a boy, change mostly described the three quarters in "walkin' around" money I may have had in my pocket. I could buy a bag of *semenses* and a bottle of pop at DiSalvo's grocery and still have change left.

As I got older, I realized that change also meant things wouldn't be the same as they were. Some changes I simply noticed in passing, like when the neighbor traded his old blue car for a newer red one. Others directly impacted me. When my best friend and nightcrawler hunting buddy moved to a new place over a hundred miles away, I was so sad I couldn't even say goodbye.

It soon became apparent that things would change whether I liked it or not. Change was constant, sometimes for the good and sometimes not so good. Sometimes I had a say in it, and sometimes I didn't.

When faced with change, I often find myself reluctant to embrace it. Those near and dear to me tend to attribute that to my innate stubbornness. I, however, maintain that all changes that may impact you should be evaluated and judged on their individual merit. Only a fool rushes headlong to embrace change without knowing the consequences, and try as I might to avoid it, I have sometimes joined the rank and file of fools.

After a bone-chilling northern Wisconsin winter, people were hoping for a little taste of warm weather in March. The old saying is, "If March comes in like a lion, it will go out like a lamb." In this case, it came in like a lion and left like one. Two days of violent windstorms knocked swathes of standing timber down like bowling pins. After the storm, it seemed like every chainsaw in Namekagon County was running at full speed. Skid steers found their way through to unblock roads and driveways. Wood was loaded on trailers and hauled away, destined to become next year's biofuel.

During the second week in April, folks were rewarded with nighttime temperatures that only occasionally touched the freezing point. Daytime temperatures reached the balmy forties and fifties and solidified hope with three sixty-degree days. The accumulated snow began to melt in earnest, recharging lakes and streams. People were out and about, and even a curmudgeon couldn't help but have a smile. Global climate change concerns were set aside, and folks just enjoyed some warm weather. When June rolled around, permanent residents and visitors were ready for the weather the north country was famous for.

Change was in the air in Namekagon County. The Chamber of Commerce had scored big this year, and the Great Wilderness Race, held every two years, was coming to the Northwoods. Top teams from across the country came to compete. The main event was still ten days away, but there was a week of activities leading up to the actual race, including fat tire bike races, kayak and canoe races, and ending with a local craft beer contest. As I walked from the sheriff's office over to Crossroads Coffee Shop to meet up with Len Bork, the soon-to-be-retired chief of the Musky Falls

Police Department, I watched as the local theater prepared their windows for the bi-annual Great Wilderness Race Film Festival with independent film producers competing for a production contract.

I got a cup of coffee and sat at a table outside in the morning sun to wait. Len had taken over as the chief during the most difficult of times, and his dedication to the community and courage had saved many lives. For Len, it was also time for a change. Over thirty years in law enforcement meant over thirty years of his wife, Martha, waiting for him to come home, and she finally put her foot down. Musky Falls was getting a new chief of police.

"Hey, John, sorry I'm a little late," Len said. "I have been stuck in the office going over everything that needs to get done before the new chief comes on board. My Lord, the piles of paperwork are two feet thick."

"Isn't the tradition to leave it for the next chief?"

"You know I could, John, but I won't. I will not leave a big mess for someone else to clean up. I want the new chief to be able to hit the ground running, not waddling around burdened with three-year-old requisition forms, budget requests, and unfounded reports."

"That's a chance you never got, Len. Man, when you took over, you had your hands full from day one. It's a miracle we all survived."

"God was sitting on our shoulders. That is the truth. Speaking of that, isn't the final duty fitness report for Jim Rawsom coming out this week?"

"It is a closed-door session at one o'clock Friday. Just me, Jim and his family, the county risk manager, and the board chairman," I explained. "Jim was offered a full medical retirement. He didn't turn them down but said he wanted to see this through to its natural end. He's been keeping up with his daily physical therapy and is making a lot of progress. He looks better than he has in a long time."

"I heard the surgeries for the head wound went very well, and the only issue is that he has to wear glasses with a corrective lens for his right eye," Len said. "Martha and I pray for him and his family every night. He is a man that deserves the best."

"That he does, Len. That he does," I replied.

We sat quietly for a moment in our own thoughts.

Then the chief spoke up. "Now that I've got you here, Martha wanted me to pump you for information about the wedding planning. How's it going?"

I was determined to handle my end of the wedding planning. My wife-to-be was a very smart, capable, wonderful person. As a result, I needed to step up and work hard to become one of those creatures known as the evolved man. To that end, I made it my goal to be involved in wedding planning every step of the way.

"Fine, Len. Just fine."

"Are you still evolving?"

"I am, and it is going well. I think Julie is happy with all my help. Just the other day, I suggested we pick a puce border for the invitations, when not too long ago, I didn't even know there was a color called puce."

Len rarely offered advice unless asked, but he decided to break that rule.

"John, my friend, your evolutionary goals are admirable and well-intentioned. But if you really want to marry Julie, butt out of the wedding plans. If she wants you to do something, she'll let you know. Otherwise, you're just in the way."

"I know you might think that, and I appreciate your advice, but with Julie and me, it's different," I replied, and then quickly changed the subject. "Any more thoughts about what you are going to do after retirement?"

"I have had some ideas. The folks at the Happy Hooker Bait and Tackle offered to set me up to guide and work at their general store part-time. Taking people out on the quiet lakes sounds like it might be fun. To start with, though, I am just going to be retired for a while and see how long Martha can stand having me underfoot. She continues to mention many potential volunteer opportunities with the Women's League at the church. It's a funny coincidence that all the shooting I have done over the years has affected my hearing, and for some reason, it just gets worse when she mentions all that. So, we'll have to see where we end up. I've got a couple of ideas of my own, but nothing for sure. For now, I am looking forward to doing some fishing this spring. Plus, a few projects are sitting in my shop waiting for some attention, like a beauty of a little Parker 20 gauge that has been halfway restored for ten years. I'd like it to be my grouse gun come next fall and am looking forward to taking it out. In my opinion, it's the best American double ever made."

"I look forward to taking you up on your promise to take me bird hunting. Depending on how it goes with Jim on Friday, I may have all sorts of time," I said.

"John, what are you going to do if Jim doesn't return to work? Are you going to stay on as sheriff?"

"I've given it a lot of thought, Len. If he doesn't return, I'll stay on the job for now. As far as becoming the real sheriff, I don't know. Among other things, I would have to run for election before too long. I have no urge whatsoever to run for any kind of political office. So, I would have to do some thinking."

"Well, if you did run for sheriff, you'd be elected in a landslide. People around here owe you an enormous debt, and they won't forget that. Would they let you stay until the end of the current term?"

"That's up to the governor. From what I know, he could call for a special election right away. I guess we'll just wait and see what happens."

A gentle fresh spring breeze was blowing, both of us keenly aware change was in the wind. We sat quietly and drank our coffee. Neither of us knew for sure what the next stop would be. Len was one of the finest law enforcement officers I had ever known. We had stood shoulder to shoulder in the face of trouble, and there was no one I would rather have backing me up. But the time had come, and he had earned a peaceful retirement. Chief Bork's radio went off, and he was summoned back to his office.

"The paperwork wars shall continue," he said. "Let me know when you hear about Jim." Then he got up and walked over to the PD.

I stayed at the table, sipping my coffee, so deep in thought that I didn't even notice when a grizzled gunfighter sort of guy snuck up on me. He put his hand on my shoulder, and I jumped back into reality.

"Man, Johnny-boy, I could have shot you dead before you even looked up," Ron Carver said. "You've got to pay attention. It's a dangerous world. Why, if something happened to you, that cute little teacher Julie Carlson would have to find some other guy to marry her. I hate to tell you, but they'd be lining up."

Julie Carlson was everything I had ever dreamed of, but the best thing about her was that I knew she truly loved me, and I truly loved her. Together we found great joy in the simplest of pleasures.

It sure didn't start out that way. The first time we met, I was at the wrong end of a shotgun pointed by her. The good news is that she decided not to shoot me. Over time, we came together. No matter how hard we resisted, it was a predestination for both of us. She moved into my cabin, and slowly but surely, we found our way. I had asked her to marry me, and while she hadn't turned me down completely, she did compare me to a pair of shoes. She had said, "John, I love you. But right now, we need to see how we work together. Kind of like buying a pair of shoes. You wouldn't buy them without trying them on, right? Let's enjoy the trying on period, and if I don't feel like shoe shopping a few months from now, we can talk about this again."

Ron Carver was a master gold and silversmith, among other things, and was charged with creating our wedding rings. Earlier this spring, Julie and I had a day off and drove up to Lake Superior. We walked hand in hand along the shore. The wind was blowing hard enough to send the waves crashing against the land with some force but not hard enough to send us back to the truck. Julie was looking down and spotted a stone. She picked it up and washed it in the water. When it was clean, she rubbed it dry against her coat and examined it closely.

"It's a Lake Superior agate, John, and by the looks of it, a real beauty," she said.

To me, it looked like a stone with reddish brown color lines, not so different from the hundred million or so other stones on the beach.

"I am going to take it home and polish it. You'll see how pretty it is."

Once polished, the stone began to show the inner beauty it held. We took the agate to Ron, who carefully sectioned it. He told us the agate was probably close to a billion years old, made of quartz reddened by iron deposited in layers to create concentric circles like the rings of a tree. This stone was a special combination of colors and hues Ron had never seen before.

"Ron, could you set a piece of this stone in each of our wedding rings?" she asked.

"No problem," he replied.

"My students and I go on an agate hunt every year.

The agate is said to have great power. It can heal inner anger and anxiety. It instills security and safety. Most importantly, it is thought to help strengthen relationships. I think it would be the perfect stone for us," Julie explained.

Ron would not show us our rings in progress. One of the women who worked at the store told us he only worked on them after hours when everyone else had gone home.

"Johnny, I saw you sitting here with Len, and I thought I would catch up with both of you, but I see I missed Len."

"He had to get back. He's trying to tidy things up before the next chief takes over. I'm sure there is plenty to do."

Earlier this spring, we interviewed three finalists for the chief's position. Musky Falls has a population of 2,500, and we didn't know what kind of applicants we would get. It was amazing to see the quality of the people who applied to a small department. One candidate, a police captain from Ohio, ran a patrol bureau five times the size of our city and county departments combined. He would have taken a sizable pay cut but said he'd always wanted to live up north and loved musky fishing.

Another was a young, energetic candidate from a small department in Dane County. He had a strong grasp of new technology, which is a bigger part of law enforcement every day, and we would eventually have to adopt advances. The candidate's tech jargon, however, left our heads spinning.

The final candidate had been a sheriff's deputy in Namekagon County for over ten years. By every measure, Mary Delzell was a top-notch officer and knew her way around a computer. The only thing she lacked for this position was supervisory experience. Sheriff Rawsom had suggested several times that she write for promotion, but each time she declined. She was more of a hands-on deputy.

During her final interview, she took the opportunity to share her version of what the future of Musky Falls PD looked like. She was bold and direct and had obviously given this a great deal of thought.

"Chief Bork and Sheriff Cabrelli, thank you for allowing me to speak openly about my plans if hired as chief. I have some priorities. First, as you know, I have been working with Becky Chali to develop a crisis intervention team. I would hope that the work we have already done at the sheriff's office could be combined with efforts at the Musky Falls Police Department, making it a joint team. The situation is critical, so we need to work diligently to get the team operational."

"I would also like to talk about filling existing vacancies. I intend to recruit the best, most qualified candidates to fill these law enforcement positions, including women and minorities. In case you haven't noticed, they are part of our community and clearly underrepresented in law enforcement. When Kristin Smith took the job with Eau Claire PD, Musky Falls lost a top officer. That needs to stop. Please do not be mistaken; I have no intention of hiring someone that is not qualified because of their gender or the color of their skin. We will continue to hire only those who meet our standards. It will require that we all have a long serious talk about the "D" word—discrimination—what it is and what it means."

That set us back on our heels, and no one said a word. The word discrimination had been shouted from podiums across the country, but the issue had not come up in our law enforcement community.

"Deputy Delzell, I object to your inference that we somehow drove her away. As a matter of fact, I personally wrote her a glowing letter of recommendation. I was truly sorry to see her go," the chief said.

"I'm sure you were, and she thought the world of you. Chief, with all due respect, that begs the question, what did you do to keep her?"

The room was quiet. Somebody had to ask the obvious question, and it had to be me. "Deputy Delzell, do you feel you've been discriminated against in your time with the sheriff's department?"

"Of course. I had to work twice as hard as the men I worked beside to get to the same place. I have done and continue to do everything I can to become proficient in law enforcement skills. During firearms qualifications, I regularly shoot in the upper ten percent. When the tactical unit was being formed, I applied, but three guys were picked because they were deer hunters. When two of them retired, I got another chance, and Sheriff Rawsom selected me. There was a lot of talk among the ranks about whether or not it was a job for a woman. Some of my coworkers questioned it just loud enough for me to hear. I am sure you remember it was not too long after that we were all put to the test. We stood together, gender aside, and prevailed—sometimes I'm not sure how—but we did."

No one would ever forget the incident. A wanted fugitive had holed up in Namekagon County. Not just any fugitive, but a professional killer working for an Eastern European organized crime syndicate. A bad man by any measure. We found out where he was and put a plan in motion to take him into custody. The killer knew we were there and came out the front door using a young woman as a shield and putting down a withering field of fire from an AK-47. Officers Malone and Holmes and Sheriff Rawsom were hit. Two were back on duty, but it was doubtful that Rawsom would ever be able to return to law enforcement. Mary Delzell was there that day and saved the sheriff and many other lives. She didn't have a clear shot on the shooter, but she did on his AK-47, and a perfectly placed bullet knocked it out of his hands.

At that moment, Deputy Delzell chose to stand up and face us. "Let's make sure we understand each other. Do not even consider giving me this job because I am the local favorite or a woman. I have earned better than that. I am a law enforcement officer and proud of what I have accomplished. I never wrote for promotion before because I did not feel I was ready. It is easy for some to pin on a new badge and take a new rank. It is not easy to do it well. I was not ready then, but I am ready now.

"Do you plan to stay with the department if you don't get the chief's job?" asked Ron.

"I will be in my car heading out on patrol tomorrow at three o'clock and will continue to do my job to the best of my ability. Then on my next day off, I will start planning my run for sheriff." She smiled at me and said, "Just kidding, John. You have to keep a sense of humor in this job."

Everyone knew Mary Delzell was the right choice for the job, but the ensuing discussion focused on the choice to hire from within. Would the other officers allow her to lead? In the end, Len was given the honor of making the offer. The citizens of Musky Falls were darn lucky to get her.

I headed out of town to run some of the back roads on the east side of the county. Somebody, most likely local kids, had been playing mailbox baseball. I'd make my presence known and wanted them to know they were on my mind.

I had just stopped to examine what appeared like a recent home run when dispatch advised me of a call. They gave me the fire number. The place I was going to was no more than a half dozen miles away. The dispatcher advised that the caller was extremely agitated.

"What's the caller's name?" I asked.

"Hugh Danna."

"The sheep farmer?"

"I believe that's correct."

"What did he say?"

"Nothing other than he wanted the sheriff out at his place right away. It was an emergency. Then he hung up."

"Did you try him back?"

"Yes, Sheriff. No answer."

"I am on it. Send another car." ▪

CHAPTER 2

I drove as fast as I dared down the back roads of Namekagon County. As is often the case, backup was a long way off.

Once close to the farm drive, I killed my warning lights and pulled in. I had met the Dannas; they volunteered with the local 4-H, working with some of Julie's students. Most recently, the local newspaper had run a two-part story about the family who had been raising Icelandic sheep, carefully crossbreeding and managing their flock to raise animals that were second to none in wool production. They had received local and national recognition. Raising sheep is not the road to riches, but a well-managed flock, cost controls, and a careful breeding program can return profits. Predators, however, were a constant threat to the sheep. Coyotes, wolves, bears, and even bobcats were always looking for a meal, especially during lambing.

I pulled into the yard and was met by two individuals armed with rifles. One carried a well-worn walnut-stocked bolt action, and the other carried a high-tech AR-15 with what looked like a night vision scope. I was not concerned for my safety. Running into someone in the north country with a gun is not uncommon. Running into someone in the north country with a gun who wants to harm others happens, but not very often.

"Sheriff, you and I have met before over at the school. I am Hugh Danna, and this is my son, Evan."

"So, how can I help you, Mr. Danna?" I asked.

"Call me Hugh, Sheriff," he said before becoming more agitated. "We got us one big problem here. A big, big problem, and we are going to do something about it, whether the law likes it or not." Without hesitation, Hugh took off toward one of his pastures. "Follow me."

Evan was on full alert as he walked with us. I followed Hugh and stopped where he did. A huge white dog covered in blood and certainly dead lay on the ground.

"That was our guard dog. A Great Pyrenes, the best one we could find. We were having wolf problems, and once we got him, they stopped. We'd still see the tracks but didn't lose one sheep. When wolves or coyotes come around, he lets them know he means business, and they don't want any part of it. He was an all-around good dog, knew his job, and was good with the family too."

"How big was he, Hugh?" I asked out of curiosity.

"Last time we were at the vet, he tipped the scales at one and a quarter."

"I'm guessing wolves did this?" I asked.

"Well, Sheriff, I don't actually know."

"Just hang on a minute, then you can tell me what happened," I said. I called into dispatch and canceled my backup. "Okay. Go ahead, Hugh."

"Although the lambing season is pretty much over, I stayed up to check the sheep once more before bed. Anyways, I was sittin' by the old stove reading. I must have dozed off for a minute 'cause I bolted up when I heard an incredible commotion, snarling and growling coming from the center pasture, the one we're in now. I grabbed my rifle, pulled on my boots, and ran out toward the noise, but I was too late. The dog was dead on the ground, blood all over the place. The sheep were all huddled into the corner over there, and that lamb," he said, pointing to another animal on the ground, "was dead. I figure all the scent from lambing must've been too much to resist, and the dog tried to take on the whole wolf pack. I'm guessin' that dog put up a whale of a fight, but they were just too much for him.

"Evan sat out all night watching the sheep, but we didn't have any more trouble. This morning we got to looking around and saw some tracks by the fence, but they were hard to figure. So, I'm telling you right now, Sheriff, and you can let everybody know that thinks this is their business, if I see a wolf on my land, it's a dead wolf, plain and simple. It's hard enough to make a living without feeding a pack of wolves. If you want to haul me off to jail, then so be it, but enough already."

"Hugh, I'm not taking anybody to jail, so settle down. But I am looking at these tracks here, and I am not sure what they are. I've seen wolf tracks, and these are not," I said.

"What are you talking about?"

"I think we might want to get an expert over here to take a look. Professor Newlin over at the college is working with a large predator expert. Some instances have happened on the other side of the county that got the local DNR and USDA people concerned."

"USDA? You mean the folks down at farm services? What do they have to do with this? Isn't this a DNR problem?" asked Hugh.

"I don't completely understand how this works either. Let me call the professor and see what he can tell us."

"I don't care, Sheriff. Call whoever you want," said Hugh.

"Sheriff, I know what you might be thinking. I think getting an expert is a good idea," Evan said.

Cell service in Namekagon County is spotty at best, but it was clear as a bell on the top of Dannas' hill. I called Professor Newlin, head of the wildlife biology program.

He answered, "*Quack*. Professor Chuck the Duck here."

"Hi, Charlie, it's John Cabrelli."

"Sheriff Cabrelli, I am pleased to hear your voice. I hope you and Julie are doing well. I am looking forward to working with her students next year. I am also looking forward to attending your pending nuptials. How can I help you?"

"I need to contact that predator specialist you've been working with."

"You mean Dr. Pederson Kouper? It is your lucky day. He is actually sitting across the table from me at this very moment, drinking my special blend tea and munching on a delicious and delightful cinnamon roll fresh from Tommye's Bakery. I will put you on speaker."

"Thanks, Professor. I need you guys to do me a favor and drive out to the Danna farm on Lang Road. The fire number is W11211."

"Okay if we come after lunch?" the professor asked.

"Well, Charlie, I'm not sure what we have here, but I need you to get here as soon as possible."

I gave them a brief description of the situation, and Dr. Kouper stopped me halfway through.

"We've heard enough, Sheriff. We will be on our way as quickly as possible," said Kouper. "One more thing, a large and potentially dangerous predator may be roaming the area. I strongly recommend that you use caution out there. Most likely, the animal has taken off for parts unknown, but then again, maybe not."

"Thanks for the info, Dr. Kouper. We'll pay attention."

The State of Wisconsin has seventy-two sheriffs, one for each county. The job description, by necessity, changes from county to county. The job of the sheriff and their deputies is much different in an urban county with a population of over a million than it is in a rural county with a population of 16,000.

Northern Wisconsin is truly wild country. Gravel roads and two-tracks are as common as paved roads. People barely outnumber bears. As a result, the types of calls for service are different and will often involve the wildlife citizens with whom we share the land.

It's a beautiful, rugged land of lakes, forests, rivers, and streams supporting wildlife species from mice to the occasional moose. It is also home to some of North America's top predators: bears, wolves, bobcats, lynxes, and cougars. People that choose to live far off the beaten path quickly find that they are part of a community where humans don't necessarily reign supreme. Most folks find that respect and coexistence is the easiest path to follow. Making a living hardscrabble farming has its own challenges. It is not uncommon for predators to show up looking for something to eat. Conflicts between wildlife and people are inevitable, whether it is hitting a deer with a car or a bear getting into the trash.

In recent years a top predator, the gray wolf, has been the focus of vigorous ongoing discussion. Some hunters and livestock producers think there are too many wolves. Some wolf advocates argue they should be on the endangered species list. Folks like the Dannas are on constant watch to keep wolves away from their livestock to prevent incidents like those that had just occurred.

A national discussion regarding the future of the gray wolf is in and out of federal court. No matter how smart these creatures are, they have no concept of their role in the national debate. It is almost certain the wolf's future will be decided far from the north country, in urban courtrooms staffed by people who most likely have never heard a wolf howl.

Wildlife becomes part and parcel of the job if you are a law enforcement officer working in a rural area—whether in the state's southern cornfields or the Northwoods.

It was just under an hour before the professor and Dr. Kouper pulled into the Dannas' farmyard.

Charlie Newlin got out of the truck and walked over to me.

"Hello, Sheriff. Let me introduce you to Dr. Pederson Kouper. Dr. Kouper is a veterinarian that specializes in the study of large predators. He is doing cutting-edge research in this field. His most recent book, *Predators of the Northern Forests*, is a must-read for anyone interested in wildlife and predator-prey relationships. I frankly could hardly put it down," Charlie said.

Kouper's boots, worn and scuffed, told the story of a man who spent his life in the backcountry. He looked fit and able with a knife on his belt and a backpack over his shoulder. He greeted us with a friendly smile and a hearty handshake.

"I work with the U.S. Department of Agriculture Animal and Plant Health Inspection and Wildlife Services. We pretty much shorten all that up and call it APHIS," Dr. Kouper began. "I specialize in problems and reoccurring conflicts between large predators and people. It is our goal to resolve conflicts that will allow people and wildlife to coexist. The vast majority of these projects are handled by our local people working in conjunction with state wildlife agencies. Sometimes, however, we have more troublesome conflicts. Then they call in someone like me to try and sort things out. That is the case here. A request for assistance came in from Sande County along the western boundary of Namekagon. There had been several instances of harassment and, eventually, predation on sheep and calves. In both cases, they were farms using rotational large pasture grazing."

"Oh yeah, I heard about that on a farm down by the river. The guy and his wife run a bunch of free-range sheep. I think some sort of critter reduced the flock pretty recently," said Hugh. "You think it was the same critter here, Dr. Kouper?"

"I have no way of knowing, but we have to consider the possibility. Mr. Danna, how about we start with you telling me what happened in as much detail as possible? Then we'll take a look around."

Evan and Hugh told their story. Kouper and Newlin listened intently.

"What do you want to do here?" Hugh asked.

"First, Mr. Danna, could you take us to see the dog?"

"Sure, he's right over there."

The body of the great white dog lay just where he died.

"If you don't mind, Professor Newlin and I would like to examine your dog and survey the site. It is important we collect and preserve any evidence we might find," said Kouper.

"Go ahead. We'll keep out of your way," Hugh said.

Dr. Kouper began to gently, almost reverently, examine the deep punctures and lacerations across the dog's body. "He was a noble beast that put up a good fight," he remarked.

After about fifteen minutes, he called us all over. "Would you all please come over here? Stay back out of the blood-stained area but come close enough to hear."

We moved in to listen.

"These wounds are not from wolves; they are typical of injuries administered by a large cat." He pulled and straightened the dog's left foreleg and pointed to four lacerations. "These would be from a forepaw. *Puma concolor* has five toes and claws on its forepaws. One claw is a dewclaw, and the other four are the ones that do the real damage. These others are puncture wounds, and, without a doubt, a bite from the cougar was the end for the dog. The cat leaped on the dog's back, holding him with its forepaws, then biting into the back of its head, crushing the base of the skull."

"*Puma concolor*? What kind of cat is that?" Hugh asked.

"It's a cougar, Dad," Evan said. "There's a perfect track over by the fence. I looked it up on the Internet. It's definitely a cougar."

"A mountain lion?" Hugh asked. "I have never heard of mountain lions in Wisconsin. He must have gotten lost to come this way."

"Yes, Mr. Danna, a mountain lion," Dr. Kouper confirmed.

"Actually, cougars are native to Wisconsin," Professor Newlin interjected. "They are not all that uncommon. In the last few years, there have been over seventy probable or confirmed sightings from all parts of the state. Just the other day, one was spotted in the far southwest part of the state around Spring Green. With the popularity of trail cameras, we are getting photographic evidence like we never have before. Recently *Wisconsin Outdoor News* ran a series of trail cam photos of a cougar biting a whitetail deer in the neck and walking away with it in its mouth. The question we should ask is, why aren't there more cougars in Wisconsin? The habitat is perfect with plenty of food, water, and cover."

Dr. Kouper spoke up. "*Puma concolor*, known by the Ojibwe as *mishibizhii,* has been here forever. In a country like this, they will dominate a range between fifty and one hundred fifty square miles. They are hard to see. Most cougar encounters are so quick people often ask themselves if they actually saw what they saw. Cougars are reclusive and extremely stealthy, allowing them to move across the land unnoticed."

The veterinarian continued his examination. Professor Newlin produced a pack of test tubes and began to capture whatever blood samples he could, carefully labeling each one. Always the teacher, the professor explained what he was doing and why.

"I am collecting these samples in the hope that we may be able to isolate some DNA from the cougar. Cougar sightings in the state are increasing. Namekagon County is wild country and could easily support a population of breeding cougars. Dr. Kouper has collected samples from several animals over the years, and through DNA testing, he has found animals that had a genetic relationship with South Dakota Black Hills cats."

After examining the dog, the two scientists thoroughly searched the ground where the dog and cat battled and found and packaged several tufts of tawny brown hair that likely had been torn from the cat. When they asked Evan about the track, he led them to a perfect pug mark in the soil just outside the pasture. They measured and photographed it before anyone said anything.

"My, my, my, this is a big fellow. A very large male would be my guess. Probably approaching two hundred pounds. A formidable predator indeed," Kouper said.

"What do you think the chances are that this cougar will be back?" asked Hugh.

"I wish I could tell you that he is long gone," the doctor began. "An individual animal will need to kill a deer about once a week. Once they make a kill, they drag it to a secluded spot under cover and begin feeding. After eating enough, they will hide the carcass in a shallow overhang or cave and cover it with leaves, grass, or brush. The cougar will return to that kill until it's fully consumed, then kill again. When it comes to dinner, a cougar is simple to understand; it will only kill something that requires less energy in pursuit than the calories produced by the meal. So penned-in livestock are a tempting dinner requiring very little energy to kill and providing lots of calories. In most cases, though, they would rather chase deer and keep the human quotient out of it. This one seems less afraid of humans than he should be, and that's where we run into trouble."

I thought they had no more use for me, and I tried to excuse myself, but Hugh grabbed me by the arm.

"Sheriff, I'm no lawbreaker, never have been anyway, but if that cat comes back here, I have got to protect my sheep, and that's just what I plan to do."

Dr. Kouper responded, "Mr. Danna, you are allowed by law to protect your life and livestock. If the cat comes back, you do what you need to. Honestly, to be blunt, sir, I think you might be doing everyone a favor if you did kill this animal. I don't believe for one second that we have seen the last of him. He will keep coming back, emboldened by each successful visit. They learn quickly. Let me caution you—this is potentially a very dangerous situation. Cougars are superb athletes and one of the fastest cats on earth. It can run short sprints between forty and fifty miles an hour and jump up to eighteen feet. The fastest human could not escape a cougar, having only the ability to run half that speed. The cougar kills its prey by leaping on its back, burying its claws in the neck and shoulders, then biting it in the back of the neck, exerting enough force to crush the skull, all happening before the prey even knows it. It is one of the greatest predators in North America."

Evan asked, "Do cougars kill a lot of people?"

"In the past one hundred fifty years in North America, there have been one hundred twenty-six documented cougar attacks on people, twenty-seven of which were fatal. The chances you will be killed by a bee sting, snake bite, or cow are far greater unless..."

"Don't leave me hanging, Dr. Kouper," I said.

"Unless the cougar decides to break the rules. In that case, livestock and humans, for that matter, may just be considered a slower source of protein than a whitetail. If you confront him, Mr. Danna, be extremely careful."

"So, what is our next step, Dr. Kouper?" I asked.

"We are going to have several enthusiastic grad students set up some trail cams that we have at the university. They will send photos back to us as soon as something crosses the camera— hopefully, a shot of our cat. I will also ask them to set up a live trap outside the pasture, near where we found the tracks. Maybe we will get lucky. In the meantime, we need to perform a most delicate task, informing residents of the situation and asking them to be on the lookout. This can work both for us and against us. Everybody you talk to is going to react differently. Some people will be scared witless, and others will make sure the rifles are loaded. Still, others will go hunting. Explain the law to them regarding the protection of your life and domestic animals."

Dr. Kouper contacted DNR wildlife biologist Jeb Barzine. He showed up at the Danna farm with Warden Asmundsen. We split up the rural area and contacted everyone we could. People living in the backcountry live out there because they don't want too many visitors. Our reception ranged from friendly and glad for conversation to wondering why we weren't gone yet. Each home had a gun or two to cover every need. It was said more than once that day, "If that cat shows up here, it's a dead cat." I couldn't help thinking that might be easier said than done.

The responsibilities of sheriff's deputies and police officers in rural areas like this are broad, and our day-to-day can get interesting. While we enforce many of the same laws, except special ordinances, it is unlikely my colleagues slugging it out on an urban beat in a major city would take a call about a cougar roaming the mean streets anytime soon. However, no doubt they have their own dangerous roamers.

On my way home, I passed a delivery truck just before I turned onto the cabin drive. As I neared, I saw Julie half carrying, half dragging a box toward the house. I got out and gave her a hand.

"John, any idea what is in this box?" she asked with a smile.

"I believe it's the deal of the day," I replied.

"What deal of what day might that be?" she asked.

I beamed with evolutionary pride. "The other night, when I was reading online about a new musky lure Doc O'Malley told me about, I saw a five-minute sale for paper plates, fifty percent off, delivered to your door. I acted quickly."

"How many are in this box?" she asked.

"A lifetime supply, enough for the wedding and then some."

She just smiled her sweet smile and looked into my eyes.

She sat at the picnic table and said, "Come over here, honey, and sit down."

I did. She kissed me on the cheek and smiled.

"John, I am so thankful that you are willing to help with the planning of our wedding. You're doing a great job."

"I am?" I asked. "I am really doing a good job?"

"You are, honey, but I think at this point, since you have all the planning for the race and everything, maybe I should take over to give you the time you need to take care of the things you need to get done."

"In other words, I might not actually be doing a good job."

"Well, John, let's just say you are the first person I would ask to plan a tactical raid on a dangerous suspect. But wedding planning is not exactly something that is front and center in your wheelhouse. If I need help, I will ask. For now, though, how about I take over? I promise to consult you on any important decisions."

"Okay, Julie, if that's the way you want it." I tried to look forlorn, but inside I was jumping with joy. Becoming an evolved man was more difficult than I had anticipated. The truth was, I would take a tactical raid over wedding planning any day.

School was out for the summer, and Julie was like a whirlwind taking care of details that would never have crossed my mind. We would be married in a small ceremony outside, with the Spider Lake Church on hold for backup in case of rain. The remaining issue was the reception. We had planned something small at our cabin. However, we found out through the grapevine that most of Julie's students, past and present, were planning to attend and would not be denied. Our guest list started to grow. ▪

CHAPTER 3

The new chief of the Musky Falls Police Department didn't waste one minute jumping into her new role. Len Bork was equally as fast at grabbing a bucket of leeches and becoming the retired chief of police. Fortunately for me, it turned out that logistic planning and coordination were among Chief Delzell's many skills, and she had well-thought-out ideas about how to improve event operations for the upcoming race.

Soon the population of Namekagon County would increase by at least 25,000 people or more, and the streets of Musky Falls would be packed. Local folks were pros at handling large crowds and events. Only half of the county's residents lived there year-round, and tourism was a major economic force. The community had made a name for itself by hosting events mostly focused on wholesome family fun tied to the outdoors. The biggest was the Nordic Cross Country Ski Race which drew over 35,000 participants and spectators. Add to that, bike, run, and snowshoe races, as well as musky fishing tournaments, and events are happening all the time.

This event, however, had a shorter-than-normal planning timeline. When the chamber put its name in the hat to host the Great Wilderness Race, they maintained their Northwoods humor, saying that there were plenty of landing spots for float planes, and smaller private jets could use the local airport, while larger planes would have to use the airport sixty miles north. Despite their regular attempts to host, it was no surprise to anyone when a McMansion community in Colorado was chosen.

However, a few weeks later, the chamber office received a surprising phone call. It seemed that the McMansion folks had not played by the rules, and our community was the next choice. The local airport had approved the selection committee's plane to land in about five hours to look things over, and they would need transport from the airport. The Namekagon County shuttle van had taken the church ladies to the casino for afternoon bingo and wasn't available. It was all hands on deck, including Len Bork and me.

The sheriff's department had a twelve-prisoner transport van with all the options: roll-up windows, extra durable vinyl-covered bench seats, rubber floor mats, and the distinct odor of old body sweat. A cardboard pine tree hung from the rearview mirror but had not been up to the challenge and long ago gave up permeating the air inside the van with that fresh pine smell. I had never used the vehicle, and the chief could only remember it being used a time or two.

After changing out of uniform, Len and I headed out in the van. We made a quick stop at the local hardware store for cleaning supplies, picked up Doc O'Malley, and drove to the self-service car wash. It was a quarter-only car wash, and combined, we had five quarters.

Doc O'Malley commented, "Well, boys, this is not a five-quarter job. You guys get started, and I will be right back." He loped across the road to the bank, returning a few minutes later with two rolls of quarters. "The teller said there was a coin shortage but gave me two rolls after I told her it was an emergency."

We gave the van cleaning task our best effort. A brown haze covered all the rear windows, leading me to believe the van had not had a good cleaning since smoking in the jail had been banned. Doc noted the rubberized van floor had screw-out drain holes. A squirt of penetrating oil to each, and they unscrewed with no problem. We hosed, scrubbed, scraped, and brushed. Soon the van was as good as it was going to get.

O'Malley checked over the vehicle while Len and I changed back into uniform, and we arrived at the airport in plenty of time. The sleek jet made a perfect landing. The pilot followed the hand signals from the airport manager to a spot off the runway and came to a stop. The engines shut down. A side door opened, and five people disembarked. They were well-toned, tanned, and wearing designer athletic wear. I feared a long day was ahead of us, but a thought about the whole "book and cover" thing gave me a nip in the backside.

We converged and were introduced to three women and two men. It was clear from the start that this was not the pretentious party I expected. They were used to working with people. What set the tone was when one of the men said we should take care of business as soon as possible because he was hoping to spend a day on the water with a musky guide if time allowed. Everybody boarded the jail van, and I acted as chauffeur. The chamber folks had mapped out a route around Namekagon County, focused mainly on the intended race course. The race committee was impressed, and frankly, so was I. Len and I left the van and the planning team at the chamber office. I handed the keys over to them.

As we were walking away, the musky fisherman called out to

us. "Hey, Sheriff, Chief, where did you get the van?"

"It is just something we keep around to transport groups of important people," I replied.

"That's what I figured," he said with a smile. Then he pointed toward the rear of the van and walked away.

Len and I hated to look, but we had to. Sure enough, stuck on the body under the rear bumper was a reflective adhesive sign that read, "Prisoner Transport Stay Back."

The second the deal was agreed upon, the race committee started the publicity wheels turning. Residents were excited about the estimated revenues it would bring. The race was big news around the community but not the biggest news.

The biggest news came with a great deal of flourish: America's sweetheart, an international celebrity born and raised in Namekagon County, was coming home. Anna MacDonald was to be the master of ceremonies for the Great Wilderness Race.

Chief Delzell and I had a meeting to do one final review of the event plans. The race company would be here in just two days to begin set up, and they had provided funding for hiring local folks for general crowd issues, which would be given bright green event security t-shirts. Chief Delzell suggested that we assign a certain number of security guards to work under the supervision of a sworn officer. Each of these groups would be given an area of responsibility, which may change based on need.

The rank-and-file law enforcement officers were well trained and didn't mind the extra work, mostly because they were on overtime. A big event promised bigger than average paychecks. Some people would be working the event, and others would be on the road taking calls, checking accidents, and other things as part of the normal routine.

My phone rang. I looked at the caller ID.

"Chief, it's Jim Rawsom. I need to take this."

"Yes, you do, John. We'll catch up later."

"Hey, Jim," I answered.

"John, I'm glad I got you. We need to talk pretty much right now if we can."

"Tell me where."

"Could you pick me up at the house in fifteen minutes?"

"I'm on the way," I said.

I pulled up in front of Jim's place, and he was waiting in the yard. He walked over to my squad and got in the passenger's side.

"John, let's head out the river road."

"Okay," I replied.

The first five miles of the trip were made in total silence, only interrupted by occasional radio chatter. We came up to a canoe landing on the west side of the road.

"Okay if we pull off at the landing, John?"

"You got it."

We pulled in and parked next to a Jeep and Subaru, each with empty rooftop kayak racks.

Jim got out and went over to look at the river. I joined him.

"You know, John, I love this place and these people, and I loved being sheriff. I know we are supposed to have a meeting to announce my fate tomorrow, but I wanted to talk to you alone. I don't want a crowd. The meeting is less about me than it is about the county being on the hook for my current and future medical bills. You can't imagine the cost so far. The chair of the county board and the risk manager want me gone, the sooner, the better. Kind of like, 'Thanks for your service; here's a plaque. Now don't let the door hit you on the way out.' They have been pushing hard to find out what I plan to do."

Jim's voice softened. "My wife and I have reached a decision. Do you have time to listen for a minute?"

"I have all the time in the world," I replied.

"Thanks, John. I needed to hear that. The doctors have done a great job patching me up, and I feel physically better every day. My wife has been a saint, and I have never loved her more. I would not have made it without her. I've been told they would approve me returning in a light-duty situation. They don't think it's the best idea, but they would approve it. I have also been offered a full medical retirement if I choose not to come back. We decided I'm not returning; I'm taking the medical."

He didn't speak anymore and looked out at the flowing river, rhythmic cascades of clear water flowing over and around boulders that had marked eons of change.

"Well, Jim, you suffered a lot of damage. It is a miracle that you came out of this as well as you did. I don't think anyone will blame you; no one at all."

"It's not the physical damage that is keeping me from coming back, John. The truth is I'm scared. I am afraid to go back to that world. I have become a coward. I can't face danger the way I used to. In another bad situation, and one will certainly come up, I don't think I could hold up my end of the bargain, and I could get someone injured or killed. I no longer have what it takes to do the job. I pray not to relive the shooting in my dreams, but it won't go away. The doctor gave me some pills to help me sleep, but I wake up in the morning feeling like I had too much beer the night before. I go to a therapist four times a month, and she put me on antidepressants, but even if I took them by the handful, it wouldn't stop the dreams, the anxiety. I am scared to death of losing my family. I am scared to death of dying. John, you got shot up, healed, and are back at it better than ever. Me, there's nothing left. Sorry to lay this on you, but I needed to tell someone who might understand."

"I hear what you're saying, Jim, but I don't believe some of it. You are no coward, never have been and never will be. I would go side by side with you into any trouble without the least bit of concern about whether or not you were up to the challenge. The problem is the devil is whispering in your ear. It never stops telling you bad things about yourself, lying to you about how you screwed up, and telling you how you should have done things differently. It wakes you up at night to make sure you're still listening. I wish I could tell you it goes away, and maybe for some, it does, but it is always there for most. I did not beat PTSD. But I'm learning to live with it a little more each day."

"John, I think I need to move away from here. I dread running into people I know, which is just about everyone in Namekagon County. They are just being kind, asking after my family and me, but I need some space."

"How does your family feel about moving?"

"Well, we took a long-term lease on a motor home and thought we might hit the road and see some new country. Make an extended family vacation out of it. Just take our time, see what we can see."

"That sounds like a pretty good idea. A little space might do you some good. I will tell you this. The better you get physically, the better you will be able to fight PTSD. I am guessing you're still going to physical therapy."

"Four days a week, two hours a day. Then I do exercises at home the other days."

"Just make sure you keep that up while you're on the road."

"No problem. The therapist already gave me a complete list of exercises along with her cell phone number."

"When are you thinking about going?"

"We're leaving tomorrow. I couldn't go until we talked. You're a good sheriff. I might even be back before you have to run for election, and I'll be your biggest cheerleader. But you won't need my help. This community thinks the world of you, and so do I. If you don't mind, I'd appreciate a lift back home."

We got in my squad, and I stopped in front of his house. The fancy motor home parked across the street took on new meaning.

I smiled at Jim. "I guess this means you aren't going to make the meeting."

"You guessed right. Jack Wheeler will appear on my behalf."

With that, Sheriff Jim Rawsom, a good man, turned to walk toward his front door. There on the front steps, his wife and daughters were waiting. They beamed love for him.

I had hoped and prayed all my life to have someone waiting on the steps for me—someone just waiting to love me, embracing the good with the not so good. I believed with all my heart that I had met that person, and I couldn't wait for Julie Carlson to be my wife.

I got back on the road. The radio was quiet, so I pulled over onto a gravel road shoulder, where I knew I would have good cell service. I gave Julie a call and told her about my talk with Jim. I began to go into his family plans when Julie stopped me. It seems that she and Becky Chali had been working with Jim's wife all along. I guess it shouldn't have been any surprise that she knew more about the situation than I did.

That evening after the end of a very long day, Julie and I finally had a moment of quiet together, sitting on the porch, looking out on the water, each of us lost in thought. She was sipping a glass of wine, and I was drinking coffee, always conscious of the pager on my belt.

Julie broke the easy silence. "I talked with Anna on the phone today. I can't wait for her to be here for a whole month. That hasn't happened in a long time. She is looking forward to meeting the love of my life and helping me with the final wedding details."

"I'm looking forward to finally meeting the famous Anna MacDonald. How long have you been friends?"

"Anna, Bud, and I have been best friends forever. I can't really remember not knowing her," she replied, becoming very distant. After a long moment, she continued. "I mean, my mom was a good person most of the time. She tried to keep things up. But anyone who lives with an angry alcoholic understands the value of having a safe place to go, and my safe place was Anna's. I kept a bag packed, and Anna's dad, Herb, fixed up a bike for me. When Mom became a drunken holy terror, I would sneak out the back door and take off to Anna's. The MacDonalds probably saved my life.

"Mom didn't drink every day, but when she did, she drank a lot and got crazy. I learned to leave her alone, and eventually, she would pass out. While there were many times she didn't come home at night, she rarely brought men home. But one night, she did. He was crude and rough. He put a bottle of whisky on the kitchen table and two glasses and began touching her right in front of me. I yelled at him to stop. He laughed and told me if I didn't shut up, he'd shut me up. Then he grabbed at me. Mom yelled at him to leave me alone, and he slapped my mom across the face so hard it knocked her to the ground, and her lip ran blood.

"He turned and came at me, spewing lewd, disgusting threats. I was terrified. I grabbed the bottle of whisky off the counter and threw it at him as hard as my skinny little arms could. It hit him right in the face. Wearing only my Barbie pajamas and without shoes, I ran out the door into the cold, pouring rain and headed toward MacDonalds'.

"I was sure the man was still chasing me, and I screamed and pounded on the door at Anna's house. Her dad answered. He took one look at me, soaking wet and terrified, picked me up, and carried me into the house. Anna's mom, Dorothy, gave me a hot shower and warm fleece pajamas with wool socks and tucked me into bed with Anna. The next morning while at breakfast, I would be fine one minute and begin shaking the next. I told them the whole story. A few minutes after listening to the events of the night, Herb, a foreman for Sayner Timber, quietly got up and said he had forgotten that he needed to pick up his log boss, Pete, and needed to get to work early that day. I did not know until I was much older that before he left, Herb checked with Dorothy to make sure he knew which house was mine. He and Pete found the man sound asleep on the couch, and the man never came around again." ■

CHAPTER 4

AMERICA'S SWEETHEART

From the time Anna was in grade school, her mother would wake her every morning before light for a family breakfast. Pancakes, double-smoked bacon, hashbrowns, and homemade toasted bread were commonly on the menu. Anna and her mom would clean up the kitchen and then walk across the alley to her mom's bakery. Her dad would jump in his truck and drive to wherever the crew was working. It was the beginning of a long day for all of them, but they didn't mind working hard.

By the time Anna and Dorothy arrived at the bakery, the ovens were already hot. Josie, their only employee, got there a half-hour earlier to see to it. Bread dough put out to rise overnight was ready to be baked. Donuts, rolls, and other baked goods went into their respective ovens. The oil was brought up to just the right temperature for fried donuts, one of the local favorites. Once the bread was out of the oven, it sat for a while, then was sliced and bagged. The fresh loaves were loaded into three big baskets bolted to Anna's bicycle, and she took off to deliver them to local restaurants.

Julie would ride her bike to the bakery most mornings to help Anna with deliveries. Herb had put two baskets on her bike. The two girls raced up the sidewalks, down alleys, and across streets. They knew every shortcut in Musky Falls and loved riding fast. The Moose Café, The Lumber Jack, and Marilyn's Pine Tree Restaurant had their back doors open for deliveries. Other people coming to work early or waiting for their favorite café to open knew the pair and called out as they blazed by. After the bread run, the girls would go back to the bakery and load up buns and rolls for the lunch and dinner menus.

Once the deliveries were made, Julie would ride home to check on her mom and leave her some fresh bread. Then she'd dress in her school clothes and ride back to the bakery at about the same time it opened to the public. People lined up to get fresh pastries and donuts packed six to a bag and thirteen to a dozen. After the rush, Anna's mom and Josie would begin baking pies filled with whatever was in season. Anna and Julie left for school, munching on donuts along the way with an extra bag for Bud.

One year during Musky Falls Fest weekend, Anna and Julie were selling hot fried donuts from a booth in front of the bakery. The crowds were huge, and business was brisk. About midday, Anna's mom came out with cold glasses of lemonade. She also held two tickets in her hand. The bakery was a sponsor for the Musky Race and got two free registrations. Dorothy offered them to the girls, and Anna jumped at the chance to run Sunday morning.

It was a big race, with over five hundred registered for the 5K or the 10K. There was a lot of good-natured talking and teasing among the runners, and Anna and Julie usually talked nonstop when they were together, but not that morning. Anna was focused. Julie worried her friend was mad at her. She said, "Nope, but Julie, I want you to know I am going to win the race, not the

5K either. I signed up for the 10K." Anna was a fast runner. She had dominated after-school flag football games but never ran in an organized race.

Julie ran shoulder to shoulder with Anna for the first third of the race. Julie was beginning to feel tired, but Anna showed no signs of fatigue. They ran past the school and then the park, where the 10K runners split off. Anna took the 10K route, and that was the last time Julie saw Anna other than her backside. Spectators said she ran like the wind, passing other conditioned racers like they were standing still. The further she got into the race, the faster she ran. Anna not only crossed the finish line first in the women's division but also beat most of the men. It was just one of a hundred small-town fun runs in Wisconsin, and for most runners, that's all it was, but for Anna, it was so much more.

Anna and Julie entered more races when they could, but mostly just ran together on the backcountry trails through the national forest along lakeshores, rivers, and streams, loving the whole experience. Julie was fast, but Anna floated over the landscape. At the start of their senior year in high school, the cross country coach encouraged them to try out for the varsity cross country team. Julie couldn't do it; she was working to save money for college and taking care of things at home. Her mother had started to drink more, and the doctor said Julie needed to keep an eye on her. Anna knew it would be impossible with her schedule at the bakery, but deep down knew it would be a dream come true if she did join the team.

Anna finally decided to ask her mom about joining the cross country team. She fully expected to hear what she already knew—she was needed at the bakery. But surprisingly, that's not what happened. Dorothy told her that she should do it and that working night and day in a bakery was a good enough way to make a living, but it was time Anna started to live her life. Julie agreed to fill in at the bakery when she could.

The minute Anna got to school the next day, she signed up. The schedule she was given had a meet set for the following afternoon. Anna asked if she could run, but the coach told her no. She had to train to ensure she was ready for competition before running an actual race. Anna was crushed, but she spent the next week doing exactly as the coach told her. The day before the next meet against Musky Falls' biggest rival, the coach gave her the go-ahead.

Dorothy picked Julie up and went to the race course. There was a pretty good crowd of spectators. Most of the runners were full of nervous energy, jumping around and waiting for the start. Not Anna. She just stood there as calmly as could be. The runners stepped up to the line. Anna was next to the best runner from the opposing school.

The referee started the countdown, the gun went off, and the race was on. The girls' race was 4,000 meters long. Most of the runners burst from the starting line immediately, jockeying for position. From the start, Anna found herself blocked at the back of the lead pack. She tried to pass other runners but was still back from the lead group when it came to the halfway point. It looked like these conditioned athletes were going to be too much for her. The pack came over the hill on the last leg, the leaders put on a burst of speed, and as a result, the field opened up.

Anna saw daylight and took off. She was not running; she was flying. She cut in and out of the runners and, with each step, picked up speed. She was gaining on the two in the lead, but the finish line came too soon.

That was the day that Anna MacDonald became Anna, the runner. The local news photographer took a picture of her as she crossed the finish line, and suddenly, the girl who delivered bread on her bike was on the front page. The Musky Falls girls' cross country team won more than it didn't. Anna learned how to run fast and smart.

In the first invitational meet, Musky Falls competed against much bigger schools. Anna's coach figured the other teams would use blockers to stop Anna from moving forward. That's just what happened, and Anna let it, giving her teammates the chance they needed. Anna finished fourth, and her teammates finished first and second. Some of the other schools' supporters good-naturedly called the kids from Musky Falls "The Musky Queens."

The high school cross country coach had been a runner in college, and she recognized a truly gifted athlete when she saw one. The day after the race, she called Anna and asked if she could come and visit her and her parents. They all sat down around the kitchen table, and the coach told them she wanted to take Anna to the University of Wisconsin in Madison. She and the head cross country coach had been teammates. She had heard about Anna and was anxious to meet her. Anna was excited, and her parents agreed that she should go. But her mom and dad couldn't get away from work, so Julie went instead.

For two girls from the far northwestern part of the state, spending a few days in the capital city was both exciting and intimidating. The university buildings were huge, with students everywhere. They parked at the track and field training facility and walked through the door into the world of Big Ten athletics. The Badger coach waved them over and embraced the Musky Falls coach. After a short tour, the Badger coach invited them to join the team for dinner that night. The coach asked Anna if she would be interested in going for a team practice run in the morning. She agreed.

The next day the girls took a bus to a local golf course. Everyone got off and immediately began stretching. The athletes were solid muscle running machines, perfectly fit, a world apart from the local girls Anna normally competed against. The trainers checked the status of any previous injuries or new complaints, then put everyone through a warmup routine, spending extra time with Anna.

The short grass golf course terrain was different than Anna's home course traversing from pavement roads, sandy fire lanes, up and down hills, and a quickly descending trail that ran along a river. Today she wasn't here for the scenery; she was here to run.

The college runners looked intimidating, but Anna was calm, almost peaceful, like a person that was where she had always wanted to be. The coach explained the goals for the training run: to learn to work together, find out where they were and where they needed to go.

The runners were called to the line in two groups of ten girls. Anna was in the second group. It was immediately clear that while this had been planned as a training run, it was a real race. Experienced runners took up positions and raced forward. Then as others tried to approach the leaders, blockers aggressively prevented them from doing so. It was nothing like running a race in Musky Falls. These girls were serious, and Anna learned how serious when she tried to make a move up the middle of the pack. One of the blockers in a well-practiced, difficult-to-see move elbowed Anna hard in the chest, and at the same time, another gave her a bump from the side, almost knocking her down. She dropped back in the pack like she had done many times before.

As they approached the last mile, the runners put on a burst of speed, and the field opened up. Anna lowered her head and ran through the crowd like a fullback, popping out near the front. This caused what the coach later called a "race to the death." Elbows, blocking, and cheap shots didn't matter anymore; it was only about who was faster. The first group finished their run and watched the race cheering on their teammates. Julie was screaming her heart out for Anna.

It was a battle. Two girls ran on each side of Anna and tried to close her off, but they weren't fast enough. Another runner stayed with her shoulder-to-shoulder, neck and neck as they crossed the finish line. Then both cruised to a stop, hands on their hips, breathing hard. Anna turned around after cooling off and walked back toward the group. The girl that had run across the finish in a too-close-to-call race stood in front of Anna and blocked her way. Then she reached out, hugged her, and with a big smile, said, "Welcome to the team." Anna was offered a full-ride scholarship. It made the front page of the hometown newspaper, above the fold.

Madison was great, but the girls were happy to get home. The state cross country meet was approaching fast, and the community was excited. Two chartered buses and a caravan of cars headed south to watch the Musky Queens run.

After warmups, the Musky Falls coach instructed the team back into the locker room, handing each a brown paper-wrapped package. When they reemerged, the crowd went silent. Then cheers erupted, led by the Namekagon County crowd. Each runner wore black and red buffalo checked shorts with an embroidered laughing musky across the backside.

Fans were on the edge of their bleacher seats when the runners lined up and the gun went off. The crowd delivered a loud cheering send-off. Anna dropped back in the pack when she recognized two blockers looking for her. The other team was well aware of her tactics and covered the middle of the pack. It was at that point Anna's teammates surprised everyone and broke to the outside and gave it everything they had, opening a spot for Anna. A reporter later wrote, "She was an unstoppable force." That day the Musky Falls cross country team smashed the Division Three state record, posting a record time that still stands today.

Anna thought she had run her last race for Musky Falls. She

was wrong. From then on, every race she ran, she ran for her home, her family, and the community that she loved and that loved her.

Fall came, and the girls had to go their separate ways. Herb and Dorothy drove Anna to Madison. Bud drove Julie to Eau Claire. Once she was in college, Anna's life became a state of constant motion. Between classes and training, she didn't get the chance to come home very often, and when she did, she could never stay long. The best friends still talked and wrote to each other.

During Anna's junior year, the Olympics were on the mind of athletes across the globe. To no one in Namekagon County's surprise, she was selected to be a member of the U.S. Olympic Team. The sports pundits covering the upcoming Olympics believed many new world records would be set. In Anna's race, she was favored to win the bronze behind a woman from Russia. A Nigerian was a strong favorite for the gold. But one commentator said that "Anna MacDonald, the Musky Queen from the Northwoods of Wisconsin, shouldn't be ruled out."

The Olympic publicity hype was at a fever pitch the first week in August when the finalists in the 5,000-meter run prepared to run for the gold. The field of runners was said to be the most talented group in Olympic history. In her heat, the woman from Nigeria had officially broken the world's record.

Most of the country, and all of Namekagon County, was glued to their TV screens. The runners began to walk to their assigned lanes. Anna was the last one. She looked directly at the camera and smiled. Cheers rang out an ocean away as Anna took off her sweats and was wearing her red and black plaid shorts, complete with the embroidered musky. Anna walked to the start and waved to her parents and Julie in the stands. The MacDonalds had insisted on paying Julie's way to attend. They were further away from home than any of them had ever been.

Competitors lining up next to her came from all over the world for this moment, hoping to bring home the sacred Olympic gold medal. Each runner had prevailed over the best of the best to get where they were. The race was an individual event just over three miles in length. Another woman from the U.S. was also in the finals.

The racers were at their marks. The gun went off, and the race began. The woman from Nigeria, Nyala Geebogu, was first off the line and ate up the track with long rapid strides. Anna was behind her from the start. When they moved out of their assigned lanes, the Russian cut in front of her, and she lost valuable seconds. The field was tight, with no room to move. Nyala was pushing the advantage. The Russian was blocking the field, looking for silver. Anna could not unleash her weapon. She was hemmed in and could not begin to fly. She watched and waited. Each time she tried to move, the Russian blocked the way, and Nyala increased her lead. This was the biggest race of her life, and she was trapped in the middle. She needed to move. She needed to run like she never had before. Julie, Dorothy, and even Herb were yelling as loudly as they could. Much of the crowd in the stadium had begun to scream for Anna.

Nyala broke further away with an unbelievable burst of speed. That gave the Russian the idea that she, too, could increase her lead and sail to silver. When she did, she opened the door for Anna. People watching at home started screaming, "Now! Anna, now! Fly, Anna, fly!" and fly she did. Anna took off. It was no longer a race for silver or bronze. She ran so hard she thought her heart would explode. Nyala seemed uncatchable, but Anna came an inch closer with every stride.

It still appeared hopeless, the distance too far to make up. Then Anna saw it. Nyala faltered. She was still running but had pushed herself at an unsustainable pace. Her strategy had been to get out in front as far as she could and make the others catch her—a good plan, except she had underestimated Anna.

One hundred fifty yards from the finish, one hundred yards, then seventy-five. They both pushed as hard as they could and charged the finish line, crossing at what appeared to be the same time. One of them would go home with gold, the other with silver. Nyala loped to the infield with Anna close behind her. They both collapsed on the soft grass, each gasping for air. The pace was so incredible that medical staff immediately attended to the two women. Anna thought there was nothing softer than the grass she lay on and wanted to stay there all day. The cheers from the crowd continued.

As the world waited for the review of the finish, the television news commentators noted that both women had unofficially broken the world's record. The Russian runner was under review. Judges had noted the possibility of illegal contact.

Nyala finally got up and walked to sit on a bench. Anna walked over and sat next to her. A news crew and interviewer were right behind them when Nyala said to Anna, "If I should die at this moment, please see that my family gets my medal."

Anna responded, "That would be fine unless I die first. I assume you will return the favor."

Everyone was on pins and needles, waiting for what seemed like an hour before the judges returned. After reviewing the video and talking to the competitors and their coaches, it was clear the Russian runner had used an illegal block on Anna. The Russians raised a challenge. Other judges viewed the video, and the violation was clear. The Russian runner was disqualified. Her coach sitting at a table was so angry he took off his shoe, pounded the table with it, and had to be quieted by the judges.

The three winners ascended the stage, each taking their place. Anna and Nyala hesitated before taking their spots, enjoying a little drama. The announcer stepped to the microphone. Winning the bronze medal: Mae Tollefson, USA. Winning the silver medal: Nyala Geebogu, Nigeria. The gold medal winner and new official world record holder in the women's 5,000, representing the United States of America, was Anna MacDonald. The cheers from Namekagon County just about shook the earth off its axis.

After the Olympics, Anna's star really began to shine. The pretty girl from a little town in northern Wisconsin who broke the world's record running in red and black plaid shorts with a musky on the butt became America's sweetheart. From product endorsements and TV ads to magazine covers, she was everywhere. She came back home thinking things would be the same. Anna's parents were ready to retire, so she bought their house in town, and Dorothy and Herb purchased a home on a nearby lake. But life for Anna had changed and now swirled around her. No one was happy when a major TV network did a story on Musky Falls and made it look like Mayberry, poking fun at some of the people of the community.

Julie was saddened but not surprised when Anna said she couldn't coordinate traveling, her work schedule, and training schedule. She was moving to L.A. to give it a try. They still talked on the phone, but one of them was always in a hurry. Pretty soon, Julie saw more of Anna on TV and in magazines than in person. ∎

CHAPTER 5

The next day I arrived early for the meeting and found Attorney Jack Wheeler waiting outside the hallway.

"Hey, Counselor. Ready for the meeting?" I asked.

"Sheriff, I'm ready. I just need to keep you updated on the most recent developments. Not five minutes ago, the county board chairman confronted me in this very hallway and asked what I was doing here. I told him that I was here to represent Jim Rawsom. For some reason, that didn't sit well with him. He walked into the meeting room and slammed the door."

"I have noted he tends to be a bit on the crabby side," I replied.

Wheeler laughed.

We found the door unlocked and walked in. Everyone took a chair around the meeting table.

It was a semiformal proceeding, and the risk manager announced that the meeting would be recorded for anyone who wanted a copy.

Although no one had put him in charge, Chairman Stewart took control of the meeting. "We might as well get started. I don't think that it has escaped anyone's notice that the individual who is the subject of this meeting has not yet arrived. Has anyone been in contact with James Rawsom?"

"I have," I replied.

"Wonderful. Now could you tell us where he is?"

"I would think western Minnesota or South Dakota by now," I replied. "What do you think, Attorney Wheeler?

"I think he is solidly in the Dakota grasslands," he answered with a straight face.

A vein began to stick out on the county board chair's neck, and it started to pulse—an accurate indicator of what was to come.

"Why is it, Sheriff Cabrelli and Attorney Wheeler, that when you two are involved in anything, it always becomes the source of great aggravation to me?"

Answers to that question were on the tip of my tongue when Jack Wheeler interceded.

"Mr. Stewart, James Rawsom has decided to accept the medical retirement. All three physicians that have examined or treated him have determined that he cannot return to active duty and have attested to that in this affidavit. Included with the affidavit is the necessary documentation to proceed with the retirement. I have corresponded with the retirement board, and they have determined that the paperwork is in order. The copy you have is just for your records."

The county board chair took the papers and handed them over to the risk manager, who began to read them word for word.

"While we are looking over your submission, I think we can stop recording the meeting. Actually, I think it is best," Stewart said and looked straight at the risk manager, who turned off the recorder. "Sheriff Cabrelli, due to Sheriff Rawsom's retirement, you will remain in the position of sheriff until the governor changes his mind about your appointment, you resign, or you are defeated in the next election. Have you made any decisions regarding your future?"

"Well, not really. I know today I am the sheriff and have all the responsibilities that come with that office. I intend to carry out those responsibilities as long as I am wearing this badge. Nothing more, nothing less."

"Sheriff, let me be blunt with you. I think you should consider stepping down for the good of the community. Maybe your big city police tactics helped us in the short term, but they are heavy-handed and have no place in Namekagon County. I think we are ready for things to return to normal. To that end, I took the initiative to contact the governor's office and asked what our options were if Jim Rawsom should retire. They indicated they would be glad to revisit your appointment if we request it. I really think it would be best, John, don't you?"

I didn't even begin to answer because Counselor Wheeler immediately stepped up to the plate.

"I am chairman of the Law Enforcement Advisory Committee. I don't recall you raising this issue with me or any other members. Did I miss something?" Wheeler questioned.

"No, Attorney Wheeler, you didn't miss anything. I was just trying to look at our options, take a little something off your plate. I know how busy you are."

"Chairman Stewart, this not the time or place to discuss this. Your conduct is out of order. I can see why you wanted to turn off the recording device. It is a good thing I left mine on." Jack pulled a tiny micro recorder out of his shirt pocket. I feared the chairman's pulsing vein might explode.

The county risk manager determined the paperwork was done to his satisfaction, and the meeting was concluded. Jack and I walked out together.

"I am not the least bit surprised that Stewart pulled a stunt like that. He has always been intimidated by the popularity of a newcomer like you."

I headed out on some back roads; I needed time to think. There are no back roads in the world like those in northern Wisconsin. Patrolling on any summer evening, you will run into cars filled with parents and kids, everyone's face glued to the windows, all out for a ride to see what they can see. I always make a point of waving or even stopping for conversation. Often the questions were from the kids. "Do you know where we can see a bear? Are there any wolves around here?" More up-north memories made every minute.

Julie and I sat on the porch relaxing. I still couldn't believe I was marrying Julie Carlson. She and I and Bud would be a family. A family of my own—something I never knew how much I wanted until it was right in front of me.

"It's not really my business, but what was the deal with Anna's marriage? I was not much up on celebrity news, but it was hard to ignore for a while," I asked.

"She called me out of the blue and said she was flying into Musky Falls and asked if Bud and I could get her parents there as a surprise. Herb, Dorothy, Bud, and I pulled in the next day just as her plane landed. When she got off, we all hugged each other. Anna kind of looked the same and kind of looked different. The clean outdoors girl look had been replaced by fancy but casual clothes, a new haircut, and a little too much makeup. I felt like a chore girl wearing jeans and a Northern Lakes Academy sweatshirt.

"A moment after Anna disembarked, another figure stepped off onto the tarmac. He was as handsome as Anna was pretty. He wore a custom-cut jogging suit, bright blue with silver trim. His hair was perfect, and his smile was almost like it was made of plastic. The man stepped forward and to the side of Anna, then put his arm around her waist, smiling all the while.

"Anna said, 'Mom, Dad, Julie, Bud, this is Stephen Cameron. He and I have something to tell you. We are engaged to be married.' We were shocked. It was the first time we even knew she was in a serious relationship, or any kind of relationship.

"None of us had met Stephen before, but we all knew of him. He won the decathlon in the same Olympics Anna competed in. You could not go by the newsstand at the end of the grocery checkout without seeing his face on a tabloid, usually romantically linked to some model or movie star. The all-American boy was engaged to the all-American girl. I was ashamed of myself when a thought about the endless marketing possibilities crept in.

"My guilt ended quickly when the next people off the plane were a film crew and a publicist. They told us to act naturally while they filmed and began to direct us in our appointed roles. The smooth-talking publicist explained how he expected things to go. He wanted the locals to meet at the park where Stephen and Anna would publicly announce their engagement, and if we could get a hundred or so people, that should work.

"If you want people to turn out in the park, throw a solstice party or community fundraiser and ask folks to bring a dish to pass. Everyone who can show up will. If it were just about seeing Anna, they would probably show up too. Locals are used to tourists and crowds, but they didn't much care for being used as background and having their pictures taken.

"I mean, John, you know as well as anyone that some people live up here to get away from something. It's big country, big enough that if someone wants to get lost, they can. Nobody around here worries much about others' pasts. After all, everyone has one. Folks around here judge you on what you are now. So having a video crew taking pictures was unnerving to some people. Others were not interested in being part of a publicity stunt, even for Anna.

"It didn't take long, and the crowd dwindled, and the curious went their separate ways. The event was a bust. Anna was completely embarrassed. She had taken advantage of her family and friends. Stephen was angry. They had planned a couple of days of filming but flew out the next day.

"The publicist used the footage from their visit on several network TV spots. The wedding was big news, and *Good Day America* interviewed the golden couple at their home overlooking the Pacific Ocean. I got together with Herb and Dorothy to watch the show. They sat cozy together on a couch, and Anna smiled a lot but didn't say much. Stephen controlled the interview. He announced that they planned to get married in a private ceremony with just a few friends and family in California. No honeymoon because their training had begun in earnest for the next Olympics. Anna, the Musky Queen, was sold as a product to the world.

"And California? We couldn't believe she wasn't getting married in Musky Falls. Even the local paper commented. Herb and Dorothy were mortified. Dorothy, again, was the voice of reason. It was Anna's life, and she gets to live it however she wants. Herb wondered if they would even be invited.

"Well, invitations came for Herb, Dorothy, Bud, and me, along with a private plane that would pick us up at the Musky Falls airport and fly us to Los Angeles. The wedding was in an open-air non-denominational church overlooking the ocean. The minister was dressed like a flower show and went on for a good while defining ancient words, then explaining their relationship to the cosmos, telling everyone how Anna and Stephen would now become one forging a cosmic bond.

"After the wedding, limousines took everyone to a restaurant, where the bride and groom had rented the top floor. Wait staff swirled through the eclectic crowd with a variety of small canapés on silver trays. Others made sure that no one's champagne flute was less than half full. One of the guests explained to the poor girl from the backwoods of Wisconsin that this was the epitome of chic with unique gourmet cuisine. The photographer and publicist were everywhere.

"One of Stephen's friends, within five minutes of meeting me, asked if I cared to join him for an evening cruise on his sailboat. I told him I would love to as long as there was room for Bud. His total time invested was less than ten minutes before he found a new target.

"Dinner was served, and another round of cocktails adorned with what appeared to be lawn grass was set in front of each guest. Dorothy noted that the bread and decorated dinner rolls were at least a day or two old. She quietly said, 'Nobody would get away with this in Namekagon County.' By the time the first course was served, the celebrity contingent, including Stephen, was clearly on the way to inebriation. Anna was more reserved and tried to keep her family and guests happy.

"After dinner, the wait staff brought out more trays of cocktails for everyone. Now loud and obnoxious, Stephen insisted that Herb drink a toast with him. Anna steered him away from her father.

"John, I would not have thought things could get any worse, but they did. This woman wearing a dress so revealing that I'm sure you would lock her up for indecent exposure if she showed up around here, set her sights on Bud, and drunkenly flirted with him. His face was as red as a beet, and he wanted nothing to do with her. Anna and I both ran interference. Anna fell all over herself, apologizing.

"Then another half-drunk celebrity of some sort approached

Herb to make conversation. When they shook hands, the celebrity commented on how strong and tough Herb's hands were. Herb told us later that it was like shaking hands with a walleye fillet. The celebrity asked Herb what he did for a living, and when Herb told him he was a logger, this guy backed up like he'd stepped on a snake and said, 'So, you're one of those people who are destroying our forests and raping our planet, then freely admit to it? You should be ashamed of yourself.'

"Herb just calmly said, 'No, that's the other guy. I'm the logger who makes sure you can wipe your silly little butt in the morning.'

"We'd had enough. Herb, Dorothy, and Bud loaded in the elevator, and I told them to hold the door. I walked across the floor to Anna, who had tears in her eyes. We both started to speak at the same time, but the three-piece band started up before we could talk, and Stephen dragged her away for the first dance. The limo drove us to our hotel, and I called the charter service to fly us home."

We called it an early night. Julie and I snuggled up together under our Hudson Bay blanket. It would soon come off the bed when the weather warmed, but for now, it was welcome on the still-cool nights.

She didn't fall asleep right away, and I could tell something was on her mind.

After a moment, she said, "You know, once Stephen and Anna were married, we rarely heard from her. She called me one night after a glass of wine, which is about her limit. Stephen became relentless about building his and Anna's brand, working on it day and night. Between that and her training, spare time didn't exist."

"Sounds like their breakup was really bad," I said.

"You have no idea how bad, but that's her story to tell. I am beat. Let's go to sleep."

We were dead to the world when the cabin phone started to ring, and my pager went off at the same time. I was up and dressed before I called in on my radio. I knew that the phone and pager going off at the same time were not meant to wish me sweet dreams. I called into dispatch and was shocked at the news. A cougar had attacked Evan Danna.

When I arrived, one of my deputies was already on the scene with EMS. All the lights were on in the house. I knocked on the door and let myself in. EMTs were cleaning and swabbing a very nasty set of what appeared to be claw marks on Evan's left shoulder.

"Evan, these are going to need some serious stitching," one of the EMTs said. "We might as well haul you to the hospital in the ambulance since we're here. I am going to call ahead and tell the doc what we have. A couple of years ago, we all took a course on treating wounds caused by animals. They talked about serious, sometimes fatal, infections caused by cat claws."

I followed the ambulance to the hospital. Lucky for Evan, a top emergency room doctor was working the end of the night shift. He had trained and worked in eastern Washington, the panhandle of Idaho, and western Montana and was well-versed in the dangers of animal attacks. He moved to Namekagon County after retirement for one reason. The inland northwest of the United States was beautiful country, but northern Wisconsin had muskies, and he was a dyed-in-the-wool musky fisherman and wanted to spend the rest of his days chasing mossback around.

I started to interview Evan, but the doctor burst into the room.

"I'm Dr. James. Tell me what happened here."

"The whole story?" asked Evan.

"Yes, the whole story, if you don't mind."

"You mind if I listen in?" I asked.

"Not if my patient doesn't," said the doctor.

"No problem, Doc," Evan replied.

"We had trouble with a cougar attacking our sheep the night before last. It killed our dog and one lamb. We were worried it would come back, so I sat in the dark corner by the barn. Must have been three or three-thirty in the morning. I had been looking hard at the dark for so long that I didn't see it at first. The cougar jumped the fence, and suddenly he was in the pasture with me. I raised my rifle to shoot, but he was right in the middle of the sheep. The cat grabbed a lamb and leaped up on a low shed roof next to the pasture. I got one round off, and it must have spooked him. He launched himself off the shed. I guess I turned away from him, and he hit me on the back and clawed at my shoulder. Then he was over the fence with the lamb and gone in the night."

"That is quite a story, young man," Dr. James said.

"Do you think your shot may have hit him?" I asked.

"Nope, it didn't. I know I missed."

The doctor gave Evan several injections of a localized anesthetic and began examining the wound. He probed deep into where the claws dug into his shoulder.

"This wound is very serious. The puncture from two of the claws is quite deep. We are going to fix this up but not here in the ER. There is a small surgical suite just down the hall from the emergency room. We'll prep it and move you down there where we can work undisturbed."

Dr. James left the room, and Hugh came in and sat next to Evan's bed. "Boy, you are lucky, real lucky. That cougar had all kinds of something to dare coming back to our place. We're going to get that devil. He has got to be stopped," he said to his son.

Ten minutes later, Evan was whisked off to surgery. An hour passed, and Dr. James came out.

"I think Evan's shoulder is going to be okay. Using moderate pressure from a large syringe and a wound irrigator, we flushed the wounds with sterile saline. We considered the options of leaving the wounds open or closing them. In the end, we decided to close the wounds and install a couple of drains. He will have to stay in the hospital for a day or two. Due to the risk of infection from wounds like this, we are giving him a super dose of IV antibiotics." ▪

CHAPTER 6

I went back home to catch some sleep. I had to sleep fast because Chief Delzell and I were supposed to meet the race organizers at ten, and before the end of the day, the race company would be arriving in Musky Falls to begin setting up. I was headed back into town by nine-thirty when the chief called me to see if I was on my way.

"Five minutes out," I said.

We agreed to meet at the park, and as I cruised into town, I couldn't believe what I saw. The Great Wilderness Race was becoming a reality. The city crew was busy putting up orange and white barricades to block off part of Main Street. Two huge semi-trucks and trailers had pulled in and were being unloaded. Any man or woman looking for a top-paying part-time job was hired. The students on summer vacation from Northern Lakes Academy saw this as a golden opportunity to line their pockets. The judges' booth, bleachers, communication center, and other essential buildings were reassembled at predetermined mapped locations.

Race promotors encouraged local businesses to advertise their services and promote the beauty of the area. Race brochures included full-color pages of things to do in Namekagon and surrounding counties. The top competitors and some celebrities were scheduled to sit and sign autographs at different businesses and visit with the crowds. It was clear that the organizers had done this before and knew how to be successful. Locals used to special events coming to town all agreed they had never quite seen anything like this before.

The color brochure clearly worked. Before the event, fishing guides—particularly musky fishing guides—found the expected new visitors excited to book a day of fishing. Fly anglers reserved time to ply the waters of the beautiful rivers in float boats guided by experts. Weeks before anyone even arrived, guides had a waiting list. A rental outfit offered pontoon boat cruises on sparkling northern lakes, serving a gourmet brew from Karin's Coffee on the sunrise trips and Out of the Woods wine for twilight adventures.

Rooms had been booked solid for the area within days of the announcement that Musky Falls was to host the race, and anybody looking for a room to rent within seventy miles was pretty much out of luck. Canny entrepreneurs fared well. On one of the lakes near Musky Run Trail, a developer had purchased a resort a couple of years earlier. His contractors remodeled the cabins into spectacular deluxe lakeside accommodations. The quiet secluded location promised the best of the Northwoods with all the comforts of home. He reached out to the production company and explained that he had a very limited number of these beautiful cabins available for the week of the race. He suspected that some of the more discriminating people attending might find these places perfect for their stay. He sent over some pictures and priced the cabins at three times the normal rate. They were all booked by two that afternoon.

Then as if on cue, when the finishing touches were applied,

people started to arrive. Within twenty-four hours, the city's population had grown over ten-fold.

The official kickoff event began early Sunday evening with a top-notch local band playing a mix of rousing country and oldies that got the crowd excited. Kids from eight to eighty were strutting their stuff and singing along.

I was in uniform, standing with Julie, Bud, and Anna's parents. After an hour of music, the race promoter took the stage, immediately engaging the audience, a mix of locals and visitors. I moved to a position at the rear of the crowd, trying to take as much in as possible. He thanked everyone in Namekagon County on behalf of the racers and support staff, mentioning several individuals by name. He explained how the race would be run and that every day the schedule of events would be posted on two different electric signs on either end of Main Street. The schedule was also available in printed form at any store that displayed the Great Wilderness Race sticker in the window.

Next, the mayor of Musky Falls and the county board chairman were asked to say a few words. Mayor Nels Robson thanked everyone from the race company and all the local folks that had put so much time and effort into this event.

After the mayor finished speaking, the county board chairman took the podium. He shared how his vision for the area was coming to fruition, humbly getting to the part about how his brilliance and forethought had guided the county to this point, and it was only the beginning. The large crowd was polite, but you could see that it wasn't long before they were ready for him to be done. The promoter graciously stepped in, thanked the dignitaries, and moved the program forward.

He rolled out the verbal red carpet. "I am honored to introduce someone you all know and love—the Voice of the North for over forty years, Tom Stockten!" The crowd gave a round of applause as Tom stepped up to the microphone.

In his booming radio voice, he said, "Hello, folks, and welcome to the opening of the Great Wilderness Race. I will be your announcer throughout the event, but my first official duty tonight is to introduce our master of ceremonies." He paused long enough for the crowd to settle. The atmosphere was electric with anticipation for the next introduction.

"There are people in every endeavor who rise to the top. However, few achieve this level of greatness. Those who do become iconic symbols of everything that is great about this country. Some people stop there, and who could blame them? Such accomplishment comes with no shortage of hard work, determination, and passion. Then there are those who are truly thankful for their success, giving back as much as they have received. Our master of ceremonies has shared her success with our community—from little league uniforms to a new roof on the public library. She has been there without expectation of praise or publicity. We would be here all night if I listed all she has done for us, so I won't. It is my sincere pleasure to introduce our master of ceremonies. Please welcome Olympic gold medal winner, our hometown girl, Anna MacDonald."

The applause and cheering were so loud it could be heard blocks away. Anna stepped up to the microphone and looked out at the crowd, her beautiful smile beaming. As soon as they quieted, she said, "I am glad to be home. Thank you so much for coming out tonight." Again, a huge round of applause.

Anna told the story of delivering bread from the bakery. How her loving family had made it possible for her to enter her first race. How the trails, lakes, rivers, and streams of northern

Wisconsin had been her playground. She told a story of hard work and determination. But mostly, she told a story of love, how the most beautiful flowers often grew from the simplest beginnings. She talked about the community always standing behind her, always supporting her. It was here she learned to love the land, our traditions, and the good people around us.

"I could never hope to give back even a small portion of the goodness I have received, but it is my goal to keep trying. So, to that end, I have a special announcement. I would like to have some people join me on the stage. Mom and Dad, could you come up here, please?"

Her father slowly worked his way to the stage showing the signs of a rough life of hard work. Still, her mother linked arms with him. They climbed the steps.

"Hi, Mom. Hi, Dad." They both smiled at Anna, but it was clear they weren't quite sure what was going on.

"Next, could Julie Carlson and Bud Treetall please join us?"

Julie was standing in front of the stage with a bunch of her students, who broke into applause and cheers. When all four were standing with her, she hugged each.

Next, she looked at Julie's students. "Could all you kids who are here from Northern Lakes Academy please come up here?"

The students looked perplexed for a second. Then Anna said jokingly, "Move it, you guys. We don't have all night." That started the kids going, and they all scrambled up on the stage.

Anna waited until everyone had settled down and then began. "When I think of goodness and giving, these four people come to mind. My mom and dad taught me the value of hard work and, more importantly, family. Bud Treetall is a man with the strength of a bear and the heart of a lamb. Then there is my best friend, Julie Carlson, who, by the way, will be getting married soon after the race is over." The crowd clapped and cheered. When it subsided, she continued, "Julie has not only taught her students at Northern Lakes Academy how to give and believe that you can make a difference, but she taught me this lesson. I lived in this beautiful place and didn't know it then, but I was building a lifelong connection with the land. It became part of me. Our natural resources are the basis of life, yet we keep moving further and further away from the very things that will sustain us.

"Tonight, I want to tell you about something near and dear to my heart. Working with some great people and using Northern Lakes Academy as a model, we have developed significant ongoing funding to develop a program that will help kids get outdoors and provide a chance to experience the wonders of nature and begin to build a connection. School district budgets are tough everywhere, and most don't have extra money to spare or even the personnel to coordinate. We have raised the money to pay for this. It was a daunting task but not impossible. My high school cross country coach told me if I dreamed, then 'dream big.' So, we dreamed big, and I am here to tell you that it worked out. The Great Wilderness Race Foundation has agreed to match dollar for dollar any donations we get in the next six months, up to—are you ready for this?—one million dollars. It will be called Field Edventures, and our goal is to capture the 'frog-catching, rock-skipping heart' in every kid."

The place went wild.

When it quieted, Anna started to speak but was interrupted by a loud voice. She ignored it at first, but the person speaking kept on and was getting closer to the stage. It was probably tabloid readers who first recognized who it was, starting a murmur that swept through the crowd like a wave. From where Anna stood on the stage, she couldn't see or make out what the loud voice was saying.

Someone in the crowd shouted, "It's Cameron, her ex-husband.

Stephen Cameron."

Anna was paralyzed. She could not move or speak.

Everyone fell silent except for Stephen. I could see him bull his way through the crowd on his way to the stage. I began to move toward Cameron, not running but moving that way.

"Hello, Anna. How are you? I am so glad to see you. It's been a long time. I know you've been busy, but a call or note would have been nice. I was excited when I found out our paths might cross in Musky Falls, and look, here we are. You look so sweet standing there with Mom and Dad, Bud, Julie, and the sweet little kiddies. Mom and Dad, would it be okay for me to get on the stage with you all? Maybe someone in the crowd could take a picture for me."

Anna managed to say, "Stephen, please don't. Please stop this."

"Oh, Anna, come on, just for old times' sake." Stephen lunged for the stage railing and almost made it. Herb MacDonald put a boot to his shoulder and pushed him off.

Trying to attack Anna MacDonald in Namekagon County was a mistake of catastrophic proportions, especially when the Weaver boys, Dennis and Daryl, were part of the civilian security team stationed at the stage. The Weavers had grown up with Anna. They both worked at the lumber mill, and physical labor was nothing to them. They were a backwoods family living off the grid. When Dennis was born, he was deprived of oxygen for a short while, which resulted in him being mentally challenged. He was sometimes the victim of cruel teasing. That never happened when Anna was around. One day some kids cornered Dennis in an alley behind the bakery, and they were throwing rocks at him as hard as they could, yelling, "Dance, stupid. Dance." The rocks hurt so much Dennis was crying his eyes out. Anna came out the back door of the bakery and saw what was going on. She picked up a bread dough pan and swung for the fence, bouncing the pan hard off the leader's head. That was enough for the bullies, and they ran off. Dennis told Anna the bullies waited for him every day. The next day Dennis showed up, and so did the bullies. However, Anna, Julie, and Bud did too, and no one ever bothered Dennis again.

The Weaver boys hit Cameron like a flying freight train, knocking him airborne into the audience. When he landed, they grabbed him and dragged him toward the exit, where the police took over. Musky Falls' finest marched him away from the crowd, gave him a shove, and told him if he came back, he'd end up in jail.

Cameron walked off and didn't say another word. Local law enforcement learned long ago that the jail would be chock full in a hurry if they arrested every loudmouth drunk at one of the festivals. Usually, a boot in the butt out the gate was all it took.

Things settled down again, and people were quiet, stunned by what had happened. Anna returned to the microphone, visibly shaken.

She began again. "I am sorry for that. I want to tell you all something—I am so glad to be home, so glad to see all of you. Nothing will spoil it. Thank you for welcoming me back, I love this place, and I love you with all my heart." Anna walked off the stage to another roaring round of applause. The band took over, and the party started anew.

Everyone got down from the stage and hovered around Anna.

"I cannot believe he's here. I always worried he might show up someplace, but he didn't, and I thought maybe, just maybe, he was out of my life," she said.

Julie wrapped her arms around her best friend's shaking body. Herb and Dorothy wanted Anna to come home with them for the night, but everyone quickly agreed that staying with Julie and me was a better choice until we could get a handle on Stephen Cameron.

I called Chief Delzell and shared the plan. The crowd was

having fun but not unruly, and Mary said that I'd probably be needed more at home than in town tonight.

Turning back to Julie and Anna, I said, "My squad is right over there," pointing to the chamber parking lot. "Let's go out to the cabin. I will still be on call, but things are pretty calm." ▪

CHAPTER 7

Our cabin was a beautiful log structure I inherited from my uncle Nick and aunt Rose. Every corner spelled comfort and usefulness. Julie and I had already begun to make it our home, and with any luck, it would be our home forever—a place where I dared to hope we may raise a family. For now, it was mostly Julie, Bud, and me, but many people stopped by, and we were happy to have them. Anna couldn't have been more welcome.

We sat quietly, drinking some of Julie's specially ordered tea.

I broke the silence. "Anna, I have to ask, do you think Stephen is a threat to you?"

"Maybe you can help me figure that out because I don't know if he's a threat to me or not," she said. "I am afraid of him, and I was terrified when I saw him tonight."

There was a long moment of silence when Anna, the Olympic hero and the pride of Namekagon County, broke down. Hiding behind that beautiful smile was heartache, and she started to tell me the story.

"One night, I got a call from the police at two in the morning.

Stephen had been in a car accident and was being taken to the hospital. His injuries were severe. By the time I got there, he had already been rushed into surgery. A nurse brought me a glass of water and said it would be sometime before they finished. I just sat there waiting when a police officer approached me and asked if I was Anna Cameron, Stephen's wife. I told him I went by MacDonald but that I was Stephen Cameron's wife."

Anna told the officer the only thing she knew was that Stephen was in an accident and was in surgery. The officer filled her in on what he knew. Stephen was on the coast highway traveling at a high rate of speed, at least ninety miles per hour, which they knew because a California highway patrolman got him on radar. The patrolman turned on his lights and siren and tried to get Stephen to pull over with no success. Instead, he accelerated.

They called off the chase because of safety concerns for other traffic. The patrolman found Stephen's car about a mile down the highway. It had gone over the guardrail and rolled over several times. He said they had no conclusive evidence that he was impaired, but they took blood samples for analysis as allowed by California state law. That was all he knew, but what he needed from Anna about did her in.

He asked if she knew the name of the woman who was riding in the car with Stephen. They had recovered no ID for her. She was unconscious when they brought her in and was also in surgery. Anna felt like she'd been slugged in the stomach and threw up in the wastebasket in the waiting room. She told the officer she had no idea who she might be.

It was at least four hours before Stephen was wheeled into recovery. There was a huge cast on his right leg with some wire and rods sticking out. He had a large bandage on his head and two sutured cuts on his cheek and above his left eye. He was groggy but awake. Before she could talk to him, the doctor came in and explained the situation to both of us. Stephen's most serious injury was two compound fractures of his right leg. He had three significant but non-life-threatening head wounds stitched up. A dose of strong pain medication and a sedative caused Stephen to drift off before Anna could speak with him.

"While I sat by Stephen's bed, I beat myself half to death, taking the blame for what had happened. I was nothing but a stupid, naïve fool. I never gave a second thought to Stephen's claim that he was working on our brand." Anna wiped her eyes, and Julie filled her teacup.

The tabloids went wild. The other person in Stephen's car was an up-and-coming actress, Cyn Taylor. Rumor had it, and it wasn't much of a rumor, that they had been involved in a romantic relationship for some time. Stephen tested positive for both alcohol and cocaine.

The real news, however, was Stephen's broken leg. The prognosis was hopeful unless you were an Olympic gold medalist. Doctors were sure he would walk again and, likely after extensive physical therapy, may even run, but his days on the podium were done.

"Then I made a big, big mistake. When I said for 'better or worse, in sickness and in health,' I meant it. I picked him up when he was released from the hospital and brought him home. I cared for him in every way I could. We hardly spoke, no casual conversation for sure. We weren't friendly to each other but not hostile either. The only time I left the house was to train, and when I did, a nurse named Ed came to stay with him."

It didn't take long for their brand to feel the repercussions. Sponsors dropped them like rats leaving a ship. To make things worse, Stephen forged Anna's name on several contracts. Lawyers were demanding repayment of advances he had received. When they got nowhere with him, they came after Anna. The young actress Cyn Taylor hired a team of lawyers who filed a multimillion-dollar lawsuit against the couple.

Stephen healed slowly physically but faster than the doctors expected. He refused to go out in public for anything other than physical therapy or to see his doctors. His overall physical condition accounted for a lot, but not enough. He became harder and harder to care for because he became angrier each day. He directed all his anger at Anna and the TV, constantly watching tabloid channels to see what they were saying about him. Eventually, they replaced the original cast with a walking cast that allowed him to watch TV and pace the floor at the same time.

"I finally got the nerve to try and discuss the situation with him, but it backfired. He didn't take any responsibility for what had happened but viciously blamed me for everything. I tried to talk to him, and he screamed at me. When I suggested we see a counselor, he exploded and smashed a glass lamp on the floor. I guess that's when I started to be afraid of him.

"His prescription of strong narcotic pain medication was empty two weeks before it should have been. The doctor refilled it but told me I needed to monitor what he was taking. When I tried to give him the prescribed dosage of two pills, he demanded four, and I refused. He took the two pills, put them in his mouth, walked to the liquor cabinet, and washed them down with bourbon.

"The next day on a major network show, *Exposé*, Stephen and I were again the leading story. I refused to watch, and when I went for the remote to turn it off, he grabbed it from me and shoved me out of the way. The show's host was joined by some prominent women—a lawyer, a film star, and a former Olympic gold medalist. They praised me and condemned those who were attacking me. Then they started on Stephen. In what world could I be held responsible for my husband's actions? It was another blatant case of sexism. Women needed to unite and stand against this type of legal terrorism. The second half of the show, they took questions and comments from the audience, the consensus of which was I was just the latest victim in generations of discrimination. Stephen was an example of everything that was wrong with society. One woman from the audience demanded that he surrender his gold medal. The show ended with yet another attack on Cameron.

"Stephen sat stoically. I took the remote control from his hand and turned off the TV. I thought that somehow the show had gotten through to him. He sat in a chair with his head down. I asked him if he was okay. He got up, turned to me, then slugged me in the face. I didn't fall, so he punched me in the ribs and head again. Finally, with blood streaming from a cut above my eye and nose, I fell. He walked over to the liquor cabinet and began to drink. I was down but conscious and smart enough to stay still. I trembled as he screamed, yelled, and threw things. Soon he settled back down in the chair, and within minutes he was snoring."

Anna went upstairs and grabbed her bag, wallet, and some cash she kept hidden for emergencies. She got in her car and drove northeast, not stopping for anything but gas, to use the restroom, and catch a little sleep in highway waysides. She called Julie on the way and told her what had happened and that she was on her way home to Musky Falls. Over two thousand miles, thirty-five hours. When Stephen tried to call her, she threw her phone off a bridge into a fast-flowing river so he couldn't track her cell phone.

When she arrived in Musky Falls, Julie called Anna's old family doctor, Dr. Krumps, who agreed to make a house call, no questions asked. Although the cut above her eye was almost two and a half days old, he still stitched it up very neatly. She had a major set of raccoon eyes and some purple bruises. Her nose was broken, but the doctor was able to straighten it and hold it in place with packing and tape.

He became concerned as he examined where Anna had been

struck in the body. The bruises were a deep dark red. As soon as he touched the affected area, she winced in pain. They needed at least an x-ray, but more likely an MRI. Dr. Krumps drove her over to the hospital using a service entrance. They went back to imaging. The mobile MRI was at another hospital, but a CT scan showed that Anna had two broken ribs. Her parents were waiting at Julie's house when they returned. Julie helped her settle in, and Anna took the pills Dr. Krumps had given her. Anna fell asleep mid-sentence.

Everybody wanted to help. Dr. Krumps made frequent house calls to check on her. Doc O'Malley put her car in the shed behind his garage. No one and everyone knew she was in town.

Stephen never reported her missing, so no one came looking. Finally, her coach and trainer got worried when she didn't show up for training. They stopped at her house in L.A. Stephen told them Anna wasn't home and slammed the door. They called the police for a welfare check. When the police showed up, Stephen told the officers that two weeks before, he had gone to bed, and when he woke up, Anna was gone, and he had no idea where.

People were asking what happened to Anna MacDonald, and there were some concerns that she had come to harm. As soon as Anna heard this, she immediately reached out to the LAPD to tell them she was alive and well and just getting a little space from all that had been happening.

Her parents went with her to a local lawyer, and Anna filed for divorce. A week after, he was served with divorce papers, and Stephen flew into Musky Falls. He tried tracking her down and was met with as ugly as Namekagon County could muster. He may have been a top athlete once, but those boys that worked at Sayner Timber were as tough as boot leather, and, if need be, they would dish out some serious punishment.

Stephen left without talking to Anna, but he did leave with a restraining order preventing any contact. He tried desperately to reclaim some of his fame and appeared in interviews with his hair perfectly a little out of place. He wasn't gaining much traction.

"Then, out of the blue, someone made a call to a credible news organization. The caller was working the night shift at a twenty-four-hour gas station. He remembered a car pulling in with California plates. I had filled the car with gas, and my broken nose started to bleed again. I went straight to the bathroom but dripped blood on the floor. I offered to clean it up, but the attendant said he would take care of it. I got cleaned up and got back on the road. He recognized me and called the police, telling them he was one hundred percent sure I was the Olympian Anna MacDonald."

The news channel contacted Anna's and Stephen's lawyers. Within a few days, Stephen's lawyer offered a quick divorce settlement. Anna's lawyer agreed but under certain conditions: Stephen had exactly seventy-two hours to surrender all film rights, book rights, and anything else regarding Anna MacDonald, and Anna would receive one hundred percent of the advances he had stolen. He had spent most of the money, and his attorney said it would bankrupt him. Anna didn't budge.

The divorce done, Anna resettled in Musky Falls in her family home across the alley from the bakery. Stories of financial problems and other misfortune followed Stephen through the media. His bad behavior was so common that it became boring. The endorsements he was getting were few, and he was old news before long. The shine had worn off the golden boy.

That wasn't the case with Anna. Her coach and sponsors helped her figure things out. Anna promised to return as soon as she was ready. In a world as cutthroat as the endorsement business, sympathy was short-lived, but they were willing to wait for her.

"Meanwhile, I trained every day, often accompanied by

girls from the high school cross country team, and made a full transition from life with Stephen to my home. There was no comparison between the concrete banks of the L.A. River and the rivers and streams of the north country. Instead of pounding my feet on pavement, I ran on trails thousands of years old. I never felt stronger, never felt better.

"Julie and I started a tradition of sorts. On Sunday mornings after church, we walked the Musky Run Trail. It was where we played and ran as children. We walked and talked, just like when we were younger. I confessed to Julie that if I had stayed, Stephen would have killed me. My nose had healed a little crooked, and the doctor was certain that it could be reset perfectly, but I chose to see it in the mirror every morning so that I would never forget.

"Then, one Sunday morning, we stopped to sit for a while on a big flat rock overlooking the stream. I told Julie it was time to go back. A few days later, after one of Mom's famous breakfasts, I left. That's pretty much the story that few people know. As far as Stephen goes, with one exception, I haven't heard a word from him."

"What's the exception?" I asked

"He called out of the blue about a year ago. I shouldn't have answered, but I did. He said he wanted to talk, so I listened. He told me how he had changed and had completely given up drinking and drugs. He said a network had approached him about a sports commentator job, and it looked like a big contract was coming his way. I wasn't talking, just listening, when it got weird. He raised his voice and asked why I hadn't said very much. After all he had accomplished, I should be proud of him and at least give him credit for the effort. Then his voice got strangely quiet, and he said, 'Anna, I did it all for you. Everything was for you. I need to see you. I need another chance. I love you, Anna. I was so stupid. Let's start over. I can't wait to see you.' At that point, I hung up the phone. I have held my breath every day since, waiting for him to show up. Today he did. Is he still a threat to me? I really don't know."

"For now, Anna, how do you think we should handle this? I mean, you're here and going to be out in public every day. Stephen didn't just show up here randomly. Him being here is not a good sign," I said.

"I honestly don't know what to do. I've committed to my role here, and I am not going to let Stephen or anyone else make me hide in a corner."

"Well, here is my thought. We have plenty of room so you should stay with us while you are visiting. In the morning, we'll go back into town, get all your stuff, and bring it back here. The other thing I am going to do is have my people note every time they see Stephen and log it. They won't make contact unless they need to, but we need to see where he's going and what he's doing. Will that work for you?"

"I don't want to put you out."

"Anna, I would love it if you stayed here. We have so much catching up to do. It'll be fun," Julie said.

"Okay, but you can kick me out any time you want. No hard feelings."

"If Julie kicks you out, you can stay at my place in town," Bud said with a smile that turned into a sheepish red-faced grin as he fumbled to explain. We all laughed. It was a poorly concealed fact that Bud had always had a crush on Anna, joining about half the eligible males in the county.

Bud headed home, and I went to bed, leaving Julie, Anna, and a bottle of wine. Sleep didn't come quickly, if at all, and I heard Julie finally come to bed. She snuggled next to me, and within a minute, she was sound asleep. ∎

CHAPTER 8

Julie and Anna took advantage of the morning's sunshine and blue skies and hiked the seldom-used trail that ran along the shore of Little Spider Lake and looped back through the forest to the starting point. A gentle breeze combined with the sunshine made the lake sparkle.

When they returned, I was well on my way to cooking up a breakfast of sauteed walleye fillets, scrambled eggs with a dash of cream, basil, and Romano cheese. I served it with Julie's homemade bread toasted and slathered with butter.

"Holy smokes, John, this is great," Anna said. "I don't think you could find a restaurant in all of L.A. where you could get a meal like this." Julie and Anna dug in like two hungry lumberjacks, and I was happy to join them.

We offered to coordinate vehicle use with Anna, but she insisted that would be too burdensome and said she'd find a rental. After the kitchen was cleaned up, I called Doc O'Malley at Bill and Jack's Garage and Guide Service. He did have a car Anna could use, his perpetual loaner, an aging Jeep Cherokee in great shape that ran like a top. It was not for rent, but she was welcome to it for as long as she needed.

On our way to town, the girls talked nonstop, mostly about our upcoming wedding and the day's plans. Anna had all sorts of event work, and Julie had mostly wedding errands. We went our separate ways.

I called Chief Delzell. "Mary, are you anywhere close to the chamber office?" I asked.

"Sheriff, this is Musky Falls; everything is close to the chamber office."

"Can you meet me in the parking lot?"

"See you in five," she said.

Although the crowd downtown was growing, they were orderly, and the sunshine put smiles on faces. Anna was meeting with budding track stars at the park to talk about running. Even this early, the ice cream wagon was the most popular venue in town, with kids' favorite flavors denoted by the color of their faces. A kayak trip to explore backwaters organized by the chamber was returning, and happy paddlers were excited about seeing twin bear cubs on the trunk of a fallen tree calling to their mom on the opposite shore.

Mary Delzell pulled in and got out of her car to talk.

"Chief, looks like you have everything under control," I said.

"This event is really something. The organizers have it well in hand. Besides the local people they hire, they also have professional security staff. I was talking to two guys today; one was retired Minneapolis PD, the other retired Chicago. Speaking of security, did you see the Weaver boys take out Cameron? Man, they really clobbered him. Maybe he learned a little lesson."

"Chief, I don't think so, and that's what I want to talk to you about. I need you to have your folks keep an eye on him. I don't know what's going on here, but something is. I am going to have my deputies do the same thing, maybe even push him a little, you know, just to make sure he knows we're watching," I explained.

"Do you have any other intel I should know about?" she asked.

"Nothing yet, but I'm keeping my eyes open."

I drove over to the podium. A fat tire bike race was about to start on the street in front of the stage. Well over a hundred cyclists would follow my squad to the edge of town, where they would jump on what was the Nordic ski trail in the winter. They would race for twenty-five miles along a circuitous route through the national forest on ski, ATV, and snowmobile trails. The route had it all: rough terrain, rocks, waterholes, steep uphills, and dangerous downhills.

Right on time, Tom Stockten fired the gun, and off they went pedaling hard for position. People lined the route and cheered for their favorites. Namekagon County was the home of some of the top riders in the country, and they were, of course, the local favorites. It was exciting. I paralleled the riders with my lights flashing until they got to the trail. Well-wishers gathered at different observation points along the way.

The bike race was just the beginning of things. Anna seemed to be everywhere—a talk to the Women's Auxiliary, local newspaper, TV, and radio interviews. She even did a sit-down with a movie star.

People were as excited about the amateur events as they were about the big race. There was a run and bike race for kids. No one rides a bike with more reckless abandon than a twelve-year-old. Celebrities mixed with locals, and everyone was having a good time.

Businesses were packed as throngs of people explored the local offerings. Ron Carver's jewelry store was sold out of sustainably harvested butterfly wing necklaces and his own rendition of a silver or gold musky charm, matching the embroidered one on Anna's running shorts. The Nordic store ordered commemorative race clothing that was flying off the shelf almost as fast as the latest book by a local mystery writer.

The size of the crowd had been underestimated and caused a long wait at every restaurant. Even the line at Dairy Queen was over three blocks long. At one point, the almost unthinkable happened: the Fisherman Bar and Grill, with a line of waiting patrons down the block, was on the verge of running out of cheese curds and walleye fillets. Although there was no staff to spare, the owner had to send his son-in-law to a town sixty miles away to resupply.

The next sporting event was a kayak race. Several of the top competitors were racing because it was a good warm-up with little chance of injury. The river was running cold, clear, and fast when the race began. Anna fired the starting gun.

That evening, Julie brought home a couple of pizzas and a six-pack of Angry Minnow beer. After a quiet, peaceful dinner, Anna shared an announcement. After the race and the wedding, she was going back to L.A. to put her house on the market, pack her stuff, and move home. She said she had never felt at home on the West Coast and couldn't wait to get back. Bud grinned from ear to ear.

The next day I went to town dressed in jeans, hikers, and my Northern Lakes Academy sweatshirt, so I could circulate downtown less conspicuously. I stopped at the co-op for a cup of coffee and ran into a group of retirees who meet daily for breakfast. It didn't take more than a minute of conversation before I found out word was officially out about the cougar attack. It was the main point of discussion with the coffee group and seemed to be led by Reverend Redberg, a retired preacher.

I had met the good reverend and his wife the winter before.

They had owned a double-wide trailer on a farm property in Namekagon County. Also on the property was a house, barn, and a couple of outbuildings that had been rented for years. The trailer was on a remote part of the reverend's family farm and had been used as a hunting shack but was rarely occupied. Local drug dealers moved in uninvited and set up a meth lab which ended up being destroyed. The Redbergs had not seen the place in a long time and drove over from their farm in Minnesota to survey the damage.

They took their time traveling across the top of Wisconsin, intent on enjoying a rare vacation away from the never-ending list of chores that are part and parcel of living in the country. They drove along two-lane roads through small towns deep in the Northwoods, stopping at cafés where the Redbergs found home-cooking and friendly conversation. At the end of the third day, they came to the fire number they were looking for. The driveway curved back and forth through giant pines, a wooden timber bridge crossed a small creek, and at the end came to a neat little yellow farmhouse with white trim the reverend remembered from his youth. His great-grandfather had homesteaded the land and had proven it with great pride. The place was nicer than they remembered. The long-term tenant had only recently moved out and kept things up. The barn was solid with a good roof, and two other outbuildings were also in good repair. Inside, the house was clean and neat as a pin. Other than the destroyed trailer, everything was better than they expected, and the Redbergs found a new home in Namekagon County.

"Reverend, have you had a direct encounter with a cat? It sounds like I may have missed a good story," I said.

"I would be glad to tell you about it," said Reverend Redberg. "The first time was about two months or so ago. I had the goats and chickens peckin' and romping around in the small pasture right behind us. I was sitting on a chair watching them, having a little taste of our homemade oak leaf wine. My wife was down at the church working with the church ladies on something. I must have dozed off for a minute when the chickens started raising a ruckus and woke me. I jumped up and ran toward the noise. Something big had gotten into the pasture, and when I yelled, it took one jump and was gone into the night. I couldn't really see what it was, but I figured it was a wolf. Well, from then on, I took my rifle with me when I watched over the animals. I am aware of the law regarding the protection of wolves, but I thought if I fired a couple of warning shots, that would send them running.

"It was just over a week later, there was a commotion in the little pasture, and it sounded like something was trying to kill every animal I owned. I ran over with my .22 rifle and flashlight, and in the Lord's truth, there in the corner of the pasture was a full-grown mountain lion with one of the goats in his mouth. Sheriff, I couldn't help it. I got so excited I shot at the animal two or three times. One bullet hit, but before I could do anything else, the big creature was gone," the reverend explained. "I'm sure mountain lions are protected, and shooting it is illegal, so throw me in jail if you have to, but I am unrepentant. I was just trying to protect my livestock."

"Cougars are protected, but you can shoot them if they are threatening people or livestock. So, I won't be slapping the cuffs on you today, Reverend. How do you know you hit him?" I asked.

"He let out a wild scream after one of the shots," the reverend replied. "I have never heard of mountain lions in Wisconsin."

North country folks like nothing better than to spin tales of a dangerous predator roaming the country, be it man or beast. Soon the number of sightings would increase significantly.

With my cup of coffee in hand, I parked myself at one of the picnic tables on Main Street, where I had a good view of people on the street. I nursed the coffee as long as I could when someone sat down across from me.

"I bet you've been looking for me, haven't you, Sheriff?" Stephen Cameron asked.

"As a matter of fact, I have," I replied.

"So here I am. You found me, or did I find you? Oh, never mind. We'll just say we found each other. Now that we have, what can I do for you?"

"Cameron, I want to know if you are here with the intention of causing Anna any problems," I asked.

"Aren't you the bold one? No beating around the bush with you. Right to the point. Well, if I intended to bother her, why would I tell you, the sheriff?"

"No harm in asking," I replied.

"I guess there is no harm in that. My answer is simple: I would never harm a hair on my lovely ex-wife's head. As a matter of fact, I am sure Anna has told Julie that we are working on reconciling. I know that sounds strange, but love is a funny thing. Who knows how something will turn out. The other night was a huge mistake, acting like a fool in front of the crowd. I had a little too much to drink. The next morning, I called Anna, and she said she had forgiven me. I know we have had our troubles, and I was the cause of most of them. I am hoping we will be able to spend some time together after the race. Did she tell you she asked me to be her date for your wedding?"

"She never mentioned it."

"I really shouldn't have said anything. She made me promise not to talk about this with you or Julie. I wouldn't miss the wedding. After all, she and Julie are closer than sisters."

"Stephen, I have got to tell you that your account of the status of your relationship is not on the same page as what I have heard from your ex-wife. While she is here, it is my duty to protect her. Anyone I even think might be a threat to her safety will get all my attention. Are we clear on that?"

"Of course, and I feel much better knowing you are serious about her safety. Sheriff Cabrelli, can I talk to you candidly?"

"Sure, go ahead," I replied.

"You and Julie are getting married. Do you love her?"

"My personal life is none of your business."

"Okay, I get it. I am sure you love her. Otherwise, you wouldn't be getting married. What if you two broke up because of something stupid you did? Wouldn't you do everything you could to find a way to get back together? Of course you would. I am no different than you, Sheriff. It's just that every time I screw up, it ends up on the news, and people recount for the zillionth time what a jerk I am. The unfortunate problem is that I mostly agree with them.

"As far as Anna facing any potential threats, well, that's a different thing altogether. Sheriff, you really don't know who Anna MacDonald is, do you? Let me help you understand. She is America's sweetheart. Everybody loves Anna, including me. Anna MacDonald gets so much fan mail that she hired two people full-time to wade through it, including love letters, marriage proposals, as well as some creepy stuff. She is a baker's daughter from nowheresville who accomplished something only a handful of people in the world will ever do. The other part of it is that she is truly nice. She should have hired private security but didn't because she was too humble and always saw herself as a little girl riding a bike around Musky Falls delivering bread. The way she thinks, why would she need security? The world loves her, and she loves them. She shows up at an event like this, and there is a pretty good chance some of her 'admirers' are here too."

"So, Stephen, why is it you are here in Namekagon County?"

"Sheriff, I can go wherever I want whenever I want, although you have given me the distinct impression that if given the chance, you would be glad to deprive me of that freedom. But I have nothing to hide. A very prestigious group has asked me to be their guest here and help them evaluate a particular team they are considering sponsoring. It's my hope that Anna and I might be able to work things out. I know I told you she had invited me to the wedding, and I may have stretched the truth. She hasn't actually asked me yet, but I'm pretty sure she will."

"Okay, Stephen, let me say this again. It is my job to keep Anna safe while she's here, and that is what I will do."

"I trust that you will. I guess we're done then. See you around, Sheriff." Cameron got up and walked away with a pronounced limp. As much as I didn't like him, I couldn't help feeling a little sympathy.

I walked around the downtown, and I could tell the excitement was increasing. The teams were here preparing for the race only three days away.

As soon as he was gone, I called Chief Delzell and brought her up to speed on things.

I disconnected and started walking through the crowd. I saw a small group over by the area reserved for competitors. Strolling over, I could immediately see the reason. Anna was in the middle of it, talking with people smiling and signing autographs, as were some of the competitors. I couldn't help but notice she now had acquired personal security. The Weaver brothers were standing on either side of her in bright green shirts. Daryl was being hospitable. Dennis, on the other hand, was giving anyone who approached Anna the stink eye. I had no doubt whatsoever that Anna was well protected. ▪

CHAPTER 9

The Great Wilderness Race required a combined law enforcement presence. But there were still other things that needed attention. The cougar was front and center for many of our county's year-round residents, so I wasn't surprised when our local reporter Bill Presser's name came up on my caller ID.

I answered. "Hey, mighty scribe. How goes the war?"

"Well, Sheriff, plenty of news this week with the big race, Anna MacDonald, and other celebrities walking around. This is quite an event, and I have got plenty of coverage on that. What I want to ask you about is the cougar. The race is a big deal, but everybody is buzzing about the attack on Evan Danna. Can you tell me what you know about the cougar?"

"Well, Bill, I am not sure it was an attack on Evan. Dr. Kouper, the predator expert, says it may have just been a push-off, the cat jumping from the top of the shed roof then jumping on Evan's shoulder. He says it appeared as though it was a hind foot but can't be sure. I'm sure it feels like an attack to Evan."

"Any thoughts on the dog hunters on the way?" he asked.

"No, I don't know what you're talking about."

"A local guy named Dewey Brewer has been running bear hounds for over thirty years. He's a licensed guide and has a place called Possum Lake Lodge. Apparently, he contacted the DNR and offered his services. Brewer said that he was certain his dogs would track the cat.

"I talked with Jeb Barzine over at the DNR as well as Dr. Kouper. They are going to get together and decide how to handle this. Sounds like the consensus is that the animal either needs to be darted and relocated or put down. Boy, that video sure got my attention. Do you have any thoughts on this, Sheriff?"

"What video?" I asked.

"The one of the cougar from the Danna place," Bill responded.

"I haven't seen it," I replied. "Have you?"

"Dr. Kouper showed it to me on his laptop. It kind of takes your breath away."

"Bill, as far as what to do, in my opinion, we need to listen to the experts and follow whatever course they recommend. I don't know about others, but Professor Newlin and Dr. Kouper are taking this quite seriously."

"It seems folks around here think that animal needs to be taken care of. I'd be willing to bet there are a lot more rifles than usual in trucks right now," Bill supposed.

"Any idea when they plan to try the hounds?" I asked.

"I don't think they figured it out yet. They'll probably decide once everyone gets together. Brewer and his crowd are not very patient about this. Brewer is a cousin to Dannas by marriage and spends a fair bit of time in the local taverns. He's got people pretty fired up. The DNR says they are getting several calls a day on cougar sightings. One came in yesterday of a cat by the daycare. Brewer is saying that if they turn the hounds loose at full light, they could have the cat treed by noon."

"Our dispatch center has been getting the same calls. We follow up on each one, but no confirmed sightings yet. You know, Bill, with the race only a couple of days away, it may be a good idea if they did chase the cougar down sooner than later."

"Sheriff, I'll keep you posted if I hear anything. If you get a chance, take a look at that video."

"Thanks, Bill. I will."

———————————

Barely an hour had passed when I got a call from Ron Carver. "John, you better get your hind end over to my store. Dewey Brewer and Hugh Danna were just on the news."

Ron had the news conference, if you could call it that, ready to go on the TV when I came into his back office. Channel 2 was a small local network affiliate. They covered local events mostly but were always looking for headlines that would prop up their network status.

The banner headline was something right out of a horror movie: "Killer Cougar Stalks Namekagon County."

The reporter was an attractive woman dressed in a light parka, utility pants, hiking boots, and a baseball cap. She started out with her best shot at a national news desk voice. "I'm Robin Rebels, roving reporter with KQALO TV. I am here in eastern Namekagon County, Wisconsin, with local sheep farmer Hugh Danna. The Dannas love life in the quiet backcountry where nothing very exciting happens, nothing very exciting until recently, that is."

The reporter turned and faced Hugh. "Can you tell us what happened, Mr. Danna?"

"It just started a few days ago. The sheep were grazing on my number two pasture that night. My dog, a Great Pyrenees, was in with them watching things. Been having some wolf trouble, so we got the dog to keep them away. Anyway, I hear this growling and snarling that sounded like a heck of a fight. Then it was quiet. All I heard was something run away. I got my rifle and went over to check things out, and there on the ground was my dog, dead, torn to shreds. I thought it was wolves that done it, but the sheriff came out and called some experts."

"Who were those experts, Mr. Danna?"

"Professor Newlin from the college and Dr. Kouper, an expert on cougars."

"What did they find?"

"They looked at my poor dog and showed me where the claws had sunk in, and he'd been bitten in the back of the neck. Then they began looking around the farmyard, and it didn't take no time at all before they found some mountain lion tracks."

"Mountain lion tracks? Are you sure?"

"That's what the two experts said, and besides that, my son Evan matched the ones in the yard with pictures on the Internet."

"Your son, Evan. Can you tell us why your son couldn't join us today?"

"Two nights after the cougar killed my dog, Evan sat out with his rifle to protect the sheep. He heard some noise and went over by the shed to see what was going on. The cat was on the shed roof with one of my lambs in its jaws, about to jump the fence. Evan must have spooked it, and it jumped on him. Its claws dug right into his shoulder. They had to do surgery at the hospital."

"In your opinion, Mr. Danna, is this animal dangerous?"

Before he could answer, a wiry fellow stepped in front of the camera. "Ah course it's dangerous, ya dern fool. I been huntin' four-legged killers all my life. When you get an animal like this that keeps comin' around, it's only a matter of time before someone else gits hurt or maybe even kilt."

The reporter jumped in. "Folks, this is Dewey Brewer of

Possum Lake Lodge. Thank you for joining us today. Mr. Brewer, you've been a professional big game hunter for quite a few years. What do you think needs to be done?"

"That cat needs to be run to ground. I've got a pack of the best dogs anyone's ever seen in the north country ready to go. That's just what we're goin' to do—run that cat to ground. I won't tell ya exactly when 'cause I don't want a big crowd of people getting my dogs all worked up, but it's goin' to be soon."

The reporter took over again. "The Department of Natural Resources has asked people to report any sightings of the cougar as quickly as they can, noting the location and, if possible, taking a photograph of the animal. Under no conditions should anyone try to approach the cougar. The animal was last encountered in eastern Namekagon County, but according to experts, it can travel quite a distance in a short period of time. Reported sightings should go to the Namekagon County Sheriff's Dispatch Center.

The news broke to a commercial.

"Welcome back. I'm Robin Rebels bringing you *your* news. I am joined by two cougar experts, Professor Newlin from the college and Dr. Pederson Kouper, a veterinarian and specialist in large predatory animals. Thank you for taking time out of your busy schedules to talk with me. First, let me ask you, Dr. Kouper, it has been reported you were already in the area when these recent attacks occurred. Is that correct?"

"Yes, I have been in the area for quite a while," Dr. Kouper replied.

"Can you please elaborate? What brought you to Namekagon County?"

"First, I was actually called to Sande County just west of Namekagon. There had been several reports of large predators or a large predator preying on domestic animals. It was initially assumed to be a wolf pack, but after further investigation, DNR and USDA field staff found some inconsistencies with that conclusion. They had gathered evidence at each site and asked if I would come and look things over. I did as asked."

"Have you made a determination?" asked the reporter.

"After reviewing the evidence, we concurred. Some of the predation was the work of wolves. In one case, it was a black bear. However, in at least three other cases, it was clearly the work of some kind of cat. One may have been a bobcat, but the other two were a cougar. In one case, there were clear tracks. In another, the cat had squeezed through a barbed wire fence and left hair behind."

"What did you do when you learned that a cougar was roaming the area?"

"Well, we would have done nothing in most cases. The cougar was likely just passing through and would continue on its way. Cougars are occasionally seen in Wisconsin. However, one of the farmers had sustained some substantial losses on two different occasions and was rightfully upset. We agreed to place some live traps around the area of his farm along with trail cameras. Ten days later, the video showed a large mature cougar walk right around the live trap and leap the pasture fence. Cows and calves put up a ruckus, and the farmer ran outside with his shotgun. He didn't get a shot off but got a good look at the animal as it jumped back over the fence and disappeared into the night."

"Is it the same animal that is now in Namekagon County?" Rebels asked.

"I don't know," Kouper replied.

"How about you, Professor Newlin? Is it the same cougar?" She pushed a little harder. "Didn't you just get a new video of a cougar at Hugh Danna's farm?"

"We did, but it is impossible to tell if it's the same animal," Newlin answered.

"How many cougars do you people think are roaming Namekagon County?" she pressed.

"Dr. Kouper, Professor, isn't it true there is a killer cougar on the loose in Namekagon County? Isn't it true you have definitive proof? How many attacks have there really been? People need to know!" she said in a feigned agitation.

Dr. Kouper, in a gesture of peace, held up his hand to the reporter. The reporter stopped speaking.

"May I ask you a question?" he asked.

The reporter looked surprised but gave an accenting nod.

"What did you have for lunch today?"

"For lunch? What did I have for lunch?" she asked.

"Yes, for lunch," he repeated.

The videographer focused in on the reporter's face.

"I had a cheeseburger, onion rings, and a glass of water," she replied.

"A meat cheeseburger, I presume?"

"Yes," she replied.

"Now, just one more question on a more personal note. Do you have any children?"

Now I could see the reporter was interested in where this was going. She answered right away. "Yes, I have two sons."

"Ah-ha. Well, Robin, you have just fulfilled the prime directive of nature. For a population to be sustainable, the members of that population need to do two things: take in adequate sustenance and procreate. If one of those is missing, the population will eventually cease to exist. You have two sons, and you ate a cheeseburger for lunch and drank water. You are no different than the cougar. Like you, the cat must catch his food and find a mate if the cougar population is to be sustainable. The big difference is that we don't demonize you for having a cheeseburger and two sons. Yet you demonize the cougar for doing what has been prescribed as survival for him and his kin for generations."

The reporter stood mouth agape.

Dr. Kouper continued, "Robin, you are a reporter. Have you ever had the misfortune of reporting on a fatal car accident?"

A sad look crossed her face. "Yes, yes, I have. It involved a drunk driver."

"Dangerous thing to be on the road with drunk drivers. Or should I call them killer drivers? Each year in this state, far too many people are killed by drunk drivers. No one in recorded history in this state has ever been killed by a cougar. Now, who is dangerous? This cougar will eventually have to pay the price for coming too close to civilization, encroaching on our carefully deeded and measured pieces of his homeland. Only an unrealistic fool anthropomorphizes wild animals. He is neither a devil nor an angel, but we are scared to death that he's waiting for us around the next corner. I have absolutely nothing else to say on the matter." Dr. Kouper and Professor Newlin walked away from the camera.

Ron shut off the screen and turned to me. "You know I've been around this community a long time. Things like this have a way of snowballing. Dewey Brewer wants to be the guy who gets that cat. He'll be down at the tavern right now telling everybody how he's the only man for the job. If he does get it, it'll be replayed around here for a decade or more. If I were the sheriff, and by the way, I'm pleased that I am not, I would call Hugh Danna and find out when they'll go after the cougar and tell him you'll be there."

"What about everyone else—Charlie, Dr. Kouper, the DNR?"

"John, they can worry about themselves. I'd give Hugh Danna a call right now if I were you."

I took Ron's advice and called him. He answered the phone.

"Hugh, John Cabrelli."

"Hi, Sheriff. I guess you must have heard. We're going after the cat first thing in the morning. If you called to try and stop us, don't.

We're going no matter what."

"No, I'm not going to try and stop you, but I am going with you," I replied.

"I'll need to check with Dewey."

"Check with him all you want, but I'll be at your place in the morning."

"I guess I'll see you then, Sheriff. We figured to head out about eight."

"See you then, Hugh."

As I left Ron Carver's store, Dr. Pederson Kouper called.

"I suppose you've heard they are going after the cougar," he said.

"Dr. Kouper, I just talked to Hugh Danna. He said they're going tomorrow morning. I invited myself to go along with them."

"Will they allow the professor and me? We really need to be there, as well as the DNR."

"It is not my dance, Pederson. I don't get to decide who gets invited. But your request illustrates a valid point. Who needs to be there? What makes this operation legal? I don't think I have the authority to authorize a cougar hunt. I don't know that I don't. Next, this thing is going forward tomorrow morning, and I am guessing this will be our best chance to find the cougar. Once those dogs get on him, he'll probably be out of our hair and start causing trouble elsewhere. You, the professor, and all sorts of other people have been discussing what to do. So, what would be your plan?"

"Valid points, Sheriff. Do you think we could locate Dewey Brewer and Hugh Danna?"

"I just talked to Hugh on his landline, so I'm guessing he's at the farm. I'm pretty sure I know where I can find Dewey."

"It would probably be beneficial if everyone involved in this got together and talked things over. Could we meet at your office?"

"That will work. Also, do me a favor, Dr. Kouper. I hate learning about things secondhand, much less third- or fourth-hand. So when might I get a look at the newest cougar video?"

"Sorry, Sheriff. One of the grad students posted it before I even saw it. It will be on its way to you immediately."

The video came over a few minutes later. While I tried to watch it with an objective mind, it was chilling. One minute there was nothing, and then an apparition-like form appeared. The apparition came closer and turned into what was no doubt a very large cougar. The high-resolution video showed loose-jointed, rippling muscles as it walked. It turned and began to walk toward the baited live trap, stopping at the entrance. Then the cat turned its head and stared at the camera. Although it sounds ridiculous, I felt like it was staring directly at me, its predatory eyes locked with mine. At that point, I had a strong feeling that we had underestimated this animal.

I got a hold of Hugh again, and he agreed to meet. He told me where Dewey might be. I stopped at a local tavern and found him holding court with a bunch of his buddies.

He looked up at me from his bar stool and said, "So, Sheriff, my cousin Hugh says you're goin' along with us. Is that right?"

"I am going with you, Dewey."

"Are you fit to chase after a pack of dogs? Pretty good shape, are ya? Once we get goin', I ain't gonna have time to look for no stragglers. Them dogs might run for a fair number of miles before we bring that cat to bay. It'll wear a man out in a hurry."

Dewey Brewer wasn't a tall man, not much over five and a half feet, and not an ounce of fat. His bare arms were long ropey muscles, his hands rough and calloused. A lifetime of chasing dogs who were chasing bears would tend to keep someone fit. My guess was that running his dogs, he left many a hunter huffing and puffing behind.

"Dewey, if you've got the time, I was wondering if you might be able to meet over at my office."

"Why and when would you want to do that, Sheriff?"

"Now, if you can," I replied.

"What's the meetin' for?"

"To figure out how all this with the cougar is going to go down."

"Sheriff, I can sure save you some time there. I'm goin' out to Hugh's place in the morning. I will get my dogs all set and let 'em go. If you're a betting man, put your money on me havin' that cat up a tree by noon. What you do then will be up to you boys. If you have any brains at all, you'll kill him right there. If he's dead, he won't come back to bother us. That's the other thing, Sheriff. If you might be the shooter, don't bother bringing that plastic .223 rifle you boys carry in your cars. Your shotgun with buckshot will work if you end up nose to nose. You might be a bit more prepared with something a little bigger. If he's up a tree and you shoot him, you better hope that he's dead when he hits the ground, 'cause if he's not, I think we are goin' have ourselves a five-gallon bucket of trouble. Nick Cabrelli was your uncle, isn't that right?"

"Yes," I replied.

"A few years ago, I tried to trade Nick out of a rifle—a model 94 Winchester lever action, a real early one, saddle ring carbine, chambered in 30-30. That would be just what we might need for tomorrow. You still have that rifle?"

"Yes, I do."

"When you get back to your place, take that old lever gun out back, nail a target to a tree stump, and make sure it's sighted in. Get it all squared away, and we should be ready for tomorrow."

I was familiar with that rifle; it was one of my uncle Nick's favorites. If I remember correctly, it was made about 1910. Uncle Nick filled the freezer with venison for many years with that gun. Dewey was right; it was a good choice. I'd blast away at a stump when I got home. ▪

CHAPTER 10

If anyone had anything planned that conflicted with the short-notice cougar meeting, they changed it. Just about everyone who had any interest in the issue showed up. Dr. Kouper led things off.

"We need to make some decisions about how we will handle this situation tomorrow. If Mr. Brewer's hounds find the cat, they will likely run it up a tree. Cougars can easily climb way up into the upper branches. Most often, they will find themselves a suitable branch and watch all the dog action from their perch. If we are going to tranquilize the animal, that will be the time to do it," Kouper explained.

Warden Asmundsen asked, "Is that our first plan? To dart him and relocate him?"

Everyone looked at Kouper. "No, it shouldn't be. As much as I regret this, I'm afraid this animal has become too dangerous. He clearly associates humans and food. After direct confrontation, he still comes back to Dannas'. The animal needs to be killed, and I will defer to the hunters here."

"I guess that means me then, don't it?" Dewey said. "Here is what I been thinkin'. I had myself a look around Hugh's place. I think that cat has been layin' low near that ravine to the back of the number two pasture. It can come and go and not be seen. It may be bedding down at the very end of that little ravine. Nobody ever really chased after it, so it figures this is as good a place as it can find. Sheep to eat, water running through the ravine, and plenty of cover. If we start with a wide loop on the other end of the ravine, he'll have to decide to run toward the farm or break cover and run for it. I think he'll run for it, and the dogs will be all over him. With all those big trees, he's got plenty of places to climb. Who is gonna be the shooters then? I want the sheriff there for sure. If things get crazy out there, he's sure not one to run."

"I'll be the other one," said Jeb Barzine.

"That'll do it then. Sheriff, you and Mr. Barzine be there all set and ready to go at eight tomorrow morning in Hugh's driveway.

"Professor Newlin and I will also be on-site," Dr. Kouper added.

"That'll be fine, but we ain't waiting for you if you can't keep up. I usually run the dogs by myself or, at the most, with one more person. So, we'll be pushin' it. You and the professor there, just don't complicate things. I don't know how this critter is going to react, but I guess we'll find out."

"Fair enough, Mr. Brewer. We'll stay out of the way," replied Kouper.

A few years ago, I would never have imagined I would be chasing a cougar behind a pack of hound dogs. Tomorrow that would change.

After the meeting, I checked in, and things seemed to be well under control. Then I drifted down one road to the next. I checked a minor accident at the edge of town and helped a group of bicyclists with directions to the path along the river. One of the cyclists asked me if the cougar had been seen anywhere near where they were headed. I told them not that I was aware of.

I stopped at Happy Hooker Bait and Tackle to pick up a copy of the *Outdoor News*. The lead story in their newest issue was about cougar habits and biology. Jeb Barzine from the DNR explained one of the main differences between mountain lions and wolves: Cougars are solitary beasts that only come into intentional contact with others of their kind during breeding and hunt using stealth, tremendous strength, and athletic ability. Wolves are very social pack animals that hunt together.

The story also quoted Dewey Brewer, who maintained that no one in Namekagon County would be safe until that cat was dead, encouraging everyone going anywhere in the back county to take a gun with them and shoot the animal on-site.

Warden Asmundsen detailed the law regarding cougar protection and the penalties. He went on to say that if you, your livestock, or any other domesticated animal were threatened or attacked by a wild animal—cougar or otherwise—it was legal to kill the animal.

I arrived home early for a change, and the house was empty. Today the quiet in the cabin and the fresh breeze off the lake seemed perfect, and I was soon asleep in my uncle's old chair.

An hour later, the rumbling noise of a four-door, four-wheel drive diesel truck shook the windows when it pulled in.

Bud jumped out and bellowed, "Hello, the cabin! Anyone home?" Bud had adopted this call once I moved into the main house with Julie to make sure the coast was clear for a visit. Next, he would knock on the front door and wait for an answer. It was a good system, although not yet perfected.

"Hey, Bud. I'm here. Come on in."

"John, what are you doing home so early? I figured you'd be tied up downtown 'til late."

"Truth is, Bud, I guess I was more tired than I thought, so I came home for a little break. Got a big day tomorrow."

"What's up tomorrow?" he asked.

"I am going along with a hound hunter to try and track down the cougar."

"You mean the one that attacked Evan Danna?"

"That's the one."

"Who has got cougar dogs around here?" Bud asked.

"A relative of Danna's, a guy named Dewey Brewer."

"Dewey Brewer?" Bud asked with an uncharacteristic skeptical tone.

"Yeah. Do you know him?" I asked.

"Yeah, I sure do. I gotta say, I don't like him very much either."

"What don't you like about him?"

"He's a goldarn poacher, that's what. He takes whatever he can get whenever he wants to. Why just last summer Lars Timson, the fish biologist, asked everybody to take it easy on Moose Lake. It's one of the best panfishing lakes around. The rulebook came out and said the panfish limit for bluegills was fifty. It was supposed to say the limit was fifteen. He put up signs and asked folks to stick to the fifteen fish a day, or soon there wouldn't be any left. Everybody did what Lars asked except for Brewer. Dewey and a couple other guys went out on the lake when the bluegills were on their beds. They caught one hundred fifty! Two other fishermen called it in to the warden. He told them there was nothing they could do. That's not the worst of it. They're always doing something. If they're chasing that cougar, it's because they want to kill it."

"Well, you're right about that, Bud. That's exactly what they intend to do," I said.

Bud dropped off a repair piece for the boat dock and headed back to town.

I grabbed my fishing rod and walked along the shore until I was just about even with a big old log, the end buried in the mud and what was left of the top just sticking out. Bud and Julie had given me some special lures for Christmas, and I had been anxious to try them out. One was a Rapala ice fishing jig that people were using in open water. I cast out toward the top of the log. It was a perfect cast, as artful as any I'd seen. The lure hit with a splash, and I worked it like a jig. A fish hit it hard on the third jig, and I set the hook. The fight was over quickly—it was a two-foot northern pike. There was no catch and release on northerns, which were considered an invasive species in Spider Lake. I carried the fish to the dock and dropped it into a bucket.

I continued to walk the shore and threw a cast at any likely-looking spots. I was doing a lot of thinking while I fished. Uncle Nick told me he'd come up with some of his best ideas when fishing.

I found myself deep in thought about the cougar. I doubt it would make much sense if I tried to explain it, but I kind of felt like I was going to betray the animal.

Uncle Nick loved to read. He always had a few books by his chair and enjoyed sharing them with me. The titles of the books frequently changed except for one. That book was well worn, the jacket intact but with creases, small rips, and tears. He sometimes took the book with us on hikes and would pull it out while we ate a campfire lunch or sat on the shore and read a section. At first, it was hard to understand the relationship between what he was reading and where I was sitting. But Uncle Nick was patient with me. The first time it sank in was when he and I cut and split a dead oak for firewood. We sat on the log to have a bite to eat.

He got out the book and said, "Johnny, listen to this. 'There are two spiritual dangers in not owning a farm. One is the danger of supposing that breakfast comes from the grocery, and the other that heat comes from the furnace.' You should think about what that means; it's important."

We worked away the afternoon before I started to understand.

Eggs come from chickens, and venison chops come from deer. The wood we were splitting came from the land. A dead oak that would no longer grow would now find its way to the woodstove to warm us on cold days and nights.

He would go on to read something that stuck with me more than anything else. "When we see land as a community to which we belong, we may begin to use it with love and respect."

When my life had taken a difficult turn, I returned to Spider Lake. When I first arrived, I gazed out across the water. It was just as I remembered it—a beautiful jewel set into a wild, untamed landscape.

Spider Lake had not changed. I, on the other hand, had. I was no longer the smiling boy catching bluegills off the dock. I was a man that had been places and done things I would never forget. I had felt heartache and sadness, made choices that had taken me down difficult paths. It was like the figure eight move of a musky lure, one more chance at catching the fish. Spider Lake was my figure eight, the same place at a different time in my life, giving me one more chance.

When I returned, I really began to understand the sense of community and the importance of being a part of the space you occupy. I had found it in the north country. I walked trails that had seen footprints thousands of years before. I shared it with all creatures, great and small. I also found it in the community sharing traditions. I had to ask myself, did I have any more right to the land than the cougar I would try to kill in the morning? Was he not a member of the same community as I was? Maybe he was, but he was potentially dangerous and looking more so every day.

Picking up my bucket, I went into the cabin. I cleaned the pike and put the bone-free fillets in a dish of cold water in the refrigerator. I walked to the bookshelf and retrieved Uncle Nick's special book, *A Sand County Almanac* by Aldo Leopold. I sat in his chair and read the same words from years before—the same words read by a different person at a different time—a figure eight.

Julie drove in, got out of her truck, and came into the cabin. She stepped behind me and gave me a wonderful hug, then she turned my head and kissed me. I stared into her irresistible blue eyes.

"Wow, what was that for?"

She smiled at me and said, "I just love you, John Cabrelli. I'm so happy I finally convinced you to be my husband."

"I thought I had to do all the convincing."

"I know, honey. I know." ∎

CHAPTER 11

I was up early and dressed in my utility uniform—tough field clothes adorned with sheriff ID patches. I grabbed Uncle Nick's Winchester rifle and two identical boxes of 30-30 cartridges. The cartridge was so named because it fired a .30-caliber bullet and contained thirty grains of smokeless powder. I was a fan of the old rifles Uncle Nick taught me to shoot. This lever action was blued steel, with an oil-finished walnut stock and forearm built by the hands of an American craftsman who took great pride in each rifle. None of Uncle Nick's rifles were less than twenty-five years old. I accepted the fact that the highly accurate AR-15 rifles made of durable component parts with high-tech optics and a thirty-round magazine offered a tactical advantage, but the 30-30 was the right rifle for today.

Instead of picking out a stump behind the cabin, I stopped at the Namekagon County Sportsman's Club range. I had a key to the gate, and there was no one else around at this hour. I put up a paper bullseye target at fifty yards and walked back to the shooting bench. With ear and eye protection in place, I settled the rifle in on some sandbags. The rifle was not equipped with a scope; top ejecting shells made that challenging. It was equipped with an aperture sight that centered the front sight. Sights like this one were common with buffalo hunters. The sight showed a mastery of machine work. I levered a round into the rifle's chamber, sighted in on the target, and squeezed the trigger—no jerk, no slap, just a squeeze that surprised me when the rifle went off. I repeated the exercise four more times. I have to say I had forgotten about the crescent steel butt plate. I think the old-timers had tougher shoulders than I do. My five shots were all within about two inches, plenty good for my purposes.

It was a short drive from the range to the Danna farm. I arrived ahead of schedule, but so did everyone else. Three dog heads were sticking out from the boxes in the bed of Dewey Brewer's truck parked in the yard. Hugh and Evan had coffee ready, along with some sweet rolls. Professor Newlin and Dr. Kouper were anxious.

"Sheriff, are you sure that Dewey Brewer knows what he is doing?" asked Professor Newlin.

"Nope. I am not sure at all. This will be my first cougar-chasing operation, and I don't have any idea what to expect. I would say that our expert here is Dewey, and we have to let him run his own show. Have you had second thoughts about having to kill the cougar?"

"Only a hundred or so. But after talking this over, we are all convinced that even relocated, the cat will likely revert to its old habits in a new location. We can't allow that to happen. I do want you to know, Sheriff, I'm glad you asked. It will bring none of us— other than the Dannas or Brewer—any happiness," the professor said.

Dewey buckled a tracking collar on each dog and then snapped a lead to the collar before they got down out of their boxes.

"These are my pals. Bob, he's the boss. Moon, he's Bob's backup man, and two-year-old Cindy here is the pup. They are good bear dogs. Bob, there, has called treed on many a bear. I don't know for sure whether they will run a cougar or not. But we're about ta find out," Dewey announced.

On our way around the ravine, Dewey talked nonstop to his hounds as if they were his children. When we reached the end of the pasture, he knelt by the dogs, petting them, and continued to talk to them softly. Whatever he was saying, it was getting the dogs excited.

Then Dewey asked us, "You boys ready?"

We nodded yes, and he let loose the hounds.

Bob cast wide and fast, looking for scent. Moon was more deliberate, sniffing here, smelling there. Cindy seemed to be partly working, partly playing. We moved further into the forest and away from Dannas' pastures and cultivated fields.

At the opposite end of the ravine, Cindy struck first with a combination of a puppy yelp and a big dog howl. Bob and Moon wasted no time in coming over for the assist. Cindy was barking and baying at a large log. She was game, her hackles up, but she was being cautious.

Dewey made short work of crossing the pasture and getting to his dogs. The log had a large area dug out underneath that looked like a den. Whatever was in there wasn't ready to come out. Bob lost his patience and tried to go into the den. Dewey grabbed the big dog by the collar, snapped the lead back on, and then snapped on Moon's. Cindy was not having any of this. She found it, so it was hers. Finally, the biologist got her by the collar, and Dewey gave him a lead. The dogs were still causing a commotion until Dewey yelled, "Quit." Bob and Moon settled right down; Cindy took a little more talking to.

Dr. Kouper, Professor Newlin, and the warden approached the den. The warden and I had our rifles ready.

"No need, gentleman. The cougar is not here," Kouper said confidently.

He then took a small flashlight out of his field vest pocket and shined the light inside the area under the log. He reached in and dragged out what was left of one of Dannas' lambs.

Then he examined a poplar tree next to the log. Long vertical gouges were cut into the trunk. He replaced his flashlight and pulled a tape measure from his pocket.

"Professor Newlin, could you please photograph the measurements?" The professor began. Dr. Kouper found measuring the height of the scratches difficult. They were finally determined to be a bit over seven feet up the trunk.

"My Lord," Kouper whispered to himself. "This is a very large animal."

"What do we have here?" I asked.

"Good question, Sheriff," Kouper responded, regaining his calm, matter-of-fact demeanor. "This is a temporary den. The cougar stashed the remains of a meal here and likely would have returned for a snack. The scratches on the tree are something altogether different. Cougars do this for several reasons. Scent is left on the trees by their paws, and that scent may be his way of advertising for a mate. Cougars' mating period is somewhat variable, especially in an area like this where there are few potential candidates. The other interesting thing about these scratches is that the cougar is likely marking his territory, and it's a warning to anyone who would trespass. By the looks of this tree, the cougar has been here many times."

The biologist looked closely. "There are a lot of tracks, and they look pretty fresh."

"Don't some look a little smaller to you?" Jeb asked Kouper.

"I suppose it's possible but hard to tell," he replied.

"I pulled my dogs back because I was expectin' a mountain lion to come boiling out of that hole and run smack dab into my dogs. That cat smell sure got them worked up. I ain't never seen Bob so itchin' for a fight. He knows his way around keepin' clear from a bear, but a big cat, who knows. Looks like we're done here, so let's turn the dogs loose again and see what they can find."

The leads off, the hounds worked their way deep into the forest. It was tough going; blowdowns crisscrossed each other. The dogs kept working but came up empty. By the time we came out of the timber, we were spent and needed a breather. About noon, Dewey called the dogs back and gave them some fresh water and a snack.

"I think we might try and run down the old logging trail below us. I've hunted this country quite a lot, and there's a low, long valley up ahead. I shot many a deer in there and a bear or two. The going is a bit easier. It leads to Old Boot Lake, a small, weedy lake with a lot of wild rice. Doesn't get many visitors; it's a long walk in."

After the dogs were rested and ready, we headed out again. We hiked toward the fire lane and stopped on a small rise to look over the land. Dewey was carefully watching his dogs. Bob was working the ground with new interest.

Dewey spoke up. "Everybody needs to pay attention here. Old Bob has got something he's trying to work out." As if on cue, Bob leaped down off the ridge and sounded off. Moon was quick to follow, with Cindy not far behind. The hounds ran downhill toward the fire lane out of sight. The chase was on—bear or cougar, no one knew yet.

Suddenly the hounds sounded almost frantic. We picked up our pace, attempting to close the gap, but they were moving rapidly away from us. Dewey guided us with GPS toward the ravine. The howling ceased, and the woods exploded with the sounds of a full-blown dogfight. Moments later, the howling dogs gave chase again.

"Whatever they's running, they's doin' it by sight," Dewey yelled while leaping through obstacles. "We gotta catch up to them dogs, or this is gonna be bad, real bad."

We reached the ravine, but the dogs seemed even further away. We had no choice but to continue to follow them. We could not take the same route they had taken and had to loop to the north and back around to the west.

Finally, the dogs cried treed. As fast as we could, we closed on them. The ruckus got louder as we neared, but before we could find the dogs, everything broke loose with the unmistakable sounds of a battle—dogs growling and fighting and a noise that could be nothing else but the snarl and scream of a cougar.

Again, the chase was on, running down slope away from us. Dewey checked his tracking collars to pinpoint the dogs. Two tracking collars were in motion, and one did not move at all.

It was almost another quarter-hour of brush busting before we came to a small clearing with a large rock backstop ringed with tall pines. Cindy lay on the ground covered in blood.

"Oh, my Lord. Not my little Cindy. Oh no, oh no. Is she dead?" cried Dewey.

Dr. Kouper had kept up with us and immediately knelt by Cindy to assess the situation. He pulled a medical kit from his backpack. Kouper had made his bones in veterinary medicine long ago and treated everything from kittens to cows, canines to equines. Only in the last few years had he developed his work on large predators. He gently looked her over.

"Dewey, she is badly injured but still alive. I will attend to her. You guys can continue to track the dogs. Charlie can assist me here," he suggested.

Dewey appeared to be in a daze but replied, "Yeah, okay. Yeah, we better get on it."

After a half-hour, we returned with both dogs on leashes. Moon looked pretty much unscathed. Bob was a warrior and showed plenty of signs of the battle. Kouper examined him and said he looked worse than he was and temporarily treated his wounds but recommended taking him to the clinic.

His major concern was Cindy. She was in tough shape. Kouper began by gently moving Cindy's front and hind legs. Her lacerations were horrible, one straight to the bone on her left shoulder. At one point, Cindy came around for a second, likely driven by pain. Charlie held her steady while the vet gave her a sedative to keep her still and treat each wound. The wounds were temporarily bound, and Cindy was slid carefully onto a partial sheet of plywood that Hugh had brought via ATV after a call from Dewey.

No one had much else to say. Everyone expected the cougar to tree. It had chosen not to, even though there were plenty of trees to choose from. Faced with the age-old decision "flight or fight," it had picked fight.

As gently as possible, we loaded Cindy on the back rack of the four-wheeler. Dewey called his vet and told her he was coming in with two hurt dogs. She said she'd be ready.

Kouper and Newlin followed Dewey to the clinic. Jeb, Warden Asmundsen, and I went our separate ways.

Exhausted, I called dispatch, who thankfully advised everything was quiet. I told her I was headed home but would keep my pager on.

The animal we were chasing had proven himself to be formidable. The big cat had likely found a home in the north country, and it could have been here for weeks, months, or years. People out hunting or hiking may have gotten a glimpse of something, but this animal had not lived to maturity by being careless. Charlie had told me, "You usually don't see a cougar unless it wants you to."

After what happened today, this cougar would be demonized, and packs of humans would hunt it to exhaustion and then kill it. The dead cat would be loaded in the bed of a pickup truck and driven to every watering hole in Namekagon County. Maybe my sympathies with the cat were because we had something in common. I, too, had fought for my life. Words can never adequately describe the experience.

Sympathy or not, there was another side to this coin. The Dannas were honest, hardworking folks, members of our community, good friends, and good neighbors. They didn't look for the cat; the cat found them. Dewey was a hunter, a predator like the cougar. His dogs were like his children, and though he knew the possibilities, he had still pursued a dangerous animal with tragic results. How do we strike a balance? It was something that had been going on since prehistory and would likely continue in some form forever.

I was sure this would end badly for the cougar. The question was what the cost would be. He knew now that he was being hunted, a situation he had probably faced before.

While I considered myself in pretty good physical shape, I woke the next morning stiff and sore with a new array of bumps and bruises I didn't specifically remember acquiring. Chasing the hounds had shown improvement was necessary. Julie and Anna were still asleep when I put on my swim trunks and walked to the water's edge next to the dock. I waded out in a sandy area with only a few foot-poking branches and immediately began to feel the rejuvenating powers of the lake. Even though it was officially summer, the waters of Spider Lake still had a chill. Once the water was waist deep, I dove in headlong and swam toward the opposite shore, with each stroke feeling better and stronger.

Reaching my destination, I hauled myself up on a rock to catch my breath and surveyed all that was before me, the untarnished natural beauty of the north country, my home. A voice called out. I looked up and saw a beautiful wooden boat row toward me. It was Jack Wheeler.

Jack had recently purchased an old lodge across the lake from my place. As part of the deal, he had gotten a 1940s vintage rowboat, still all there but badly in need of tender loving care. Sheamus Ruwall, a local craftsman specializing in wooden boat restoration, had worked magic to bring the boat back to life. Weather permitting, Jack rowed the boat back and forth each morning between the two points. Sometimes he fished. Sometimes, he didn't.

"Hello, John. How are you doing on this wonderful day?" Jack asked.

"Counselor, I am doing just fine, a little stiff and sore from yesterday's adventures, but all-in-all, in one piece," I replied.

"What were you up to yesterday?" Jack asked.

I filled him in on the previous day's events.

"Does the predator expert seem to know what he's doing?"

"Between Dr. Kouper, Professor Newlin, and the DNR biologist, there is an amazing amount of knowledge and experience. That's what concerns me a little bit," I replied.

"How so?"

"Well, Counselor, the predator expert has dealt with things like this all over North America. I think this one has him worried."

We talked for a few minutes more. Jack started to row off to throw some casts for muskies when I noticed a big lure on his line. Until then, I knew he mostly fished with spinners, number four and five bucktail Mepps.

"What is that big plug you have on the end of your rod, Jack?"

"It's a Suick, made right here in Wisconsin. This one is perch colored. There is a school of thought regarding musky fishing that says for bigger fish, use bigger lures. I am a fan of bigger fish, so here I am."

"Any luck so far?"

"Actually, yes. I have raised a big fish off the end of the point twice, both times while I was casting this Suick. My technique may have been a little flawed. I got a few pointers from the guy down at Happy Hooker. He said the way to work this bait is to cast as far as I can past where the fish has come up, let the lure sit on the surface for a while, then jerk it, reel up the slack, and repeat. I believe it will be a sound strategy. If you hear me yelling, bring a bigger net."

"I'll listen for you, Jack," I chuckled.

He rowed in one direction, and I swam off in the other, propelling myself along with a leisurely breaststroke. Halfway back, I saw two heads coming toward me. Seems Anna and Julie also decided a swim was a good way to start the day. When I reached them, they turned around and swam back with me. We toweled off on the dock.

Anna whipped up some tea, I brewed dark roast coffee, and we sat on the porch discussing the day. Anna was booked solid for the next couple of days. The race would start tomorrow morning at seven and would end with the medal ceremony on Sunday.

Julie was helping her students in the Northern Lakes booth, selling school logo t-shirts, sweatshirts, and the new addition Northern Lakes Academy caps. They were also in the home stretch of taking donations to support their ongoing partnership with DNR Fish Biologist Lars Timson putting PIT transponders in musky fingerlings. The kids had made a real eye-catching Adopt a Musky sign, and as a result, sales and donations were booming.

Later that morning, I met Chief Delzell at a park in the middle of town. We had almost everything taken care of with less than twenty-four hours to go. However, there were always details and brush fires to stamp out.

"John, I think all the fill-in officers and deputies have checked in. They are attending to anything that might require a sworn person's attention. The 'green shirts' are doing a great job with everyone else, keeping things moving."

"I warned Anna and Julie to keep a lookout for Stephen Cameron. Have you seen him?" I asked.

"As a matter of fact, yes, I have. He has been very visible, hanging out and partying with some of his celebrity buddies, laughing it up. I've been walking around, and whenever I get close to him, he gives me that phony smile," the chief said.

"Do you know where he's staying?" I asked.

"I am almost positive he is staying in one of those fancy lodges on Big Buck Lake. I ran into Christi from the Catering Corner, and she said they have her booked solid, requesting local fare, so the first meal she served them was cheeseburgers, walleye cheeks, and beer. She said they loved it."

"If I get the chance, I need to check that out," I said.

"He hasn't been any trouble that I know of, but that could change. Speaking of trouble, what is going on with that cougar? Is it really some sort of crazed wildcat?" Delzell asked.

"I'm sure if you asked some folks, they would swear it is. Dewey Brewer brought his dogs over, and we tried to catch up with the cat. That did not work out like we thought it would."

"I hate to ask, John, but is there any risk to the racers? At one point, the course runs close to Dannas' farm."

"I never thought about it, and you're right. According to Dr. Kouper, those cats can cover a lot of ground quickly. Let me call him."

Kouper answered right away. "Anything for me, Sheriff?" he asked anxiously.

"No. How about you?"

"The agency people have attempted to track the cat again

around Dannas' farm with no success. I don't think they had the best dogs. After what happened to Brewer's dogs, most local hound hunters seemed to have lost interest in risking their valuable bear dogs. Some folks in their summer cabin over a dozen miles away from the Dannas got several pictures of a cougar on their trail camera. They sent the photos over, and while it was impossible to be sure, it was likely the same animal.

"The houndsmen are going to that location in the morning to see if they can get something. In the meantime, there have been several reports of cougar sightings; most have been unfounded. We keep trying to follow up on each as best we can. People are getting spooked. Sheriff, I really hope that cat has moved on," Kouper said.

"Dr. Kouper, I need to ask you something."

"Go ahead, Sheriff."

"We have the race tomorrow. One part of the planned course goes in the direction of Dannas' farm. Any chance that we might have trouble with this cat attacking a runner or spectator?"

"Not likely. Never say never, but not likely. If the trail cam photos are the same animal, that puts him twelve miles further away from where the race is, not a great distance, but some space anyway. I also think the cat would hesitate to attack a person in a large group. They prefer solitary prey. But again, with this one, who knows," he said. ▪

CHAPTER 12

The Great Wilderness Race was held in a different location with a course designed to offer unique challenges based on terrain and culture. The racecourse approved by the race committee was a rugged one through the Chequamegon-Nicolet National Forest.

This year, teams of four—two men, two women—would begin in tandem kayaks, paddling for twenty-five miles on a fast-flowing river where skill would be required to navigate without flipping over. They would use a compass and map to get to a location where the river splits and takes two directions. There the team had to make their choice—no turning back. Each choice would have its challenges. If they successfully followed either course, they would come to a small landing. At the landing would be an eight-foot-long poplar log, one cant hook, two blocks to set the log on, and a crosscut saw. Using the cant hook as a lever, teams needed to set the log onto the blocks so two people, one on each end of the crosscut saw, could cut through the eighteen-inch thick log. The cut piece would be handed to one of the judges standing by, who would sign it and write the time on it.

Then next leg of the race was on foot, using a map and compass to cover twenty or more miles and find their way to the next checkpoint and lumberjack challenge where another log awaited. One team member would chop through a ten-inch thick log using an axe. They were allowed to call "switch" once and have another team member take over without penalty. Once the log was cut through, the judge would mark the time again and send them off.

The final leg was thought to be the most challenging. Teams headed off on mountain bikes across terrain ranging from a flat fire lane to up and down extreme hills. For twenty-five miles, they would traverse the landscape. It was about speed but also required highly technical riding skills. At every downhill, racers were tempted to make up time, knowing that if they did, they increased the risk exponentially. The mountain bike leg brought them to the last lumberjack challenge, boom running. Floating logs were chained together, end to end, and tired legs had to carry each team member across the boom to the finish line. The time would not be recorded until the last team member crossed. The estimated time to complete the race was a grueling thirty hours.

A lot of people couldn't believe that others would choose to put themselves through such torture. But when the time came to sign up, top qualifying teams were registering from all across North America. The team with the best time and fewest deductions would win a substantial cash prize and product endorsements. Maybe that was enough incentive, but not likely. It was all about the challenge.

The competitors were tough and fit, ranging from brawny lumberjacks to running speedsters. Each team had a strategy they hoped to employ, and every team member was an expert at some aspect of the race. Everyone was welcome to attempt to qualify for the race, amateurs and professionals. Teams traveled across the country during the previous two years, competing to earn points that would get them to the championship. With one exception, the sponsoring community was allowed to enter one team that had not accumulated the number of points required of the other teams. The promoters figured it would bring the community out for the event. It did that and then some. Four years before, a local team with no qualification points had won the championship. Now it was billed as the ultimate test of strength and endurance, where anything could happen. Musky Falls fielded a tough team: a fourteen-time Ironman competitor, an experienced wilderness racer, a world-champion lumberjack, and a high school coach.

The race's media team worked overtime, interviewing competitors, past winners, celebrities, and sponsors. Twelve teams would start the race, and no one had any idea how many would finish. Some on the inside said it was the most demanding course they'd seen in several years. However, there had been over fifty entries for the twelve spots. Because of how the course was laid out, there were plenty of opportunities for spectators to watch different portions of the event and then move on to another leg or the finish line.

The race teams were all standing in front of the stage. It was unlikely that any group could be more diverse. As the teams were introduced, each seemed to have its own cheering section. The Voice of the North introduced Anna MacDonald. She talked about the difficulty of the course and how people had come from all over the United States to compete.

She said, "I can't help but point out that not one, but two teams from Wisconsin qualified for this race—one of them homegrown right here in Namekagon County. Whether competing on their home ground will make any difference will remain to be seen. Now, if the captain of each team will come forward." The Voice of the North handed Anna a red bucket with "FIRE" in big letters on the side.

Anna explained to the crowd, "Each captain will pull a slip from the bucket, and the slip will have a number. That number will be the order in which the teams begin, with fifteen-minute start-time intervals. Teams will have their total time individually recorded— how long it takes to get from start to finish and complete all the tasks on the way."

Anna climbed down the steps from the stage. The team captains were all lined up. Each pulled a number from the bucket. Teams expressed little displeasure from the starting numbers. It was a fair process. A team from Colorado drew number one. They handed the number over to a judge and stepped to the start. The crowd waited with anticipation. Anna raised a blank revolver in the air and pulled the trigger. The Colorado team took off at top speed, racing to the river landing. One member braced the kayaks for the others to get in, then jumped in himself. They wasted no time and headed downriver with powerful strokes, rounding the river bend into the rapids within five minutes.

It was fast-paced action from then on. The Alabama team lost one of their kayaks at the landing only to be saved by a powerful swimmer among them who caught the rope before the boat went downstream sans crew.

It was clear to those watching that each team had developed its own strategy, and a good part of that was the selection of team members. Cameras were set up at each lumberjack challenge, and live video was transmitted to a bank of jumbo screens so people at the stage area could watch. The kayaking went well despite the challenges of maneuvering a tandem kayak.

A couple of teams began to fall behind during the trekking. Other teams had members with expertise in orienteering and moved as quickly as possible, walking fast and jogging.

Halfway through the race, three teams had dropped out due to sustained injuries and two more from exhaustion. Both Wisconsin teams were still in it, jockeying for position. Teams had to make critical choices—they had to eat, drink and rest. Without doing those things, unless they were superheroes, they could not finish. Stopping was a double-edged sword. Too long and the fatigue catches up and muscles begin to tighten and cramp; too short and the steam needed to finish will not be there.

Twenty-four hours after the starting gun, the Colorado and Wisconsin teams were neck and neck. A sunny morning greeted the racers' weariness, and determination pushed them on. The Colorado team was gaining time. The Wisconsin team got to the log run and dumped their bikes. Then began the precarious journey across the logs. No one was running; they were carefully walking and trying to keep their balance. One team member crossed over without a hitch. All the others splashed into the water and had to start over. The more attempts they made, the harder it was, but finally, they all finished.

Colorado figured on making up time through the mountain bike leg. The four team members came down the hill as fast as possible. They were riding with reckless abandon, hitting the staging area for the bikes at almost the same time. They flew off their bikes and started on the logs. Halfway across, one of the team members took a nasty fall that resulted in what is known as a banana split. He could not again regain the logs, and the team finished one short.

Over the next two and a half hours, the teams that were going to finish had. Racers were kept back from the crowd and given the opportunity to rest, eat something, and rehydrate. The medical team led by Dr. James from Musky Falls Hospital attended to injuries and evaluated the racers' overall condition.

The winning time was 28 hours 37 minutes, posted by the team from Wisconsin. Second went to the team from Minnesota, and third to Alabama. To everyone's elation, the local Namekagon

County team took a solid fourth and finished to a round of foot-stomping applause and cheers.

Once all the official times were posted, the three placing teams climbed onto the podium. Anna gave a great speech interrupted twice by applause. Then she presented the medals. The Voice of the North came up next to Anna and announced the beginning of the post-race celebration and the winners of the craft beer contest and the movie festival awards. Taproom exit polls had Happy Minnow as the local favorite brew and *Return of Mossback* as the film festival winner.

After watching the end of the medal ceremony, Chief Delzell and I met in town. Although the event was not quite wrapped up yet, we hadn't had one serious incident, and it looked like we would come in under budget. The chief was already formulating a plan for big events like this in the future.

"John, we should put together special event teams with the sheriff's personnel and city PD working together. Four deputies and four city officers per team. The race reimbursed us for security costs. They willingly overpaid, and we came in enough under budget that we could use the extra funds to start to put this together. What do you think?"

"It sounds like a good plan. I knew it was a good idea for the others on the board to insist we hire you over my objections."

"Funny, John. Very funny."

Our pagers went off simultaneously—an emergency call.

I connected with dispatch just as I heard an ambulance screaming out of town, seeming propelled by the exigency of the situation. A child hiking with her parents on the Musky Run Trail by the Big Bluff overlook sign had been attacked by a cougar. That's all dispatch got from the screaming mother before the call was lost.

I drove as fast as possible toward the trailhead. I was familiar with the victim's location. It was on a rocky, narrow stretch. A sign with an arrow showed where a "one person at a time" footpath would take you up to the top of the big bluff for a spectacular view of the river and surrounding area. No way was it wide enough for my squad or an ambulance. There was a Nordic ski trail crossing about three miles from the bluff. I would have to try to bushwhack my way through. Maybe I could get to them with four-wheel drive and a little luck. The ambulance, however, could not. I talked with the EMTs on the radio. The two of them would jump in with me, and we would try to make our way to the victim. I cut across a meadow and came out at the trail crossing. The ambulance came in behind me.

A quick assessment was all we needed—no way we could use our big vehicles on the trail. We agreed to hike down the trail and, in the meantime, ask Spider Lake Fire to respond with an ATV. I had seen the cougar. A child or adult, for that matter, would have no chance of surviving an attack. Minutes ticked away like heartbeats.

Before we reached the trail, the relatively unmuffled exhaust announced the arrival of a first responder on call for both Spider Lake Fire and Namekagon County Search and Rescue. Locally he was known as Jimmy the Jeep, and he often spent his free time exploring the back roads and fire lanes in his hopped-up, all-terrain Jeep with the top off and his Labrador Bronco riding shotgun.

Jimmy jumped out and asked, "Sheriff, what have you got here?"

"Somewhere down by Big Bluff, a little girl was attacked by a cougar. That's all we have. Fire is on the way with a UTV. We are going to hike in."

"Forget hiking; my Jeep can make it. Let's get the gear loaded and go," he said.

Gear flew in, a backboard was tied to the roll bar, and Jimmy took off.

"Keep your hands and feet inside the vehicle at all times," Jimmy said, half smiling.

He ran the Jeep hard through a clear cut that paralleled the trail, then jumped on a small clearing and popped out on Musky Run. Jimmy hit the gas. The EMTs and I were white-knuckling the roll bar. Bronco must have been used to this because he just seemed to roll with the ride.

The Jeep was up to the task, and so was the driver. We drove as fast as possible, sometimes with the driver's side wheels halfway up the embankment. A turn signal broke off on a tree, he bent his fender when the trail got too tight, and a mirror went. Finally, we came around a bend and saw the family. The Jeep slid and came to a stop two feet from a very narrow spot in the trail between boulders.

I jumped out first. An adult female carrying a child ran to the EMTs. An adult male remained on guard, holding something in his hand.

I drew my weapon and approached the man. "Is the cat still here?"

He pointed toward the top of a six-foot-high outcropping with a can of wasp and hornet spray he was holding. I brought my gun to bear and approached the rock, and the man gamely came along. By the looks of things, if I stepped around the back of the rock, I would have a clear shot at anything sitting on top. I quietly slipped around the edge, the man backing me up with his bug spray.

I jumped out from behind the rock, ready to fire. There was nothing to shoot at. The only thing left of the cougar was its tracks. The animal was long gone.

I went to the child and was relieved to find she was uninjured, as were her mother and father. The Bayens family, Ric, Mary, and seven-year-old Claire, was visiting from Milwaukee.

Mr. Bayens explained what happened. "We rented a cabin for two weeks on the lake. There was a map inside that showed local hiking and biking trails. After being cooped up in the car, we decided a hike was just what we needed. On the map, I saw where we could get on this trail by cutting through the woods behind the cabin. Actually, there was an easy-to-follow path that led to it. We walked along the river. Claire got a bit ahead of us, but not far. That's when I heard a low rumbling noise, not like a growl, more like a deep, menacing hum. I looked up, and there was a mountain lion crouched on the rock. I swear it looked like it was ready to spring.

"This is our first time up north, and I was worried about running into a bear. I tried to buy some bear spray at that little store down the road, but the owner didn't have any. Instead, he gave me this can of wasp and hornet spray. When I saw the wild cat, I didn't know what to do, so I sprayed him in the nose. He let out a horrible growl, and I thought he was going to attack. It must have been enough to send the animal on its way. I have heard about bears around here, but I have never heard of mountain lions."

"I'm glad nothing more serious happened, Mr. Bayens. I think you did the right thing when you sprayed the cat. You probably put a stop to his intentions and kept things here from being a whole lot worse."

I hiked out with the Bayenses on the trail they came in on. Jimmy took his fellow first responders back to where we started, then picked me up at the Bayenses' cabin.

"Jimmy, thanks for the help. That was some kind of driving back there. There were a couple of times I thought we might go over. Glad you had things under control," I said.

"Holy smokes, Sheriff. You weren't the only one who was a

little nervous. I think I will have permanent dents in my steering wheel."

Jimmy headed for home, and I gave Dr. Kouper a call.

"Dr. Kouper, I think the cougar may have just stalked a family." I relayed the story. He was silent.

"Sheriff, cougars generally won't attack groups. That little girl separated from her family, even for a moment, could have represented prey to him. Had the father not sprayed the cat, I hate to think what would have happened," Kouper said. His voice took on a somber tone. "John, I need to say something."

"Go ahead," I replied.

"I am aware of all the local talk about this animal. In situations like these, exaggerations are the rule of the day. We will have our hands full when word gets out about this little girl. It could very well make national news. The tabloids love this kind of thing. You know, 'Killer cougar stalks the north country.'"

"I know. Things are already heating up. The county board chairman wants to call a special meeting under the Public Safety Committee."

"Ah, yes. He called Professor Newlin and me and asked us to make ourselves available."

"I am sure this incident will move that meeting date up."

"Likely so. Well, whenever or wherever it is, Charlie and I will be there."

"I will too."

"Sheriff, that cat was last sighted at least twenty miles from Dannas', which puts it at least twenty miles from the trailhead. It sounds like he's on the move. Something may be inhibiting his ability to hunt normally—first lambs, and now this. Deer, of which there are plenty, should be his first choice. If he's injured in some way, that could complicate things. He will have to eat, and he may have to choose slower, easier-to-catch sources of sustenance."

"Like a little girl?" I asked

"I pray that is not the case."

"Me too, Dr. Kouper. We have to get this cougar."

"Sheriff, I agree. I am not confused about prioritizing the value of human life."

Chairman Stewart immediately called a public meeting set for the next evening. He was on the local radio channel, and the electric sign at the bank broadcast the time and date. The *Namekagon County News* put the information out on their e-news. ∎

CHAPTER 13

The day after the completion of the Great Wilderness Race, everything was packed up and ready to head down the road to wherever it was going. The green-shirted security staff had now turned into a maintenance crew and worked with the city to make sure Musky Falls was as clean as when they found it.

The county board meeting room was packed. Locals, tourists, and reporters all turned out. The Dannas and Dewey Brewer stood along the wall. The county board chairman walked over and shook their hands. I recognized several others in the crowd, including the Bayens family.

The county board chair stepped to the podium, called the meeting to order, and got right to it.

"I don't believe in beating around the bush," he said in a loud voice. "Those of us who live in and visit the north country are used to an occasional encounter with wild animals. In fact, it is one of the charms of living where we do. Most of these encounters are harmless, and it is extremely rare that anyone would be injured. However, now we seem to be faced with an animal far more aggressive than usual. I have demanded some answers from the DNR, and they have sent the local wildlife biologist to answer our questions if he will come up here."

The biologist, Jeb, walked up to the podium and faced Scott Stewart.

"Thank you for letting me come here tonight to talk about cougars," he began. "In the last few years, there have been several documented sightings of cougars in Wisconsin—from the urbanized southeastern part of the state all the way up here to the Northwoods. They are all most likely members of the Black Hills cougar community that is expanding its range. We have no evidence that they are breeding in Wisconsin.

"There are some important things to be aware of here. There have been nine bear attacks recorded since 2013, but no cougar attacks. In fact, there has never been a cougar attack on a human in Wisconsin. Not once. Considering the number of encounters with these animals that occur every year, the risk is very, very low. I have some suggestions about how we may—"

"Bullpucky," bellowed Dewey Brewer from the audience. "Jeb here is a pretty good guy, but he's gotta follow orders. Anyway, here we go again, the DNR up to their old tricks. We got a killer lion running loose in Namekagon County, and he's been told to cover up for those fat cats sitting in downtown Madison. Everybody knows DNR trapped these cougars out west and let them out around here. It was all funded by the insurance companies. Cougars eat deer, so more cougars, fewer deer; fewer deer, fewer car-deer crashes, and the less money they have to pay out. It's simple arithmetic.

"The other day, a guy I'd trust with my life—he don't want me to use his name—and I were sittin' down at the Log Cabin Tavern talkin'. One night he was lettin' his dogs out before he hit the sack. A truck with its lights off drove real slow down a two-track that runs next to his house. He followed the truck, and when it came to a clearing, two guys got out. They put down the tailgate, and there was a cage in the truck bed. One of them guys stepped out to the side with a rifle while the other guy opened the cage door. A full-grown cougar let out an awful growl, jumped out of the cage, and ran off into the night. I wouldn't be surprised if it's the same one we're chasin' now. It's easy for you to talk about how harmless these animals are, but my dog is laying in a cage at the vet hospital just a breath or two away from death, thanks to your harmless cougar. What about Evan Danna's shoulder? These cats are natural-born killers. They live to kill."

The crowd joined in, and a good number of the louder ones were with Dewey. Finally, the chairman had to quiet them down, but not until they were sufficiently riled up.

The wildlife biologist started to speak again, but the chairman cut him off, saying, "We've heard enough from you," and dismissed him.

The chairman started again. "We need to do something about this mountain lion now before it's too late."

The crowd rumbled in agreement. He was about to start again when a big man called out from the back of the room.

"Mr. Stewart, mind if I talk for a minute?"

Stewart recognized the speaker. It was Senator Sholz representing Namekagon County. By most accounts, people don't have much time for politicians, and maybe rightly so. That was not the case with this senator. He had been elected year after year; no opponent stood a chance. Folks from both sides of the aisle voted for Senator Sholz. He hunted, fished, and farmed. He could often be found having breakfast at one of the local cafés. When he was in Madison, Senator Sholz was a relentless supporter of his constituents. When he spoke, folks listened. He joined many others in the opinion that Scott Stewart was a windbag.

"Go ahead, Senator, you have the floor."

"Thanks, Mr. Stewart. My question is for you. How do you propose we get rid of this cougar?"

"Kill it. We need to kill that animal," Stewart replied with certainty.

"How do you plan to do that?"

"By whatever means necessary!"

"What does that mean?" the senator calmly asked.

"I know you're a hunter, Senator. I mean, shoot it."

"So that's the plan, Mr. Chairman? How do you intend to get this accomplished? It seems this is a canny and cautious animal. So far, attempts to catch him have not really worked. What do you intend to do differently?"

Stewart puffed out his chest, preparing for yet another proclamation of greatness and demonstrated brilliance. "We are putting up a $5,000 bounty on that cougar. Some of the finest hunters in the Northwoods are right here in Namekagon County. They will take care of business and eliminate this dangerous animal. The crowd roared a menacing cheer.

"Excuse me, Mr. Stewart. May I speak?" Pederson Kouper asked from the audience.

"Why, of course, Dr. Kouper. Ladies and gentlemen, if you don't know who this is, it is the so-called cougar expert sent over here to take care of this problem. It is readily apparent to everyone just how unsuccessful he has been. But Dr. Kouper, by all means, go ahead."

"What if there is more than one cougar?" Kouper asked.

"Is there more than one? Are you withholding information from the public?" Stewart responded.

"At a scratch log we found, there were smaller tracks along with the ones from a big animal. They were hard to see because they were, at the very least, a few days old. It could have been another animal. However, scratch logs are one way cougars leave their scent to attract a possible mate. So, if hunters come upon that animal, will they also kill it? If they do so intentionally, they would be violating the law. I believe the penalty is several thousand dollars in fines, nine months in jail, and the loss of their hunting license for three years. Sounds like a hefty penalty. I doubt your proposed bounty would cover the legal fees. Not to mention, by the way, that I believe it is illegal to offer a bounty on a protected species," Kouper said.

A response came from the back of the room, "I got a shovel." The crowd again rumbled in agreement, this time louder and more sustained.

"We got a right to protect ourselves!" yelled another from the back of the room.

"No judge will convict us for protecting our families," shouted someone else.

More shouts came from around the room. "Go back to where you came from. We can handle it ourselves!"

Dewey stepped up again and told everyone to shut up and sit down. "Don't go getting all over Dr. Kouper there. My little Cindy girl would surely be dead if it weren't for him. I owe him for savin' her. He sure did bring up a point. Now you all know I'm a man of the law. You never catch me poachin'."

The crowd laughed a little, and the woman in the front said, "'Catch' is the word, Dewey."

"Never mind that kinda talk," he replied. "What I want to know from the warden is if someone goes out and kills a cougar, what are you going to do about it? Are you going to arrest the person?"

Warden Asmundsen answered, "Unless the animal poses an imminent threat to the safety of you or one of the animals you own, you can't kill it. You can only kill the cat if it is a threat. Otherwise, my answer is simple. Kill a protected species, and I will absolutely arrest you. For the record, I don't write the laws; I only enforce them. I would guess that goes for Sheriff Cabrelli as well.

"I'm not looking to cause anybody extra trouble, and I know this cat has plenty of people spooked, but I am not going to stand by and watch a dangerous situation unfold and not do something about it. I know most of you, and I bet not one doesn't have a gun in their pocket or a rifle or shotgun in their truck. That reward money isn't going to happen. If somebody does get that cat and violates the law, then we will end up in court. If I were you, I'd let the professionals see what they can do. They have a whole bunch of real experience with cougars," said Warden Asmundsen.

A woman in the first couple of rows raised her hand.

The chairman was back in charge. "Yes, ma'am. Do you have a question?"

"Yes, I do. My family and I are here visiting from Chicago. We had planned to do a lot of hiking and biking on the local trails. What should we do if we do encounter a cougar?"

"That's a very good question. Maybe Dr. Kouper could answer that."

"I would be glad to. If you run into a cougar, face it directly but stare at its feet, not its eyes. Staring at its eyes may cause aggressive behavior. If the animal appears aggressive, raise your arms, pull up your coat, and do anything to make yourself look bigger. If the cougar does not leave, make noise—shout, yell, or do anything to break the cat's attention. If the cat still doesn't leave, throw rocks at it. One thing is for sure, never ever try to run away from a cougar. If you're jogging, stop. Otherwise, there is a good chance that will shift them into predator mode, and the cat will likely chase you. If you are attacked, fight back any way you can," Kouper replied.

"What about a gun?" the woman asked. "Should I take a gun hiking with us?"

"Sheriff, would you like to take that?" asked Kouper.

"Do you have any experience with firearms?" I asked.

"No, none at all," she replied.

"When you are facing a cougar would not be the time to learn. In a stressful situation, even someone with a high level of training finds it difficult to hit the target. The chance of wounding the animal or missing altogether and hitting something you don't intend to is very good. If you want to carry a gun, the first thing you should do is get some expert training. There are firearms safety courses available at many places. I'm sure there are some close to you."

"Sheriff, I live in Chicago. The only people who have guns there are the criminals. What about bear spray?"

Dr. Kouper replied, "Bear spray is just as effective on cougars as it is on bears, in some regards even more so. You may have recently heard a family of hikers ran into an aggressive cougar. They had wasp and hornet spray, the type that shoots over thirty feet. They used it to good effect."

The meeting broke up after several more questions from the audience. The wildlife professionals, working with grad students and four local hunters, set out three more large live traps baited with fresh beef liver and cat food.

I walked out of the building and ran right into Len Bork.

"Hey, Len. What are you up to?" I asked.

"I had planned to attend the meeting, but when I saw all these people and who some of them were, I decided against it. Instead, Ron Carver and I stopped at the Fisherman for a beer. How did the meeting go?"

"I don't know. I can't imagine that anyone can pinpoint the location of that cougar. From what Kouper told me, it could already be fifty miles from here. I just don't know. What I do know is that this has people's attention. It might have a negative impact on tourism if something doesn't change."

"I think you'd be surprised, John. People come here to experience the wild country. Something like a mountain lion sharing the woods with them is all part of the adventure and becomes part of a long list of scary stories around the campfire. Kids are probably already sneaking up behind people, grabbing a leg, and growling at the same time. It'll be all part of the fun. By the way, Martha and I will be over tomorrow night. What's a good time?"

"Julie wants everyone there at five. She'll run us through the wedding plans and then dinner."

"Not that it matters, but what are you guys serving?"

"Marcy's goose stew along with homemade hashbrowns and cornbread."

"I intend to starve myself all day just to make sure I get as much of that food as I can shove in."

"You should be fine, Len, unless you get in Bud's way."

"I may get over to your place a little early just to get a jump start on him."

"Good luck with that, Len. When it comes to dinner, he has perfected the art. The good news is that Julie has been feeding him for years and knows how much to make."

"Who all is coming?"

"Just you and Martha, Bud, Anna, and Julie and me," I said.

"Ah, the wedding tactical unit."

"Pretty much that's what it is."

Tuesday morning, I was gone at first light. I knew I had a bunch of paperwork to do. Among other things, I followed up on cougar sightings, which yielded little until a family had been hiking and got a glimpse of what might be the cat. A teenage girl snapped a quick cell phone photo. Although not the best quality, Dr. Kouper took one look and confirmed it was a cougar. They took the picture at least twenty miles from the Danna farm and ten more miles from Musky Falls.

Julie asked me to try to get home early for our small dinner gathering. On my way there, I thought about how lucky I was to live in one of the most beautiful places on earth. I remembered the commute in the city, lines of traffic and billboards, impersonal structures of poured concrete, every space full, visually overwhelming. Yet, most people could not recall what they had driven past unless it was some notable event, like an accident.

Traveling a north country road is a new experience with every trip. There is much to see, and each traveler fills their own mental north country notebook. It is also something we love to share.

Saw that big old three-footed bear loping down Murphy Road on my way in this morning.

Out on the highway Doc O'Malley was winching old man Jefferd's beat-to-death Suburban onto his flatbed again. Wonder when Doc is gonna get tired of working on it.

We valued these simple shared stories of daily events.

I drove in that afternoon and realized that just about everyone expected had already arrived. Julie, Bud, Len, and Martha were sitting on the porch taking in the afternoon.

Everyone was there except for Anna, who had told Julie she had one morning meeting, after which she was going for a run and planned to be back at the cabin around three for a swim and a shower before dinner. Anna's decision to move back to Musky Falls had added some short-term complications to her life, so her being delayed was completely understandable. She was probably sitting somewhere on a phone call.

At six o'clock, Julie and Bud started expressing concerns about her whereabouts.

"Julie, did she say where she was going for a run?" I asked.

"Musky Run," she replied.

"Musky Run? You're kidding me. What was she thinking?"

"What are you talking about, John? We run and walk that trail all the time."

"That's where the cougar was last seen, Julie—where it stalked a little girl two days ago," I said. "Didn't we talk about this?"

"No, John, we've been like ships passing in the night and have barely seen each other. I didn't hear anything about a cougar at Musky Run, and I doubt Anna did either," Julie said, her voice strained.

We waited a few minutes more, but by six-thirty, Len, Bud, and I were in my squad heading for Musky Run. Julie and Martha stayed at the house in case Anna showed up.

We pulled into the parking lot, and the only vehicle there was Doc O'Malley's Jeep Cherokee—the one Anna had been using. ▪

CHAPTER 14

Musky Run was a rough up-and-down trail that followed the river. It was the favorite of Julie and Anna—few people and beautiful scenery.

I faced Len. "What do you think?"

"She likely sprained an ankle or took a fall. Probably waiting for help to come along. It is anyone's call. My first inclination is that we go looking for her. Any idea which way she might have taken the trail?"

"Julie and Anna run a loop. Let me find out where that goes, exactly."

Julie answered our house phone on the first ring. "John, did you find Anna?"

"No, honey. We are at the trailhead parking lot, and the Jeep is here, but no Anna. What is the loop you run?"

"We take the main trail for about a mile, then take off on a narrow path that goes west up a big hill overlooking the river. We stay on that path until it connects back to the main trail and then to the parking lot. John, I am coming over there right now."

"Julie, stay put. I will let you know what we're going to do. She probably just sprained an ankle. We're going to get this figured out, and I promise once we do, I'll call you and let you know what's going on."

"Okay, fine. But please let me know."

"I will, honey. Don't worry," I answered.

The conundrum we faced required an immediate decision. Light was fading, and we had to decide what to do. Did we take off and try to locate Anna or call for a canine unit? If we tracked up the trail, we risked destroying any scent or ground disturbance that may help the dog. I checked in with dispatch, and they advised that K-9 handler Chad Wichs and his dog Rosie were about a half-hour away. I called the communication center on the phone.

"This is the sheriff. Tell Deputy Wichs to head over to the Musky Run trailhead parking area. Tell him no lights or sirens but to move right along."

"Ten-four, Sheriff. We'll relay your message. Can you advise what you have there?"

"A jogger is a couple of hours late, and we are going to attempt to locate her."

"Do you want additional help?" the dispatcher asked.

"At this point, no. I have Len Bork and Bud Treetall with me, and I want to keep the number of people here to a minimum to give the K-9 the best chance of success."

"Ten-four, Sheriff. Deputy Wichs and Rosie are en route."

As I stood in the parking area and looked out over the Northwoods landscape, an overwhelming feeling of dread washed over me. Len called me over to an area of soft sand by the beginning of the trail.

"Look what we've got here, John. Anna's not the only one on the trail."

There were two distinct cougar tracks in a small patch of sand.

They were pointed in the same direction Julie indicated they most often ran, the same loop where the cougar threatened the little girl. We cautiously tried to follow the tracks, but from the sand, the area turned to rock and had no additional sign tracks we could see.

"We need to wait for the canine, Len. Once he's here, we'll run the track. I'll take my shotgun, and you take my rifle. If we see the cat while looking for Anna, we need to kill it. Every fiber in my body wants to charge off and find her, but the dog is our best chance."

"John, I'll go down and start searching the lower trail right now while you guys wait for the dog," Bud said, clearly anxious to do something.

"Can't do it, Bud. We need to be smart and wait for the K-9 unit. I don't like waiting any more than you."

It seemed like forever before Deputy Wichs pulled in. I explained the situation to him.

"Okay, Sheriff. If you, the chief, and Bud will flank me and give me cover, I'll work the dog. I'll keep her on the long lead."

Wichs opened the rear door of his squad and out jumped a beautiful German Shepard. The dog immediately came to a sit in front of Chad and looked up. The deputy outfitted her with a tracking harness, all the time talking to her calmly, reassuringly. He snapped on the lead and gave her a quiet command. "Good girl, Rosie. Good girl. *Sucken, sucken.*"

The dog began to use its uncanny olfactory senses to survey the area and record the information in her canine brain. Wichs played out the lead as she worked, not restraining her but with enough pressure to let her know she was still attached to her partner.

Rosie walked onto the trail and stopped straight-legged at the pug marks. She bristled not in fear but in the challenge mode, noted by a low and dangerous-sounding growl. The deputy calmed her and knelt beside her. He again spoke to her softly and put her back on the track.

"I hope you guys are paying attention. I don't want to lose my dog to a mountain lion. Those tracks look fresh." Chad was typical of K-9 handlers. These dogs were their partners, friends, and family members. The K-9 deputy's mantra: Don't worry about me; protect my dog.

"We've got you covered, Chad," Len confirmed.

It didn't take Rosie long to get solidly back on task and follow a track. She began to pull at her harness a little when she came to the path that split off to the loop. Then she stopped and laid down, holding still. The deputy shined a light on what had caused the dog to stop.

"Sheriff, we have blood here. You'd better come take a look." As we approached, the K-9 deputy's phone gave an alert tone. He took a quick look at the screen. "Rain moving in any minute. It looks like a lot," he said.

As we looked at a significant amount of blood on the trail, Bud noted something else—drag marks. Something had been dragged across the ground, down the trail loop. Mixed with the drag marks was what looked like another cougar track. I got down close to the marks, blood, and tracks, taking several pictures moments before the rain came. I removed my uniform windbreaker and covered the blood as best I could. Then we were deluged by a downpour the like of which you only get in lake country. Evidence of any sort would now become harder and, in most cases, impossible to find. Tracks would be washed away as if they never existed. It didn't matter. We continued to search, even though the conditions made it difficult. Then the soaking wet dog lay down at the top of the hill overlooking the river. It was a running shoe, the same brand that sponsored Anna—the brand Anna wore.

I contacted dispatch, and they paged out the Spider Lake fire chief. He called me within a couple of minutes. I explained the situation and confidentially shared what we had found. The evidence suggested Anna was still moving, whether under her own power or being dragged. She was alive, and we had to find her.

The population in the Northwoods is small, and most folks like it that way. A small population does not mean small challenges. It is big country and one of the few places left where you can wander just about forever. The first responders are law enforcement and fire when a situation like this presents itself. Each brings a different skill set to the table, working hand in hand. No one wanted to be called out to search on a rainy, miserable night, but they would come anyway.

"Sheriff, I have three firefighters on first responder call, so with me, that is four people we can have on-site pretty quick."

"Pack rain gear."

"We are on the way, Sheriff."

"Thanks, Chief," I replied.

I called Julie to let her know what we had planned.

"Julie, I need you to do a couple of things for me."

"I'm coming out there," she said.

"You can, but first, I need you to do something. You need to go out to Spirit Lake and let Anna's parents know what is happening. Can you do that for me?"

"What should I tell them?"

"Tell them Anna is missing, and we are searching and will not stop until we find her."

Bud, the fire chief, three firefighters, Len, and I formed a line, spreading out along the trail, each of us responsible for the ground immediately to our front and sides. The rain had changed to a drizzle. Deputy Wichs and Rosie took the lead as we headed off. Darkness was quickly closing in on us, and our hand-held searchlights illuminated well but cast shadows. The more tired we became, the more each shadow looked like someone on the ground. We checked out each one. After several miles, the trail loop had been covered, and we sat on the damp ground for a break. Rosie laid her head on her paws. A few minutes later, we were back at it. Predawn arrived, and we were wet, exhausted, and needed to rest. Bud and I stayed where the search stopped, waiting for the fire chief to show up with relief searchers.

Clouds covered the sun, and drizzle continued as the next group of trained searchers relieved us. The intermittent heavy downpours during the night had most likely obliterated any sign or tracks. I was faced with a stark reality. Anna MacDonald had come to some harm, perhaps a bad fall on the rocks or an encounter with a wild animal, but some type of harm.

The search would continue. Now I asked searchers to not only look for Anna but also to watch carefully for anything that might be construed as evidence. They would use the technique of going over something meticulously but as fast as possible.

Anything found now—a piece of cloth, a speck of blood, a candy wrapper that may look like nothing—could be a critical piece of a bigger puzzle. It was not yet a crime scene, but we needed to handle it as if it was. We could not keep this quiet for very long. Eventually, at best, we would have to keep things under control.

Julie and Martha Bork were at the MacDonalds'. I called Julie and gave her a progress report. She said Dorothy insisted on putting together some food and drinks for the searchers. She thought they would be on the way within the hour.

Rural Wisconsin fire departments are manned primarily by

well-trained volunteers, many with extensive search and rescue training. The fire chief started to go down his list of volunteer firefighters calling each and bringing them up to speed. Most of his men and women worked regular jobs, and a callout meant they wouldn't show up for work until the callout was over. Their employers were used to the idea that they would lose an employee or two for a while when a pager went off. Everybody agreed to agree on this because the next call might be at their house.

I called Tim Stewart, the director of Namekagon County Emergency Management and the cousin of County Board Chairman Scott Stewart. He answered the phone groggily.

"Tim, this is Sheriff Cabrelli. I need you to immediately activate emergency status, fire up the Emergency Command Center, and drive it to the Musky Run trailhead."

The emergency command center (ECC) was an aluminum-sided, brown and white behemoth Winnebago motor home. When Jim Rawsom was sheriff, he seized it as part of a rolling drug house investigation. Once it was awarded to Namekagon County by the court, Jim drove it over to Doc O'Malley's garage. Doc went over it stem to stern, doing maintenance and repairs. When he was done, he determined that while it was an older vehicle, it was in pretty good shape. Working with the local Lions Club and Habitat for Humanity, the inside of the Winnebago was outfitted into a first-rate emergency command center. One of the jobs the emergency management director was paid to do was make certain that the ECC was always ready to go. While rarely used, it would become the center of any emergency situation when needed.

Stewart still sounded like he'd spent a long night in the tavern when he asked, "What emergency? What are you talking about, Sheriff?"

"Tim, drive the ECC to the trailhead parking lot at Musky Run. Once you're there, I'll brief you," I said.

"Well, I will have to check with Scott first. His policy is that ECC doesn't move without his approval."

"Okay, Tim, let me help you with this. You will get your butt out of the house, take the keys to the motor home, get in it, and drive it out here right now. We have an emergency. Do you understand me?"

"I'm going to hang up and call my cousin."

Enough was enough. Another minute wasted got us no closer to Anna. The ECC would allow my worn-out crew to get inside and out of the drizzle. There were four bunks in the back, and they could stretch out for a minute. It would also provide a central location to coordinate the search.

I put my phone on speaker and called Deputy Pave over. "Tim, before you hang up on me, listen closely to what I am going to say. I want to be clear. This is an emergency! I am the chief law enforcement officer in Namekagon County." He started to talk again, and I shut him up. "Deputy Pave, I am going to contact the city police. I want you to drive into town as fast as you can and meet them at Tim Stewart's house. Once there, retrieve the keys to the emergency command center. If Tim Stewart resists you in any way, take him into custody and put him in jail. That is a direct order. If he calls anyone else and they are stupid enough to show up and interfere, they go to jail too."

"Got it, Sheriff. I'm on my way," Pave said, smiling.

"Cabrelli, if you try anything that stupid, I will make sure my cousin has your badge."

"You're not the first who wanted my badge and most likely not the last. Funny thing, I am still wearing it."

"Wait, wait, Sheriff. Just wait—you can't take the ECC."

"I can, and I will, and you along with it if need be."

"No, you can't. You see... it won't start. The battery is dead."

"The battery is dead? The emergency command center won't

start because the battery is dead?"

The previously indignant Tim Stewart now became sheepish. "Scott used the command center to take a group of people up the road to the hill overlooking the racecourse. When we got back to town and parked the motor home, everyone got off. I guess some people had been drinking a little. Well, someone must have gotten back on to get something they forgot or to use the bathroom and left the interior lights on. The next morning the battery was dead."

"Didn't the emergency generator kick on to charge the battery?"

"No. Scott had me turn the bypass switch. He said the noise from the generator was bothering his friends while they were watching the race."

"Tim, be out front of your house with the keys."

"Am I going to jail?" he whined.

"I can't spare the people to arrest you right now. But you listen to me. We are not done."

I disconnected and called dispatch. "Lois, get a hold of Doc O'Malley. Tell him the battery is dead on the emergency command center. I'll have Pave meet him at the lot where it's parked."

"Will do, Sheriff. What do you want to do with calling people in?"

"I am calling Chief Delzell next. The fire department people have relieved the first search crew. They are out now. Julie is bringing out food. Conditions are miserable right now, but we are going to have to tough this out. We need to find her. If we are wet and cold, she is wetter and colder."

"I will pray, Sheriff." Lois, the ultimate calm in the storm, a dispatcher's dispatcher, one of the unsung heroes of emergency services.

"We need it, Lois."

Although morning was not fully upon us, Mary Delzell sounded wide awake and ready to go when she answered.

"Chief, here is what I've got. Anna MacDonald went for a jog on Musky Run. She never returned to her car. We have been searching all night. We called in Chad Wichs and the K-9 unit, and the dog indicated on a large patch of blood on the trail near what looked like drag marks. The marks were consistent with what you would expect if someone held a person under the arms and dragged them across the ground. At another location, we recovered what we believe to be one of her running shoes. With one glaring exception, we found nothing else.

"What's the exception, John?"

"In two places on the trail, we found cougar tracks."

"A cougar? You're sure?"

"In the very recent past, I have become more educated than I care to be about cougars. I am positive it is a cougar track."

"Sheriff, I am going to come out to the trailhead if that is okay," said Chief Delzell.

"Thanks. I'd appreciate that, Chief." ∎

CHAPTER 15

The rain stopped as the early sun rose in the sky like a beacon of hope. Julie drove in, her Suburban loaded with food. The searchers had worked up quite an appetite and dug right in. Most were still wet, and the shelter of the ECC was a long way off. Bud rose to the challenge. Moving wet logs from the top of dry, he found enough suitable wood, and with a little help from "Boy Scout in a Can," the fire was burning. Bud continued to add wood until it was a warming blaze on the line of a small bonfire. Sheriff's deputies and firefighters who had been called in began to pull into the trailhead parking lot.

A howling noise hit Rosie's canine ears first, then ours. Shortly after that, the ECC appeared in the distance, siren wailing and driving at maximum speed for a barge of its size.

Doc O'Malley was behind the wheel with a determined look on his face. He turned sharply into the trailhead parking lot. Deputy Pave followed closely behind and put down his window as he neared me.

"I told Doc O'Malley he couldn't hit the siren until he got to the old iron bridge. Didn't want to attract a bunch of rubberneckers. Not many houses between there and here."

"Get some food, Deputy, and thanks." Once everyone was together, I got their attention. "Here is the situation. Anna MacDonald came out here sometime yesterday afternoon for a run. She was supposed to be at our cabin for dinner, but she didn't show up. Several of us began to look for her immediately, assisted by Deputy Wichs and his dog, Rosie. We have not yet located Anna MacDonald. As soon as you're ready, we will begin a grid search of the area. Searchers go quickly but carefully. If you come upon anything unusual or anything that may be of interest, stop, call back to the ECC, and we will send someone to you to collect the evidence."

"Sheriff, do you think she is the victim of foul play?" asked one of the firefighters.

"I have no reason to think that, but we need to cover all our bases. I do believe that she is out there somewhere, alive and waiting to be found by us. The fire chief will coordinate search teams to start. Additional searchers will be arriving throughout the day. We need to have a coordinated and organized search.

"Before we get rolling here, I need to say something, and I hope you will listen. This operation will get way more complicated as soon as the press finds out that it's Anna MacDonald who's missing. They may already know. We all know Anna as a hometown girl. The world knows her as Anna MacDonald, the pride of America. When the media shows up, ignore them, and stick to your job. I hope you will have the good judgment not to give the media information. Any law enforcement officers here understand not to share sensitive information. The rest of you will have to make that decision for yourself. Just remember what you say might mean the difference in whether Anna makes it home. As for sheriff's personnel, I would like everyone to call home and explain to their significant other what the circumstances are. Everyone is on emergency status. Any questions?"

Deputy Pave spoke up. "Sheriff, it was the cougar, wasn't it? It was probably the cougar that got her."

No one had dared to ask, but everyone had the same thought. They stared at me, waiting for an answer. I tried not to look at their eyes, and when I did look up, I saw only Julie's beautiful blue eyes. She wanted me to tell her this would be alright. She wanted me to tell her that two weeks from now, we would get married as we'd planned with Anna by her side. I looked her square in the eye and said, "I believe completely that Anna MacDonald will be found safe and alive. We will find her."

Chief Delzell arrived and deployed two squad cars to block each end of the road. I soon learned why. Not more than five minutes after they got set up, a big network news van arrived, followed by another.

I ignored them and went over to talk with Doc O'Malley. As always, he proved very useful. The ECC was equipped with a shower, and he worked on the water heater and got it fired up. There were no kitchen facilities, but once he got the generator powered up, the outlets worked.

"Doc, I don't know what we would do without you around here. Not just today but always. If you're ready, I have a car that will take you back to town."

"Sheriff, I want to stay. I want to be here to help if you need me. I want to help find Anna."

"Thanks, Doc."

My next call was to my old police partner.

The rough, gruff voice answered, "Commander Malone."

"Bear, it's John."

"Ah, the groom-to-be. Did Julie finally come to her senses, and you want to cry on my shoulder?"

"No, Bear, we have trouble. I need some resources, and I need them now."

It must have been the tone in my voice or Bear's intuition. All he said was, "What's happened?"

I told him as much as I could as fast as I could, knowing that every minute counted. The challenges with the weather, the cougar, Stephen Cameron, and everything else I could think of.

"Where is the ex-husband?"

"I don't know," I replied.

"Find him."

"I need some help right now on the ground. What can you do? The only evidence we have is on that trail. We need to find her."

"I'll check with Liz Masters and her team. They've spent at least half of their time over the last several months putting together a drone program. It's designed for lots of applications, including situations like this. Their record for locating things by drones is impressive. Let me check in with them, and I'll get back to you."

"Call me when you find out their status."

"Will do, John, and find the ex."

I went back to where everyone gathered. I could see that they were all antsy and frustrated by the delay. No one was more frustrated than I was.

There are over seventeen million acres of woodland in Wisconsin. Sixty percent of it is in the northern part of the state. It never seemed bigger to me than at this moment. I felt like a speck of dust on a giant's thumbnail. Insurmountable is a word that causes me a great deal of irritation when someone uses it in my company. I had to push this word out of my head.

My people, men and women, were perfectly suited for this task. This wild north country was their backyard. Most of them had been hiking trails, plying rivers and lakes since they could walk. I couldn't have handpicked better. As Uncle Nick used to say,

"They all carry pocketknives."

Volunteer firefighters from the Spider Lake Fire Department and a couple of others showed up, ready to go. All the deputies I had available reported in and were either on-site or on the way.

"Okay, folks gather around," Len called as he walked toward them. "The sheriff has something to say."

I looked at the small group waiting for leadership, waiting for wisdom. I started to speak when my phone rang; it was Malone.

"Sheriff, Liz and crew will be en route to your location shortly," Malone said.

"Thanks, Bear," I said.

I faced the group again. "Here is my imperfect plan, and I am ready to accept any comments or criticism. I know you are ready to go. That was Commander Malone on the phone, a man many of you know. He is sending the state's top crime scene unit to assist us immediately. Dr. Masters' team has helped us before. Asking for them does not imply that we have a crime scene; that is not the case at all. The team is highly skilled in many fields and is currently involved in cutting-edge technology regarding using drones for law enforcement purposes. I don't know where they are at this moment, but they are on their way. In the meantime, we will continue to search."

No one said anything.

"We are short of people to do this search, but we can do our best to confine our area to the places where we found evidence. Deputy Holmes recently attended a training course put on by the FAA. It involved developing a search grid map on your cell phone. You can add as many grids as you have searchers. These areas will be confined enough that we will not walk past anything of importance. I will not pretend I know how to do this, so I won't waste your time before I turn it over to Holmes. But before he briefs you, I want to talk about the cougar. My deputies and municipal officers will carry rifles while they search. I am sure just about every one of you is skilled at tracking and trailing in this country and know how to shoot a rifle. For now, though, we are keeping it to sworn officers to make sure we don't run into an issue regarding the protected status of the cougar. There is a good chance that you may come upon the mountain lion you've all heard about. Deputies and officers, if you have a good clean shot, take it. Wounding the animal will complicate this situation even more, but take the shot.

"I am not going to desert you, but I need to go back to Musky Falls to try and locate Stephen Cameron, Anna's former husband. I think he is still in the area. If any of you have seen him or know someone else who has, let me know now. While I am gone, because of the joint effort by different agencies, I have asked Chief Delzell to take charge. Is everybody okay with that?"

Without exception, everyone nodded their head in agreement.

"All of you who were up all night with me need to take a break. There are fold-down bunks in the command center. Get some sleep. I wish I could let you go home to your beds, but we need to stay together right now."

Hearing no more questions or comments, Holmes herded everyone over to the beginning of the trail and got things going. With millions of acres of tough country and barely over a couple of dozen searchers, luck needed to be on our side.

The searchers were set up in no time and began to run the first grid slowly. The chief and I both were anxiously awaiting Masters' team's ETA. We had worked with her team before, and they were the best of the best. I was thankful that Malone was sending them.

I reconnected with Bear, and he agreed to check whether Stephen Cameron had used his credit card, bought a plane ticket, or anything else.

At the same time I was doing that, the chief got a call.

"John, we made the national news," she said. "'America's Sweetheart Anna MacDonald Lost in the Wilderness.'"

A minute later, my phone rang. It was Jack Wheeler. "John, is Anna MacDonald really missing?"

"Yes, Counselor, she is. We've been looking all night and nothing. My deputies, some city officers, and volunteer firefighters are starting a search grid right now. Malone sent a drone team that is on the way."

"Is it the cougar?" Jack asked.

"Well, Counselor, you are the second person to ask me that. The truth is I don't know, but the evidence points to the animal. It's an aggressive, mature male cougar with a well-established territory around here. It stalked a little girl on the same trail that Anna was running. We found clear tracks at the trailhead. Further up the trail, we found blood and drag marks. That was when the rain started coming down in buckets. We kept going and found one of Anna's shoes on the trail loop. I'm afraid the rain washed away most of our hopes of tracking her or the animal. I can tell you that if we see it, we're going to shoot it before it gets someone else."

"What about the cougar expert? Does he know what's going on yet?

"Jack, I have been searching all night. I don't have time to track down someone who wants to take scat samples for DNA comparison. Anna MacDonald is missing, and every minute the chance for survival gets worse and worse," I snapped.

"I'm sorry. I didn't mean to push."

"Sorry, Counselor. I am tired and edgy."

"Do you want me to come out there to help?"

"No, Jack, not right now."

"Okay, if you need me, just let me—"

"Jack, wait, I do need you to do something. It looks to me like, before too long, the media vans will be stacked up like cordwood. I need a spokesperson. I can't do what I need to do and placate the media. Will you be the spokesperson?"

"I can help with that. What would you like me to do?"

"The story is out. To keep things under control, we will need to brief the media and the public. Anna is much loved in this community and the country, and I'm sure the story is already running wild. If we don't say something, I'm afraid one of these news anchors will make something up. I want to get ahead of that kind of thing."

"I think that's a good idea. I will grant myself some authority because of my position as the Law Enforcement Advisory Committee chairman. That would be completely appropriate."

"Sounds like a good plan."

"When were you thinking for the first statement, Sheriff?"

"Later this afternoon, around four or five? Hopefully, we'll be announcing she has been found safe and sound. I'll let the chief know. Thanks, Jack."

The next call, in what soon would be an endless stream of calls, was Liz Masters.

"Sheriff Cabrelli, we are on the way," she said.

"Liz, it's good to hear your voice. Where are you?"

"About one hundred thirty miles east of you. We just blasted through Three Lakes, called ahead to the Pine Isle Bar and Grill, and they delivered brunch to the curb. Burgers, fries, and deep-fried cheese curds really hit the spot. After our last great northern adventure with you, my doctor ended up putting me on cholesterol medication. Even mentioned I should lose a pound or two, but a girl has got to eat. Choices are limited while you're flying across Wisconsin. Anyway, Malone filled me in, and we have the drones ready to go. According to our new tracking system, our ETA is about two and a half hours. Your current location is locked in," she said.

"Regarding our current search efforts, I have people in the field running a grid search now. Can I keep them going?"

"Absolutely, Sheriff. It won't cause us any problems. I do need you to do us a favor. Contact the Musky Falls airport and advise them of our beginning point of the search. I tried to reach them and didn't get through. They will be able to monitor our flights on AirMap. We may be flying high- and low-altitude flights day and night."

"Got it, Liz. I'll make sure they know."

"Will you be on-site when we arrive?"

"I don't know. I am going into town to try and find the lost party's ex-husband. I don't know that he's involved, but I need to see."

"Ex-husband, huh? For my money, he did it."

"What makes you think that?" I asked, hoping she had information I didn't.

"Sheriff, I divorced that worthless husband of mine over ten years ago and haven't laid eyes on him for nine. The other day I went to the grocery store and forgot to get milk; I blamed him. Speaking of which, I would guess that wedding plans are now a little up in the air."

"I just don't know, Liz."

"John, you tell Julie not to worry. This equipment we're using is the best available. Visual, motion, heat, 3D imagery, overlay, mapping, and elevation are just the beginning of what these things can do. Give her a hug for me. Be there in a jiffy."

I went over to talk with Julie. The day was warming, and Bud had let the fire die down.

"Honey, you look completely worn out. Come over here and get something to eat and drink," she said.

"I can't. I have got to go. I need to try and locate Stephen

Cameron."

"Do you think he has something to do with this?"

"Every stone turned, every possibility investigated, everything taken until its natural end. We can't ignore anything."

"Has anyone seen him?" she asked.

"Not that I know of."

"Be careful, John. Please be careful."

"Careful is my middle name, sweetheart."

Just then, Len walked over. "Sheriff, didn't you say you were headed to town to find Cameron?"

"I'm going right now."

"If I'm not mistaken, he has saved you a trip. That fellow over by the roadblock arguing with two of Musky Falls' finest followed by reporters looks an awful lot like Stephen Cameron." ■

CHAPTER 16

I walked over to Cameron, and everyone quieted except him. "Who do you think you are, Cabrelli? My wife is missing, and you don't even have enough of a thread of common decency to let me know? I demand to know what has happened; I have a right to know."

At that point, Cameron got in my face close enough that we were nose to nose. The troops started to move up for what would surely be trouble. I waved them off.

"Stephen, come on over to the ECC, and we'll talk." I didn't wait for him and started toward the motor home. Our conversation would be important. By my way of thinking, he was here for one of two reasons. Maybe he was truly concerned about his former wife and hoped she would be okay. Then again, maybe he had something to do with her disappearance, and he was pretending to be the grieving ex-husband, hoping to get some information from us. Either way, he was one of my two prime suspects.

We went into the command center and sat down across from each other at the table, away from the bunk areas.

"Can I get you some water, Stephen, or a cup of coffee?"

Cameron was clearly agitated and, for just a minute, looked like he might come at me. "Cabrelli, just cut the crap. I don't want your coffee or water. The only thing I want from you is information about my wife. What happened? Is she okay?" he shouted.

I waited until he settled and answered him in a calm voice. "Stephen, the truth is I don't know. We have been actively searching since early last night and will continue to search until we find her. I have requested additional personnel to help."

"I'm sorry, Sheriff. I'm sure you're doing your best. I just lost it for a minute. No one told me she was missing. I had to hear about it on the news. You can imagine how shocked I was. I thought someone would at least let me know. I am her husband, after all."

"Actually, we have released no information other than that she is missing. As far as calling you, well, you are her ex-husband, not her husband."

"As her ex-husband, I would guess I am already high on the suspect list."

"Right now, there is no suspect list or suspects to put on it. Anna is missing. Priority one is finding her. But I have a couple of questions I'd like to ask, if you don't mind."

"I don't mind, Sheriff, if you think it will help."

"You never know what ends up helping," I replied.

"When was the last time you saw Anna?" I asked.

"Yesterday. She and I met at a coffee trailer. We sat at an outdoor picnic table and talked."

"Do you remember the name of the place?"

"Kelly's or something like that."

"Maybe Karin's?" I asked.

"That's it. Karin's."

"How long were you there?"

"A couple of hours, at least. We had a lot to talk about."

"Like what?"

"We mainly talked about our past, present, and future relationship. I told you I was trying to convince her to give us another chance."

"Did you leave the coffee trailer together?"

"No, she had some post-race stuff to do, and I had some things of my own to take care of," he replied.

"Did you two see or talk to anyone else?"

"A couple of young girls asked Anna for autographs. Oh yeah, and the owner or worker had Anna sign a couple of coffee cups."

"What time was this?"

"I'm not sure. I think about ten in the morning."

"Have you seen her since?"

"We had planned to meet again, and I expected her to call, but I never heard from her. I thought maybe she got tied up with race sponsors. I tried calling her several times, but it went to voicemail."

"Do you have your cell phone with you, Stephen?"

"No, I'm afraid I don't. I was so upset when I heard Anna was missing, I took off and left my phone. You know, Sheriff, I can see you're confused. Everyone is convinced that Anna hates me, and for a while, she did. But things have changed between us. She just wanted it to be kept quiet until we figured things out. I can't think of anything else to tell you. If you need me, I won't be hard to find. Now, if you don't mind, I would like to join one of the search teams. I need to help look for her."

"I appreciate how you feel, Stephen, but joining a search team won't be possible. You'll have to stay behind the perimeter with everyone else."

Back when I was just starting in law enforcement, I was part of a search and rescue effort in a rural area. All the neighbors helped with the search, including a local guy who was a definite person of interest. At one point, he bent down quickly, grabbed something off the ground, and stuffed it in his pocket. My sergeant saw him and asked to see what he had. He replied, "Just litter." The sergeant demanded to see it when the subject pushed him aside and took off running. He was quickly tackled by other searchers. In his pocket was a cigarette butt, his brand.

"Stephen, do you have anything else to tell me?"

"Not that I can think of, Sheriff."

I handed him a small notebook I always carried, a remnant of the old days.

"Stephen, if you don't mind, would you write down your cell number and where you are staying." He wrote everything down and handed the pad back to me.

"Thank you, Sheriff Cabrelli. I'll stay out of your way. Just let me know if anything happens."

Stephen limped out of the command center and back to where he had left his car. A throng of reporters accosted him. He just walked through them like they weren't there, and I lost sight of him. He returned a minute later with a folding camping chair, opened it up, and sat down at the perimeter.

I started back toward the search area and was intercepted by Julie.

"What does he want?" she asked.

"He says he's worried about Anna. He was blindsided by her disappearance and heard about it on the national news."

"He has never been blindsided by anything. Stephen Cameron is nothing but trouble, and he has caused Anna no end of pain," she said angrily.

"Julie, did Anna say anything about meeting up with Cameron a couple of days ago?"

"No, she didn't. I can't imagine she would ever agree to do that."

"He says they met at ten at Karin's coffee trailer. Sat at one of the picnic tables."

"John, he is lying. Anna doesn't scare easily, but she is scared to death of Stephen."

"I have to check it out. That may put him as the last person to see her yesterday before she drove out to Musky Run. She is somewhere, and we need to find her. That means no stone unturned."

"I'm sorry, John. I didn't mean to jump down your throat."

"I know, Julie. I know. Everyone is on edge."

"What can I do?" she asked.

"Well, one thing for sure, you can help Anna's parents. Len told me that Dorothy found Herb wearing out the linoleum and pacing the floor when she got home from bringing all the food. He is bound and determined to get in his truck and look for his daughter. Herb had a heart incident a while ago, and Dorothy is scared to death he'll have another. Maybe you could take Martha and go back over there to calm things down a little."

"That's the least I can do, honey." Julie kissed me on the cheek and took off to do her appointed job. Julie didn't really want to go, but there was no other choice at the moment. I didn't blame her one bit. I promised she would be my first call if there was any news.

Any help anyone could provide was welcome. I needed to turn all my efforts and resources into coordinating effective search efforts. Time was not on our side or Anna's. In every respect, the search for Anna was going to ramp up. I needed to focus and ensure everything was going in the right direction.

I checked in with Deputy Holmes, who was leading the search team. He was in good physical shape but was breathing hard when he answered.

"How goes the search?" I asked.

"Sheriff, we are going, but it's slow. All these blowdowns make taking a straight path almost impossible. We are keeping the grid, though it's harder than I thought. We've jumped some deer and a small bear but nothing else. According to the GPS, we are about a mile from a fire lane. It's my plan to stop there for a break."

"Do you need anything?" I asked.

"We have water bottles and protein bars. Everybody is holding up pretty well, so I guess we're good."

"Okay, Deputy, keep me advised. I have to check on something in town, but I will be available."

"Ten-four, Sheriff."

I drove into town and stopped at Karin's coffee trailer. The owner was working.

"Hey, Karin, I have a question to ask you. Do you have a minute?"

"I will as soon as my daughter gets back. How about a cup of coffee, and you go sit at one of the tables for a minute or two?"

"Fine, thanks." I sat and started to drink yet another cup of coffee, certainly not my first of the day. I acquired my coffee habit on the night shift. To support my coffee excesses, I only read health articles that said drinking coffee was good for you.

Karin came over to join me. "How can I help you, Sheriff?"

"Karin, did you happen to see Anna MacDonald here yesterday?"

"Yes, I did."

"Was she with anyone?"

"Her ex-husband."

"Stephen Cameron?"

"That was him. It started quite a buzz with our customers and crew."

"Were they arguing or anything like that?"

"No, not that I saw. They sat at the table furthest away from the trailer, but if there was shouting, I would have heard it."

"How long did they stay?"

"They left at the same time I left for the day, about noon. I saw them go. She walked to a Jeep, got in, and took off. Her ex walked toward downtown. I didn't pay any more attention than that. Sorry, Sheriff."

"Thanks, Karin. You've been a big help."

I drove back to the trailhead to find the number of news crews had grown significantly, and a large, white utility van was trying to wind its way through the parked vehicles but to no avail. The road directly passing the trailhead was hopelessly blocked by news trucks, even though the county highway department had set up detour signs to route traffic to a county road, down a town road, then back onto the highway. Someone had to move. One news crew driver tried to be courteous and moved over as far as he could and ended up stuck in the ditch. It accomplished the purpose and allowed plenty of room for the utility van to get through. Doc O'Malley again demonstrated his constant usefulness and ingenuity to Namekagon County by using a fire department pickup to pull the heavy vehicle slowly out of the ditch.

The front and side doors of the utility van opened, and the crime scene team exited. Liz stretched and walked over.

"Sheriff Cabrelli, how have you been?"

"Good, Liz, but I've got my hands full."

"Is that giant Winnebago your ECC?" she inquired.

"Yup, Jim Rawsom got it in a drug bust."

"Where was it parked? Next to the shuffleboard court in Sun City?" she joked.

"Before we even get started, I need to thank you. Dropping everything and coming over here probably disrupted everything else you were doing. So, thanks."

"Actually, John, when Commander Malone—the same Commander Malone who controls our funding, the same Commander Malone who decides whether we are working crime scenes or searching through dumpsters—calls, we tend to do exactly what he tells us to do. It's not that we don't like you folks or the area. It's just that we have been around long enough to know which side of the bread the butter is on. The truth is you guys are good to work with. So, what's going on?"

I began to fill her in, but it was obvious that her arrival had gotten the interest of the headline hunters.

"How about we all go into the command center?" I suggested.

"Good plan," said one of Liz's techs. "The dumb-looking reporter over there with the huge nose has got a parabolic microphone aimed right at us."

Hearing the comments through his high-tech headset made the reporter jerk his head up.

Inside the command center, everybody found a space.

"Where should I start?" I asked.

"At the beginning, Sheriff Cabrelli," Liz said.

"Anna MacDonald, Olympic gold medalist, planned to go for a run yesterday afternoon. She thought she'd be back at our place around three, enough time to be ready for a five o'clock dinner where we were going to finalize wedding plans and assign tasks."

"By the way, Sheriff, my crew just RSVP'd your wedding. Keep going."

"When she didn't show up by six-thirty, Len Bork, Bud Treetall, and I went looking and found the Jeep she was driving parked here at the Musky Run trailhead. We began to look for her and called in a K-9. The K-9 found a large spot of blood and what appeared to be drag marks on the trail. I covered them with my parka and put rocks down to hold it in place. It was at that point the clouds let loose with a gully washer, and for the rest of the night, we searched in the rain. Farther down the trail, we found what appears to be one of her shoes. That's it."

"Anything else?" asked Liz.

"Yeah, there is something else, and this may be a real issue," I said.

"What's that?"

"Locally, we've been plagued as of late by a cougar."

"A cougar, mountain lion, wild cat, catamount kind of cougar?" asked one of her people.

"A cougar, and a big one at that. It killed a huge dog and a couple of sheep and gave the local reverend a moment to ponder heaven. Three days ago, the cat stalked a little girl on this trail, the same trail we think Anna was running on. The K-9 alerted on pug tracks right at the edge of the parking lot. The cougar does not seem to be afraid of people."

"Were you able to follow them?" Liz asked.

"No, we stuck with the K-9, and then the rain washed us out."

"Good sense to stick with the dog."

"I figured it was our best chance," I said.

"I agree, Sheriff."

"I have a team out searching now. Deputy Holmes just finished some training on setting up coordinated grid search lines using cell phones. That's what they are doing. I believe they are locking in the searched grids."

"John, tell me more about the cougar."

"The cat moved into the area and was seen on some trail cams. The DNR received several reports of disappearing pets and livestock. Then there were a couple of cases where people out hiking ran into it and reported that the cougar was not interested in giving them the right of way. Cougars aren't common in Wisconsin but are not unknown, either. The DNR says they are reclusive and avoid human contact most of the time. Not the case with this one. The county was able to get a predator specialist sent here, a veterinarian named Pederson Kouper, who is doing a study in the area on large predatory animals."

"What does he think about the cougar?"

"He thinks it needs to go, and I have got to say I agree with him."

"Do you have a gut feeling on this, John?"

"Liz, a large predator has been raising trouble around here. The last sighting was on Musky Run. The last place we can put Anna MacDonald is Musky Run. I hate to think of this possibility, but we have to consider it."

"If it turns out to be a cougar attack, what would be left? Do they eat the whole body? I understand some predators will cover the body and come back to feed later. From our aerial point of view, what should we be looking for?" asked Liz.

"I hope and pray it's an alive and well Anna MacDonald."

"I know, but we have to cover all the bases."

"Stand by. I will call Dr. Kouper right now."

The vet picked up on the second ring. "Sheriff Cabrelli, I was just going to call you." ▪

CHAPTER 17

"Dr. Kouper, I have got you on speaker with Dr. Liz Masters from the crime scene unit."

"Hello, Dr. Kouper. Nice to meet you."

"Hello, Dr. Masters. We need to talk, Sheriff. Rumors are running rampant that Anna MacDonald is missing, and the prime suspect in the disappearance is *puma concolor*. Is that correct?"

Kouper was unusually rattled; I could hear it in his voice. "Sheriff, Dr. Masters, is that correct?" he asked again in a demanding tone. "Sheriff Cabrelli, I asked you a question, and I expect an answer," he said this time, his voice uncharacteristically raised.

Liz stepped in. "Let's get off on the right foot, Dr. Kouper. We are all on the same team here. People are under stress and tired, but we need to work together. We need to know, if the cougar, in fact, killed her, what would we be looking for? A body out in the open? Covered with brush and other debris?"

I could hear Dr. Kouper take a deep breath, and the line was silent for a moment. "Of course, Dr. Masters, I apologize. This is such a stressful situation. I am afraid that I am already stretched very thin. Reporters have chased me all over town. We would expect the body to be hidden with brush and other debris. If it is okay, I would like to come to the scene and see if I can be of any help. Professor Newlin would like to come with me."

"Stand by, Dr. Kouper," I said. "Liz, I am trying to give us the best chance of finding a clue. The search team is going to meet us on a fire lane close to where they are right now. I don't want any more people than can be useful. I think Kouper and Newlin might have something to offer. What do you think?"

"Here is what I think. By the time the evening news comes on tonight, the idea that a wild animal might have killed Olympic gold medalist Anna MacDonald will fuel the news fire. The best chance you have is now. I think Dr. Kouper and Professor Newlin should come ahead. Now I need to get with my people and help set up. We have some daylight left and shouldn't waste it."

I confirmed Dr. Kouper and Professor Newlin's arrival time while Liz's crew were busy unpacking a drone and what appeared to be some sort of launch pad. The drone resembled a combination of a flying saucer, a jet fighter, and a spider. It was much larger than other drones I had seen.

Liz must have read my mind, saying, "One of the reasons the drone is so large is that it has extra battery capacity. Usual maximum flight time is just under an hour. With the unit we are testing, we can switch over to another set of batteries and get another fifty-five minutes. The challenge here is weight versus power. The more batteries we carry, the more the craft weighs, so the shorter the flight time. However, we can switch the unit to a lower power setting and stretch things if necessary. In addition to the standard cameras, we have thermal imaging, low light imagery, and night vision capability. The best thing about this beauty is the range. On a clear day, we can work up to nine miles away and home it right back to base."

Liz changed the subject. "So, you have Deputy Holmes running the current search?"

"I do," I replied.

"I was the lead teacher in that class he just took."

"He told me he did well," I replied.

"He definitely leans toward the technical side. He was practically leading the class by the second day. We can really use him with the search."

Liz and her crew continued setting up their gear. Once completely assembled, they began to perform a series of systems tests, the results of which were confirmed by another team member.

"All systems are checked and confirmed. We are ready to go," said one of her techs.

"Sheriff, how tired are the people you have out in the search right now?" Liz asked.

"Some are nearing exhaustion. We're going to meet up at the fire road and drive them back to the ECC."

"Even though they are tired, they are already out there, so let's get going with the drone. We can quickly find their location and begin the aerial search as well. I don't have to tell you time is a critical issue here. Ask Deputy Holmes for the coordinates of where they will come out on the fire lane."

I handed Liz my phone, and after a brief discussion, they were ready to launch. The drone took off at an amazing speed but was surprisingly quiet. Two of Liz's team members began the surveillance. In less than five minutes, the techs advised they were on location with the searchers.

"We are going to fly the grid lines they have already walked. We'll double-check to make sure we have cleared those areas before we proceed again. We have learned in both practical application and training that it is very easy for a searcher to walk past a person, particularly if they are lying on the ground in heavy cover like we have here. We will turn on the thermal imaging device, which will show every warm place. The difficulty in the country is the abundance of wildlife and the size of the trees and canopy. But this setup has really worked well. Each time we get a thermal hit, we will also try to get a visual. That way, your people aren't chasing deer."

"This will pick up a cougar?" I asked.

"Absolutely. Sheriff, do you have any coffee in that mobile command center?"

"I sure hope so. Let me check."

We almost made it to the door of the Winnebago before a reporter and a video crew almost ran us down.

"Sheriff Cabrelli, Sheriff Cabrelli, is it true that you believe Anna MacDonald was killed and eaten by a mountain lion? Have you found a body? Is it Anna MacDonald?" shouted the reporter.

Sensing some new information, other news crews started to run toward us. I did the only thing I could do; I stopped and waited for them to catch up. Everyone saw their opportunity, and within minutes we were surrounded by media. They fired questions at us while Liz and I stood silent. Eventually, they wore down.

"I will gladly tell you what I can as long as you settle down. First, I want you to understand that we are all in this together. Anna MacDonald is missing. We need to find her, and that is what we intend to do. I hope I can count on you folks if we need you. Time is of the essence, especially if she is injured. We currently have a significant search party on the ground and a state-of-the-art drone in the air. Dr. Masters is the head of the crime scene and search unit. They are the most experienced team available. We all need to let them do their work with minimum interference. I will be glad to answer a few questions right now, but I need to get back to the job at hand."

"Sheriff, could you at least confirm that there is a dangerous animal out there? Is that true? We have a report that a cougar attacked a young girl on this same trail," asked a reporter.

"First off, let me say that there are potentially dangerous animals everywhere out here, but we have nothing to support that Anna MacDonald has been the victim of a wild animal attack. We have asked wildlife specialists to join us at this location so we can use their expertise if we need it. Right now, however, I have to keep things moving and arrange for additional ground searchers. Jack Wheeler, chair of the Law Enforcement Advisory Committee, will be handling all press releases and issues. I promise to keep him up to date."

The drone had been operational for just under an hour. Liz and I were walking over to the ECC when one of the techs yelled, "Liz, we've got the cougar. It's about fifty feet behind the line of searchers, heading toward them! The cougar is on their transect five."

That was all we needed, and the media stampede began. I ran across the lot, away from the crowd, and grabbed my radio.

"Deputy Holmes, the cougar is about fifty feet behind you following on transect five. Advise all your people to turn around and get ready to shoot the cougar."

"Ten-four, Sheriff."

"Is it still on tract five?" I yelled to the tech.

"Affirmative, maintaining a distance of fifty feet."

Then we heard it, a gunshot and another. The tech zoomed in, and the cougar was no longer visible.

"Deputy Holmes, did someone shoot the cougar?"

"Stand by, Sheriff. I am still trying to figure out what happened here."

"Ten-four, standing by."

The response came back quickly. "Deputy Pave shot the cougar. It is down. It tumbled off a rock outcropping and fell into a shallow valley. Pave is certain that he hit it twice."

"Do what you need to do to confirm it's dead. We'll stand by."

"Sheriff, it's no more than thirty-five yards from where we are. We will wait a half-hour or so, then go down and find it. Pave is sure he hit it right."

Deputy Pave was a hunter and one heck of a rifle shot. The press was going crazy, and the only thing I could do was wait.

I was looking at the drone images with the tech when someone tapped me on the shoulder. I jumped a mile. It was Dr. Kouper and the professor.

"Has the cougar been shot, Sheriff? The reporters are saying the cougar has been killed. Is that true?" Kouper asked.

I have learned the hard way that sometimes running the show requires difficult choices. Now was one of those times. Maybe we had killed the cougar, maybe we didn't, but we were looking for Anna, and that was priority number one.

I turned to face the crowd of reporters. I tried to settle them down, but this was happening news. They were all hoping that Anna's body was found in the jaws of a cougar. I had no idea that so many people had gathered, and just when I thought we were getting somewhere, things changed. One of the network trucks launched its own drone. It paused in the air above us.

"It's orienting. It will take a minute," Liz said.

They didn't have a minute. I got my shotgun from the squad and pointed the short barrel in the sky. I let go with a blast. It had the same effect as the old west shot in the air. The crowd quieted and stared at the sheriff with the crazed look in his eyes, holding a

Remington 870 pump shotgun with an extended magazine. They didn't know who or what was next, and for a moment, neither did I. The drone was unharmed because I had intentionally missed, but my point was made.

"Enough, enough! This stops now! Right now, whether you like it or not. I have a human being, Anna MacDonald, who is missing. This is just the next best story for you, and you will most certainly be thrilled to pack up at a moment's notice and get back to civilization. For us, this is our home. Anna is part of our family, and we must move heaven and earth to find her. I don't care if you file every possible complaint against me with every possible person that will listen; it won't matter. I am here to find Anna and will stay until I do."

"You shot at our drone!" yelled one of the people from CBN.

"If I'd shot at your drone, it would be a pile of electronic space-age rubble laying on the ground. I strongly suggest, however, that you take the hint and land it. Dr. Kouper and Professor Newlin, I want you to follow Dr. Masters' techs to the location of our people and the dead cougar. This is a distraction. Our goal has been to find Anna, so please move along. Press people, you can stay here, but unless you have something to offer, you need to stay out of our way. If you don't, I'll move the border of our restricted area to the limits of Namekagon County and arrest anyone who crosses that boundary."

"You can't do that, Sheriff!" shouted a reporter.

"I can, and I will do it. Bet every last nickel you have on it. Besides arresting those who don't cooperate, I will tell the whole world how your network interfered in our attempts to rescue an American hero."

That seemed to have put a damper on their overenthusiastic search for the truth.

Newlin and Kouper took off with a handheld GPS. I let Holmes and Pave know that they were on the way. The time ticked off slowly. Deputy Pave called me on the radio.

"Sheriff, we have a significant blood trail. Dr. Kouper suggests we wait for at least an hour before we begin tracking. He says that dead cougars have a way of attacking people."

"Can we continue with the drone and see if we can locate it that way?" I asked.

"Negative, Sheriff. The drone may keep the animal moving if it's just wounded. The blood is bright red, which means it is probably hit good. I think we should just wait it out," Pave said.

I called Jack Wheeler and asked if he could come out to the trailhead. He advised he was on the way. It is important when there is a significant press presence on any case to try and control the flow of information as much as possible. One point person is the first best way. Jack was an experienced litigator, and he would handle this well.

Time always passes slowly when you are waiting for something. When Aunt Rose was making pasta, I would stare at the pot in anticipation. She would sweetly admonish me. "Johnny, a watched pot never boils." I was definitely watching the pot.

Although I had given it much thought—probably too much—I could not for the life of me figure out how I ended up in the places I ended up in. I never imagined I would be part of chasing down a two-hundred-pound mountain lion. The danger was real, and this search could result in someone injured or killed.

I adopted a rule the day I became sheriff. I had observed this rule working with the best of law enforcement supervisors: never send people into a situation you would not go into. I was not about to change that. I told the people at the cougar site to stand by.

This would be a close-quarters fight, so I grabbed the shotgun from my squad for the second time that day. I replaced the round I had fired earlier with the same kind of double oo buckshot. Each shot would send twelve .33 caliber pellets hopefully to the target. As of late, the shotgun had its detractors, who spoke loudly about the perceived deficiencies of that type of weapon. Maybe so, but many experienced law officers grab the shotgun at the first sign of real trouble.

The tech gave me another handheld GPS and sent me on my way. The moment I took my first step in the direction of my men, I felt better. They were hunters and competent and would do fine without me, but I needed to be there.

Upon my I arrival, Deputy Pave gave a little chuckle as he said to everyone present, "I told you he would come out here. Sheriff, you're a good man, even if you do get eaten by this cougar." ▪

CHAPTER 18

We lined up together on the ridge overlooking a little valley. It was choked with vegetation. As often happens, these little valleys accumulate more water, and the plant communities thrive. The plants provided an obstructed view in every direction.

Dr. Kouper advised us that if the animal was alive and wounded, it may very well be at the stage of giving up flight and choosing to fight. In that case, he will likely conserve his energy and wait under cover until the last moment, then spring to the attack. Even badly wounded, a mature cougar can move incredibly fast and do a great deal of damage to a thin-skinned human in a matter of seconds. He told us to try for a center chest shot or a front shoulder shot if the opportunity presented itself. The shoulder shot will hopefully immobilize the front legs. Do not stop shooting until the animal is down and not moving.

We started slowly, a few feet apart, our weapons at ready. Pave was in the center following the blood sign, I was on the right side, and Holmes was on the left. We were veteran lawmen, and each of us had faced danger many times. It was nothing like this, looking for something that would fight to the death with every ounce of its strength. We tried to be silent, but walking through heavy cover is a noisy process. I figured, like any animal that lives by its wits, it already knew we were coming and was waiting.

We came to the edge of a clearing, and a brown flash crashed through the brush. Pave yelled, "Deer!" before we fired, and we watched the flags of a doe and her fawn disappear in front of us. I don't mind saying that those deer cost each of us a year of our lives.

Pave said, "The blood sign is much heavier here. Pay attention."

A minute later, a rifle shot. Pave yelled, "Cougar!"

Everyone froze, weapons at ready. No one but Pave could see the animal, and all he could see was a brown patch of fur. Nothing was moving. The silence of the Northwoods I so loved was now oppressive. We moved in cautiously. Dr. Kouper, although unarmed, somehow got in the lead.

"Hold up, Pederson," I said. There was no stopping him. When he arrived, Deputy Pave was already standing over the animal. In an experienced move, Pave touched the muzzle of his rifle to the cat's eye—no reaction.

Dr. Kouper knelt next to the cat. Again, like when he was looking over Dannas' dog and treating Brewer's hound, he examined the animal with a sort of reverence. His hand stroked the coat, examining the wounds.

"I am sorry this happened. It couldn't be avoided, but I am sorry, nonetheless," he said quietly.

"Dr. Kouper, the animal had become too dangerous. You said so yourself. It had to be dealt with," I said.

"Sheriff, I have not changed my mind. I feel that every time we end up killing a large predator in a situation like this, we have failed. It's always exciting to see a mountain lion, and we coexist well with them, until we don't. Deputy Pave, you did a good job here. Thank you," Kouper said.

Dr. Kouper stayed with the animal, and I returned to the trailhead lot to get a blanket we could carry the body back on. The parking lot was a barely restrained group of reporters joined by local folks and tourists. Jack Wheeler was standing in front of them, hands raised, palms out, trying to get their attention. My appearance didn't help one bit. Questions came at me like a full auto Thompson. I don't know how he did it, but Jack settled them.

"Sheriff, can I talk with you for a second?"

"Sure, Jack," I replied. Then I followed him over to the ECC.

"I strongly suggest you give them something. They already know almost everything you can tell them, but they are like a pack of dogs waiting for scraps. Let's give them some scraps. I will get them organized and lay out a few ground rules. Then you can talk to them before you head back into the bush."

"Okay, Jack."

I grabbed an old wool surplus blanket out of my squad and a length of rope and walked back to the crowd.

"As many of you know, this is Sheriff John Cabrelli. I'm sure you can imagine the sheriff has his hands full at this moment. You have been so patient and cooperative that Sheriff Cabrelli has agreed to give a brief statement. Sheriff, go ahead," Jack said.

"Folks, here is where we are at. The search for Anna MacDonald is going well. Not as fast as we hoped, but it is going well. As many of you saw, the tech team from the crime lab has arrived and launched a drone to help with the search. That drone is one of the most sophisticated search instruments in existence, and Liz Masters and her team are nationally known. Dr. Pederson Kouper and Professor Newlin are wildlife experts. Dr. Kouper is one of the leading researchers on large terrestrial predators in North America. They are all here for one purpose: to help us locate Anna MacDonald. Now I hope you will help us do that.

Here is what we know: Anna parked the Jeep Cherokee you see over in the corner of the trailhead lot, sometime probably early afternoon on Tuesday. It is the best estimate of time we have. That would have given her enough time to get her run in, shower, and change for a dinner commitment at five. This trail is called Musky Run, one of her favorites."

"Wasn't this dinner at your house, Sheriff?" asked an anemic-looking reporter.

"It was. Anna MacDonald grew up with my wife-to-be and was joining us for dinner. She didn't show up, and we became concerned. We found the Jeep at the trailhead and immediately began to try and locate her."

"Who is 'we,' Sheriff? You said 'we' began to try and locate her," another reporter asked.

"Retired Chief Len Bork was also an invited dinner guest, as was Bud Treetall, and they came with me. Our initial search attempts were unsuccessful, and I called in a K-9 unit. Shortly after the dog started working, we were hit with a torrential downpour. It made the situation significantly more difficult, but I called in more help, and we continued to search through the night. The first thing this morning, I contacted JJ Malone, commander of the Department of Criminal Investigation, and he sent Dr. Masters and her team."

A reporter known for his sensational spin on things jumped to the front. "Sheriff, thank you for talking with us. It's frustrating when the people in smaller communities don't recognize the importance of our job. My investigative news team interviewed someone who has been a key member of the team trying to locate a killer cougar in Namekagon County. He told us that a mountain lion recently stalked a family on this very trail. He told us that you had not let anyone know there was another close cougar encounter in the area. That included Anna MacDonald. Sheriff, if you were aware that Anna enjoyed running on Musky Run

Trail, shouldn't you have let her know of the imminent potential for danger? Aren't you somewhat responsible if she has been the victim of a wild animal attack? We all want to know what the gunshots were about. Will you tell us?"

Jack Wheeler started to jump in, and I stopped him.

"This is wild country, and every one of us who lives here rubs shoulders with bears, wolves, and yes, mountain lions. Ninety-nine percent of the time, nothing happens. I have no reason to believe that this case is any different. However, we have to consider the possibility. We are prepared should we run into an aggressive animal. During our search, we had to be on the lookout for the cougar that has been roaming the area. I gave my people the order to dispatch it if they came upon the cougar."

"You mean kill it, right, Sheriff? Kill an innocent animal because you didn't adequately warn the public."

"I talked a great deal with Dr. Kouper. We made a decision we felt was the best for the community. No one takes any of this lightly. The drone located an adult mountain lion in close proximity to the searchers. When it approached even closer in very heavy cover, one of my deputies dispatched the animal in accordance with my orders."

"Where is the cougar now? Is it the killer cat we've heard about? How will you know?" yelled someone from the back of the crowd.

A network reporter in the front was on his phone immediately, "Stand by for immediate hookup. They got the killer cougar. Stand by." Another reporter was doing the same.

At that point, Stephen Cameron barged through the crowd of reporters and onlookers, knocking a female videographer to the ground. When he got to the front of the pack, he was livid.

"Cabrelli, there was a killer mountain lion on this very trail, and you didn't let anyone know? You let my wife go jogging on this trail, knowing her life would be at risk? You found the killer.

Anna is lying out there, dead or wounded from the cougar. Did you ever think about the ramifications of such a poor decision? I am not going to stand here and do nothing. I will not watch what is surely to come. I will not watch when your people carry out my wife's mangled body." Cameron ran back through the crowd, got in his car, and fishtailed away down the driveway, squealing the tires when he hit the paved road.

Members of the press were increasing quickly. The story of an American hero killed by a lion was too good to pass up. At this point, I was done with the press conference. Jack, always astute, recognized I had reached the end of my rope and quickly took over. He assured the reporters that the search would continue night and day until Anna was found.

I gathered my supplies and walked to Kouper's location. The cat, thank goodness, had not moved. We placed the animal on the blanket, rolled it up, tucked it in, and tied the ends. Then Newlin and Dr. Kouper carried it out. The crowd wanted to see the cat. Dr. Kouper refused, and when a reporter stood in his way, he almost walked right over him and would have if he hadn't moved. They loaded the cougar in the vet's vehicle.

"Dr. Kouper, what is your plan from here?" I asked.

"I plan to do a complete necropsy on the cougar, including DNA sampling. The animal's death is sad, but we can still learn a great deal about him, including where he came from, his age, and overall health. Professor Newlin arranged for me to use an operating suite at a local veterinary clinic, and the vet there agreed to assist."

"Just so I have an idea, how long will all this take?" I asked.

"The actual exam should take a few hours. Much of that time will be involved with taking and labeling tissue samples to be sent off for analysis. The analysis of those samples will take from days up to six months. I am assuming one of us will have to make a public statement about the overall health and condition of the cat. I think by noon tomorrow, we should have some information we could share. We will need to wait and see."

"Okay, Dr. Kouper. Let me know."

They left, and I checked in with the search team.

"Sheriff, the grid search is working well," Liz said. "While it is impossible to cover everything perfectly, using the drone and trained personnel is effective. We are approaching the end of the day, and I am sure your people are close to exhaustion. It is my thought we should close the boundaries of the area searched and then have everyone return here to debrief."

My hesitation spoke loudly.

"John, I am well aware that time is of the essence in a search like this. I have no intention of suggesting we reduce our efforts. One of my team members thinks we should activate a drone thermal search tonight and follow up immediately if we get a heat signal. What do you think?"

"Liz, I am not as familiar with drone technology as you are. I am going to have to defer to you."

"Let's close the map and get everyone back here. They can catch a breather, and we can find out what they have to say."

"Okay."

I got on the radio and asked everyone to return to the ECC. Each acknowledged.

My people came back with ripped coats, torn pant knees, and overall scuffed and dirty. Search and rescue people are a unique breed. Television shows have been based on the trials and tribulations of their lives; some are even quite accurate, but none are real. Real is putting purpose and need beyond yourself. Real is cold coffee, torn pants, and physical exhaustion, but continuing anyway.

I watched them gather around. I was so very, very proud of

these people who accepted and lived the life of first responders. We could not all fit in the ECC, so we circled up at the far end of the parking area. I asked Jack Wheeler to join us.

"Before we start, I want to thank you all for your dedication and efforts. I can see some uniforms that have rips and tears. I know normally you would wait until your uniform allowance came out or pay out of pocket to replace them. In this case, send an email to Lois, and we will replace what needs replacing." This announcement was met with an exhausted rumble of approval. "Anyone want to comment on what and how we are doing?" I asked.

Deputy Plums spoke. "Sheriff, I think we're doing a good job. The drone has been amazing. This country is rough. Other than the trail, we are bushwhacking the rest. The trees that came down in that windstorm this past spring are not making things any easier. That said, we are still covering ground and doing a thorough search. I do know where I'm going deer hunting this fall. By the way, I think I speak for all of us when I say the whole cougar thing made walking up on a deer a lot more interesting."

"With regard to the cougar," I began, "Dr. Kouper is over at Ghost Lake Veterinary necropsying the animal right now. I don't believe he is looking for anything that will help us in the search. Remember, he was brought in to deal with the cougar, not a missing person. So, while he has been extremely helpful, his priorities are what they are. Everyone is worn thin. We will have to make some decisions about what we do next. It has been suggested we do a thermal imaging search tonight, and when we get an image, check it."

"So far, everything with the drone has worked well, but if we keep going in the same direction we're headed, we will come to some dense, tall timber. Will the drone be effective there?" Deputy Plums asked.

Liz jumped in. "The drones are a good tool, and they are getting better and better every day. One of the places they have some difficulty is big timber country like this. Sometimes it is just a temporary loss of GPS signal. Other times, the cover or canopy is heavy, and we can't see the ground where it's most likely that a lost person might be. The situation we have now is the best: eyes on the ground and eyes in the air. Still, it's not perfect."

"What do you think about continuing the search tonight?" I asked Liz.

"The sooner we find Anna, the better her chances of being found alive. She grew up in this country, and while anyone can get lost, it seems unlikely that she got turned around in daylight on a trail that is familiar to her. In my opinion, it's more likely she is injured. These trails aren't paved city jogging trails. Even the best ones are full of things that anyone could trip on. She might have fallen and hit her head, becoming disoriented. We won't know until we find her."

I looked at my people, some had already been here since before sunrise, but there was no doubt that we would continue the search through the night. Liz and her people worked with the volunteer firefighters and law enforcement to do a three-grid search.

Rough country and downed timber made the night search difficult and slow going. Tired searchers became less observant, stumbled and fell more, and the chance of injury increased. By the early morning hours, we were all exhausted. Finally, we called it a night.

Once back at the ECC, people dropped down where they were. I sat on the ground with my back on one of the big tires. It is surprising how welcoming a truck tire backrest can be when you're worn out. Pave, Plums, Bud, and I would stay on-site while everyone else would go home to get some rest. Although Liz and crew were determined to stay, I convinced them to head off to the

Cedar Inn. They would be back and ready to go at eight when a fresh crew of searchers would be here. I crawled into one of the bunks in the ECC. Pave, Plums, and Bud grabbed the others. ▪

CHAPTER 19

It was hard to believe morning had come already and harder to believe we even slept. The blaring of a truck horn was our alarm clock as we rolled out of the bunks. The horn belonged to a full-size school bus under the command of none other than Ron Carver, who was telling a news crew to move. The driver of the news van said he couldn't move because Ron was an idiot and had blocked him in.

Ron could put on ugly second to none, and he was many things, but an idiot was not one of them. By the time I got there, he had already jumped down from the driver's seat and was busy telling the reporter that he fully intended to back up to get a running start and drive his school bus through, not around, the news vans. It was no idle threat. Once he made up his mind, he would most certainly do as he proposed.

I stepped in, and after some cajoling and threatening to have Doc O'Malley show up with his truck and move vehicles out of the way at their expense, the news crew got the hint. We started to untangle the mess of haphazardly parked cars and vans on a one-lane gravel trail road. Then two Musky Falls officers showed up and took over, directing the trucks and vans off the main road to areas with widened gravel shoulders and a small trailhead parking area. Carver finally drove through to where the ECC was located.

Once in the parking lot, he opened the bus exit door. Stella and Amber Lockridge came out first, followed by Tim the plumber, a logging crew from Sayner Timber, a contingent of church ladies, and a couple dozen more community members. Citizens of all ages pitched in and immediately began to set up what can only be described as a tent city. Out of the back of the bus came chairs, folding tables, and a canvas wall tent on loan from Big Top Music. Bud and the logging crew took charge of the tent. Everyone else pitched in setting up tables and chairs. Community coming together—one of theirs was missing, and everyone would do what they could to bring her home.

Jack Wheeler arrived on-site and, in his attempt to stay out of the way of the tent crew, he ended up standing next to a recognizable national reporter who had been one of the most outspoken and always at the front of the press line. His reports included dramatic delivery and more than a tinge of sensationalism. To Jack, it seemed to be a countdown to finding Anna dead.

His camera went live, and he said to the listening audience, "Now we have breaking news from Namekagon County, Wisconsin."

Jack listened as the reporter gave his report, repeating previously reported details and adding anything new. He signed off and walked toward me. Jack intercepted him. Like all of us, he was tired. The man of calm and reason had enough for the moment.

He said to the reporter, "By listening to your report, it almost sounds to me like it would make your day to find a wild animal had eaten Anna. Too bad you're missing the real story unfolding right in front of you. This community—my community—is coming together to bring one of ours home safe and sound."

He looked at Jack with world-weary eyes and, after a long moment, said, "You know something, Jack? It is Jack, right?"

"Yes, Jack."

"You're right. Tragedy sells more shampoo. I've been at this a long time. I have been behind the lines in war zones and tracked down more crooked politicians than I can remember. I've reported on too much sorrow, too much heartache. Jack, I'm tired, but no one pays me for good news. Do you know what the last community event story I did was?"

"No, I don't," Jack replied.

I stood just close enough to hear his story. "It was just a month ago in a city about a thousand miles from here. A protest was planned to take place in an urban neighborhood, and I was assigned to cover it. Things started out peacefully enough with lots of speeches, indignation, and righteousness, and then lots of cheering and clapping. Almost like one of those old-time church gatherings, kind of fun in a way. The local minister gave a wonderful speech about peace, love, and commitment.

"When it got dark, it all changed. The minister was the first of two people killed when he stood with a store owner and tried to stop looters who had smashed through the front glass window. A sixteen-year-old boy from the neighborhood he had baptized was charged with the murder.

"Before it was all over, the very businesses owned by their friends and neighbors, the stores they shopped at, were all looted and burned to the ground. Fire companies' lights and hose lines crisscrossed through the night. Ambulances were coming and going. I don't even remember how many were injured. Police were finally able to get things calmed down at about three in the morning.

"The next day, I went back to where this had all occurred. If it's true that a community requires a place to be, a place to grow, then this community no longer existed. It was nothing but charred rubble and memories of what was. Nothing gained, but so much lost.

"Then I watched as it happened. An elderly man came out on the street with a shovel and began to clean up the debris. Soon he was joined by another and another. I watched as a community just like yours came together. Soon the street was full of good people starting over again. The news about death, fire, and destruction was all the network wanted. The old man with the shovel never made the news.

"You're right, Jack. I need to tell this story the way it should be told. The sheriff was dead on when he said we are all in this thing together. We all want Anna McDonald found alive and well. Tell us what we can do to help."

The tents were up, and tables and chairs were moved in. Even the reporters pitched in to help. Then out came the food, enough to feed this small army. I went to get a cup of coffee, and when I bent down, I was dizzy for a minute, almost asleep on my feet. The searchers were headed back out and would return in three hours when another crew would take over through the day.

I was deciding what I should do when my cell phone rang. "Sheriff Cabrelli," I answered.

"Sheriff, this is Pederson Kouper. I need you to come to the Ghost Lake Veterinary Clinic as quickly as you can."

"Hold on, Dr. Kouper, while I shake my brain awake. You need me where?"

"The Ghost Lake Veterinary Clinic. It is important."

"I am on my way."

"Sheriff, if I may, I suggest you contact the medical examiner and ask him to respond, too."

A chill ran through my body, and for a second, I lost my breath.

Through a premonition, or from the hard road of experience, I knew what this meant. It doesn't happen to everyone, but it does happen. I don't believe any law enforcement officer ever forgets it; I never did.

My first was years ago. I started out on patrol at eleven at night. It was a beautiful May night with a full moon, and I was assigned to a rural farming area in the northern part of the county. The farms were few and far between. Most folks were sound asleep. I came around a sharp curve on a narrow country road made more for hay wagons and tractors than high-speed travel. There at the sharpest bend in the curve was a car, rolled over and sitting on its top. I advised dispatch of what I had, and they sent another unit. I walked up to the car and shined my flashlight around. There was one person in the car. He was pinned inside. I could detect no pulse or respirations. I hollered into the radio for an ambulance and Jaws of Life. I didn't need to wonder how old he was, how many brothers or sisters he had, or where he lived. I already knew all that because we had been friends and classmates since kindergarten. His body was crushed, but his face was untouched. I had seen him only a week or so before the accident. Once things were taken care of at the scene, the officer in charge asked if I wished to notify his family, and I said I would. So in the wee hours of the morning, I found myself knocking on the door of a house where I had often been a guest. His father answered the door. He must have known when he saw me in uniform because the only thing he said was his son's name. He gathered the family but asked to speak with me alone on the front porch. I told him what had happened while he listened without saying a word. He was a strong, tough man, a combat veteran. He placed his hand gently on my shoulder. Tears streamed down his face, and he thanked me for coming. He thanked me for being a good enough friend to deliver the worst of all news. He told me that he wished I would go now.

Cops want to portray a tough image, and they do a pretty good job of it. The reality is even the toughest ones have a heart, feel sympathy and compassion. They hide behind a hard shell erected to protect themselves. But they never forget when the victim is someone they know. It will be with them forever.

Dr. Chali responded on his radio, then asked me to switch to the secure channel.

"Sheriff, any idea what this callout is about?"

"I have got an idea, but I don't think I should speculate over the air, secure or not."

"Got it, Sheriff. I am on my way."

Our ME, Mike Chali, had only recently moved to Namekagon County with his wife. She was a crisis counselor and had become a close friend of Julie's. The Chalis had moved away from financially rewarding jobs and big careers to live where they could raise a family and live with the lakes and the loons. They wanted to find a place where community and values still mattered. But mostly, they wanted a place where they could catch muskies. Like generations before them, the beauty of Namekagon County captured the Chalis, and they never looked back.

As I pulled into the veterinary clinic, I could see one end of the building was completely lit up. The door was unlocked, and I walked in. Following the lights down to an operating suite, I found Pederson Kouper, Charlie Newlin, and the clinic's owner, Dr. Connel. Under the lights was the body of the cougar. Sample jars were arranged on a tray, each neatly labeled. Several tubes of blood were also on the tray. Larger organs were in stainless steel pans. They were so involved in what they were doing that they didn't even notice when I came in.

Finally, Dr. Kouper looked up at me. "Oh, Sheriff, my gosh. I didn't see you."

The other two in the room did not greet me; they only stared.

When you walk into a room of people you know, and they say nothing, guaranteed it is a harbinger of bad news. Bad in a way that no one wanted to deliver it, bad in a way that no one wanted to receive it. I had seen Dr. Kouper's kind and gentle side when he was examining the animals. I could see it coming out now.

"John, I am sorry to share what I have to share with you. I am not certain how to do this or what to say. Is the ME on his way?"

"He is."

Kouper took a breath and looked at me. "Sheriff, we should talk before we go forward. Better yet, let's wait for the ME. I am certain that he will have his own procedures to follow. You may as well."

At that moment, a vehicle pulled up to the clinic. I walked outside to meet Dr. Chali as he got out of his restored FJ55 Land Cruiser.

"Hi, Sheriff. What do we have?" he asked.

"I'm not sure, but I have a very bad feeling about this. Dr. Kouper wanted to wait for you before they explained."

"Okay, we better not keep him waiting any longer."

Hellos were still subdued.

"Thank you for coming so promptly. We are entering into some not unknown but uncommon circumstances. Sheriff, I need you to know before we proceed that the animal before you likely has a direct connection with the missing person Anna MacDonald. I cannot advise you on how you may choose to proceed. Understandably, your close personal relationship might make this difficult."

I had already known the minute I got the call.

"John, what do you think?" asked Dr. Chali.

"I think this is my job. I'm here, so let's get on with this," I said.

"Okay then. We shall begin. I will try and keep the scientific jargon to a minimum. There will be plenty of that in the final report. I do, however, want to record my report to you. Is that acceptable to everyone?"

We agreed. Dr. Kouper, Professor Newlin, and Dr. Connel had on face masks. Dr. Chali put one on and handed one to me.

Kouper began. "This animal is a fully mature *puma concolor*. It weighs 87.62 kilograms. We have removed most of the organs and prepared them for future study. During the course of our necropsy, we examined the contents of the digestive system. First, the stomach, then the colon, and lastly, the small intestine. Like all carnivores, the cougar has a short digestive system. The full digestion should occur in twelve to twenty-four hours, depending on what is eaten.

"We isolated contents of these three areas immediately upon removing them. First, we examined the stomach. Upon close inspection, we found several pieces of black cloth consistent with some sort of elasticized fabric. The pieces were ripped and torn. We also found and removed several bone fragments as well as some smaller intact bones with flesh still attached. In addition, we removed the entire contents of the stomach, which was mostly partially digested flesh of some kind, as well as small pieces of bone."

Dr. Kouper showed us three stainless steel pans containing the bone fragments, the pieces of cloth, and the stomach contents.

"The reason for all the bone fragments is a cougar has very strong jaws and will easily crush and break bones, as you see here," he explained.

Then he reached for another pan and avoided looking at me. "In this pan, we have intact bone segments, some with flesh attached. Dr. Chali, I am assuming you will want to examine these more closely. Dr. Connel has an excellent magnifier and projection PC that he will gladly assist you with.

"The entire contents of the digestive system have been labeled and isolated, again mostly partially digested food and bone fragments. Of note, when we examined the colon, we found bone fragments, more black cloth, and this."

Kouper showed us a pan that contained another piece of cloth, red this time with a snap-type fastener attached, like the kind you might find on a windbreaker or jogging jacket.

"Protein from other animals make up almost all of a cougar's diet," the vet continued. "They are efficient hunters but have a fairly low success rate even in the best of circumstances. A mature animal will try to make a significant kill every seven days or so, but if unable to do that, it will feed on anything it can catch. After a kill, the lion will feed and then cover the remains with sticks and brush. This will likely occur in proximity to where the kill was made, often within one hundred yards. It will pick a spot that will shade the kill to slow spoilage and allow the cat some privacy when it returns to feed on the carcass again.

"In this case, we have another circumstance that would impact the cougar's ability to pursue its natural prey. The animal's front right paw was abscessed and extremely swollen. An x-ray showed two broken bones, both attempting to heal poorly. Lodged tightly in those bones between the toes, we found this."

Kouper held up a specimen jar that held a small metallic object. He handed it to me.

"Looks like a small caliber bullet, maybe a .22," I said. My thoughts flashed back to Reverend Redberg's story of the cougar's visit.

"I would concur, Sheriff. It would have made hunting very difficult for this animal. Yet the cat, while a little thin, shows no signs of malnourishment. In fact, based on the stomach contents, I would say it fed only a few hours before it was killed," Kouper said.

"In other words, even with a badly injured forepaw, it found something it could catch and eat?" I asked.

"I would have to agree with that, and likely more than one meal," Professor Newlin said.

"The paw could also explain why he didn't tree to get away from Brewer's dogs. He probably had limited use of the injured paw," Dr. Kouper said.

No one knew what to say. This situation was beyond anyone's comprehension, but I was faced with the blunt reality of what had likely occurred. A cougar was shot and killed in the same area where Anna had disappeared. The same area where a child and her family had been stalked. The cougar was badly injured and couldn't hunt its normal prey. It needed to survive and would have been very clever in finding food—it had found Anna.

"Sheriff, it is consistent with the evidence you recovered," Dr. Kouper continued. "Tracks at the beginning of the trail. Anna would have been running, which could have triggered the predator-prey response in a hungry animal. Blood and drag marks are just the way a cougar hunts. Maybe she tried to kick at the animal with her foot, but the cougar grabbed her shoe."

While Dr. Chali was listening, he was also doing his job. He had donned a pair of surgical gloves and was looking through the stomach contents. No one was really watching him until he said, "Dr. Connel or someone, can I get a specimen bottle?"

Dr. Connel removed the cap of the bottle and held it for the ME. He was holding an item with a forceps and carefully dropped it into the bottle. Dr. Connel put the cap on.

"What is it, Mike? What did you find?" I asked.

"John, I'm sorry. What I found was a human bone."

"You're sure?" Kouper asked.

"I am positive," Chali replied. "I have also examined several other fragments. They, too, came from a human. I do have a question, Dr. Kouper. You said that a cougar will eat, digest, and excrete in twelve to twenty-four hours, correct?"

"Yes, that's correct," Kouper replied.

"Is there anything in a cougar's system that accelerates the breakdown of consumed tissue?"

"I am aware of some research that shows a change in the digestive acid of a cougar based on the abundance of food or lack thereof. For example, some cougars may eat certain types of vegetation when deer or elk are not as plentiful in their home territory. It will take longer for that vegetation to break down than meat. That's really all I know. It is a very specialized field of study. I can check around with others. Why do you ask?"

"Just a question," replied Dr. Chali.

I think that we were all stunned by the realization. Unfortunately, being stunned into nonaction is not allowed in situations like this. Again, Dr. Kouper spoke up.

"There is a course of action here that will give us a good chance of recovering Anna MacDonald's body."

We had now changed course. We were no longer trying to rescue Anna from unknown harm. We were now planning on how to recover her body. From rescue to recovery, a giant and heartbreaking step for the searchers. For us. ∎

CHAPTER 20

"What do you suggest we do, Dr. Kouper?" I asked.

"It is very likely that the cougar was only a short distance from its feeding site when it was killed. The injury to the right front paw would have kept the cougar from going further than necessary. If we started at the spot the cougar was killed and did a shoulder-to-shoulder slow search, there is a good chance we would find something."

"The searchers will be starting again in an hour or so. I have another idea. I need to call Liz Masters and run something by her. In the meantime, I'll contact my deputies and the search team this morning and ask them to hold things up. Professor Newlin, Dr. Kouper, Dr. Connel, what is your plan now?"

"I plan to get these old bones home and catch a little shuteye if I am no longer needed," Dr. Connel said.

"Charlie and I will finish up here, recording the information and cataloging the samples. Then we will put the cougar in Dr. Connel's freezer until we know the next step."

"Dr. Chali, if it's okay with you, I would like you to accompany me to the trailhead parking lot and meet with Liz Masters," I said.

"Sure, Sheriff," Chali agreed.

"I will keep everyone advised on the situation as soon as I know something worth saying."

Chali jumped in his vehicle and followed me to Musky Run.

While nothing much had changed at the trailhead, everything had changed for us. We followed Liz Masters' van into the parking area. Searchers were getting geared up and organized under the direction of the Spider Lake fire chief and Chief Delzell.

As soon as Liz got out of the van, I asked her to come over to the ECC. When we stepped inside, the aroma of the command center was distinctly different from the fresh northern air.

Liz, Dr. Chali, and I sat at the small table covered with different maps of the area.

"Good morning, Liz. Get any sleep last night?" I asked.

"I slept very well. My team and I checked in at the Cedar Inn. An hour in the hot tub, good food, and then to bed. I learned a long time ago that sleeping in the van or on the ground is a poor second choice to getting a good night's sleep and hitting all cylinders in the morning. By the way, John, you look like you haven't slept in a month, and Dr. Chali, you don't look much better."

"Dr. Kouper just paged us out," I said.

"If it wasn't an offer to meet for early coffee, I'm guessing it has something to do with why you called this meeting," said Liz.

"Dr. Kouper necropsied the—" Then the door burst open.

"Sheriff, are we calling off the search? We've got two dozen people ready to go, and they're all wondering what's holding everything up," Deputy Plums inquired.

"Plums, I need you to stand by out there. We are working on something at the moment that is critical to the recovery of Anna MacDonald," I said.

"Sheriff, you just said recovery, not rescue," Plums observed.

"Deputy, you have got to help me out here. No search until I say so. Don't get these people worked up; keep them calm."

Plums was a good man and went out to do his job.

I looked at Liz. "I need your help."

It was Dr. Masters who stared back at me.

"Last night, Dr. Kouper, Professor Newlin, and Dr. Connel, owner of the vet clinic, performed a necropsy on the cougar. During the course of the necropsy, they discovered pieces of cloth and human remains."

Dr. Chali interjected, "I examined several bone fragments. They are from a human. One was a finger with flesh still attached. Dr. Kouper and Professor Newlin have collected all the samples, and they will be maintained at the Ghost Lake Clinic until we need them moved."

"So, your theory is that the cougar killed and ate Anna MacDonald, correct?"

"Pretty hard to ignore the evidence," I said.

"That it is," she replied. "How can I help?"

"Do you know Tony Eagen?" I asked.

"Yes, I know Tony well. We've worked together on several cases," she replied.

"I know him too, and he's the best there is, and he is who I need here. I want you to put in a priority mutual aid request. I want Eagen here as soon as possible."

"John, I don't know his schedule, what he has going. He is still a working deputy sheriff, so it's not like he can just take off at a moment's notice. Have you talked with Malone?"

"I figured I'd hit you up first."

"Oh my gosh, your wedding—Malone's coming for the wedding. What about the wedding? Have you told Julie what you suspect?"

"Liz, I haven't had two minutes to do anything since last night. Anna is her best friend in the world. I will go home and tell her as soon as we get squared away."

"Sheriff, you need to be her best friend in the world. She'll need you right now, maybe more than she ever has. Dr. Chali being here is bound to catch someone's notice. You need to go now."

"Liz, I have got to—" She cut me off.

"You have got nothing to do until you see Julie. We can handle things here. Now get going." Liz turned to Dr. Chali. "What is your plan for the moment?"

"I'm not sure."

"How about you dictate a report that explains your preliminary findings? Basically, what led you to think there may be a corpse. I will include your narrative with my request for Tony Eagen and his dog," Liz suggested.

"Okay, I'll do that right now."

"After you're done with that, I'll send a couple of my techs to follow you back out to the vet clinic. Once you get there, make sure everything is bagged and tagged, just as if it were a crime scene. When you get that done, you should probably head home and get some sleep. I've got a feeling that we're in for a long haul. I don't have to tell you that even if the cougar consumed a corpse, we might still be a long way from a cause of death."

"I know, I know," responded Chali.

I hadn't moved. Liz turned to look at me. "What are you still doing here? Get going, now!"

I got in my squad and headed home to break the love of my life's heart.

I knew I would find Julie at home. She had been with the MacDonalds all yesterday and convinced them they should not go back out to the search area. They agreed to stay put and finally went off to bed, and Julie called me and said she was heading home.

I pulled into our drive, and my heart was leaden. Sadness permeated my entire being. It was like that night long ago, telling my friend's father the last words he ever wanted to hear. My words would bring such pain. There was nothing I could do, nothing I could say that would soften the blow. It was a story of sadness I needed to tell, and it challenged my courage.

I walked in, and Julie was sitting in her chair, a magazine on her lap, staring out the picture window. She had on her reading glasses that made her look so cute and so scholarly at the same time. She looked up at me and tried to smile, but it wasn't there.

"Hi, honey. I'm glad you're home. I'm sure you could use a break. You look so tired. Can I get you something? Anything you want. Just stop looking at me that way. Please stop."

"Julie, come over and sit by me."

She put her head on my shoulder, and her tears soon soaked my shirt. We didn't say a word. Words didn't need to be said.

"Have you found Anna? Is she gone?" she sobbed.

"I am so sorry, honey. I'm afraid it looks that way. We have not yet located Anna. But Dr. Chali has examined the evidence, and it's conclusive."

"You have not found her body?"

"No, we haven't. I have asked for a specialist from Dane County to come and help locate it."

"With all the searchers, the drone, and everything else, you have not found her body?"

"No, we haven't, but I believe we will soon."

"John, you have not found Anna's body because it is not there. She is not dead, John. I am sure of it."

"Julie, honey, I know this is hard. I can't imagine how hard it is. You're going to need some time. I'm here for you. I know you two were like sisters and, well, you know, sometimes people have trouble processing things like this."

At that moment, Julie laughed, and at the same time, tears poured from her eyes. "John Cabrelli, I know she's alive. You know how I know?"

"No, Julie, I don't."

"Anna MacDonald would never miss our wedding. Now I would appreciate it if my handsome, strong, super sleuth of a husband-to-be would stop wasting his time here and get out there and find Anna. I love you, John. Now get going."

Julie was a woman of resolve, and I had learned that sometimes nothing I could say or do would change her mind. It is just best to leave things alone. Eventually, she would find her way to the reality of loss. I would be by her side forever, including when that happened.

As soon as I pulled out, I called her friend, Becky Chali, and explained the situation with Julie. She promised to stop by and see her.

I was back at the trailhead in time to keep Liz Masters from clobbering Stephen Cameron. As I pulled up, he ran over to my squad.

"Cabrelli, get over here," Cameron ordered. "Why aren't these people searching for my wife? I came down here, and everyone said you canceled the search. How could that be? Why would you cancel a search when you haven't found who you are looking for? I demand an explanation."

I let him burn all his considerable fuel, and then I walked over to the searchers. Before I spoke, a flash of Shakespeare came to mind. Everyone, including Cameron, quieted, waiting for me.

"Folks, we are not searching today. Your support has been critical in our attempts to locate Anna MacDonald. You are welcome to stay here if you like, but some of you have other things that need doing. Most of you have been here day and night. The bus is coming back. I suggest you head home, get some rest, and get caught up on things. This situation is not over by any stretch, and I may have to call on you again. It would work better for all of us if you were well-rested.

"We have requested special assistance from Dane County. I do not yet know the status of that assistance. Dr. Masters, can you help me with that?"

"Sheriff, the request from Dane County has been honored, and the person you requested is en route."

The bus rumbled in, and the crowd began to disperse.

A reporter boldly stepped up to the front and shouted, "Is it true, Sheriff, that you have requested the assistance of a cadaver dog from Dane County?"

The crowd stopped moving, and all eyes were fixed on me.

"Yes, it is true. I am so sorry to say that, but yes, it's true. We have recovered evidence that has led us to this next step."

It was like sticking a pin in a balloon. The searchers raring to go a minute ago were now deflated. They had all understood this might be the outcome, but no one wanted to believe it.

"We are not going back into the search area again until the dog has had a chance. This is one of the most successful K-9 teams in the country. We need to give them every advantage."

"It's the cougar. The cougar got her, didn't it? That's the evidence you found. The cougar got Anna MacDonald," he shouted. The questions and statements came fast and furious after that. The barrage was relentless.

I was so news weary I could have cried. Tonight, people across the country would watch this story unfold on the news: "Olympic gold medalist gets eaten by a mountain lion." Reporters would comb the town with new vigor to find barstool experts willing to say anything for a crack at their fifteen minutes. Our community would not find the reports interesting or entertaining. Most wouldn't even watch.

As enthusiasm and energy waned after the hours of searching without results, the hope of finding one near and dear to our hearts kept people going. Now, a stranger with a camera and microphone had burst their bubble. They knew the possibility existed, but they chose the half-full glass. All but a handful of volunteers took the bus back home.

In mid-afternoon, a marked Ford Explorer emblazoned with a K-9 unit banner and a colorful emblem depicting anglers, education, farming, and the state capitol arrived. The driver ignored everyone and drove slowly through the crowd, intent on reaching his destination. When he stopped the car, reporters tried to move in. The deputy got out and turned to them.

"Ladies and gentlemen, we have come a long way. I would like to let my dog Ty out because he has to pee. I am sure that would not offend your sensibilities, but there is one other problem—my dog bites. I have tried to keep him from doing it, but he just won't stop. Normally, that would disqualify him from the job, but he is so darn good at what he does, we've decided to overlook that one little problem. So, our lawyer has suggested that we simply warn people and give them plenty of time to get out of his way. So, here's the warning: If I don't let him out, he probably won't, but he may very well pee in the car. Aside from his shortcomings, he is a dignified gentleman, and peeing in the car would offend his sensibilities. Then there is no telling who he might bite. I am going to let him out now, so please stay back."

The deputy opened the rear door and out jumped seventy pounds of black Labrador. He shook himself back into shape and then walked deliberately toward the crowd. People started to back up. The Lab stopped when he came to a reporter's black gear bag on the ground. The owner of the bag tried to move it, but the dog either growled or burped; it was impossible to tell. Then he lifted his leg and let go with a stream that would make a racehorse proud.

I approached the deputy. "Hey, Tony, thank you so much for dropping everything and heading up here." I knew Tony from my previous law enforcement service. He and his dog were legendary. He was a professional who did a daunting task while maintaining a good sense of humor.

"It's not like I had much choice seeing how it seems as everyone who has any clout," Tony said, pointing at Liz who had just joined us, "told me this was where I needed to be, so I have arrived."

"We have a situation, and we likely have a body somewhere out there. Liz and her crew have been flying the drone, along with coordinated searchers on the ground. We have suspended the search pending your arrival."

"I would like to sit down with you, Liz, the ME, and anyone else you think needs to be there to talk this thing through," Tony replied. "The information I have right now is kind of sketchy. I have been following the news, and when I heard about the celebrity status of the lost person, I wondered if I might be called here."

We crowded into the ECC and tried to get comfortable, which was an impossible task, compounded by the big Lab, whose wagging tail immediately swept several empty soda cans off a small table.

"Tony, he doesn't look like a biter to me," I commented.

"John, he's never bitten anyone in his life, and I don't expect he ever will. You actually have a better chance of me biting you. I just say that to scare people enough that they leave us alone. Pissing on the camera bag, though, was all his idea. He has an indignant streak and rarely, but sometimes, uses those nonviolent forms of protest to express himself. I find it pretty funny—an inside joke Ty and I share. Could we go someplace else? I need to be able to concentrate, and I would like to give Ty a chance to work out the kinks after the long drive," Tony requested.

"Will you begin the search today?" asked Liz.

"I don't think so. I want both Ty and me to be fresh. That will give us a chance to get all the information I need. I'm sure you're anxious to get going, but I want the best chance of a rapid recovery. So where should we meet up?"

"Normally, I would suggest my place," I said, "but it won't work under the circumstances. I have an idea, though. Let me make a call." ∎

CHAPTER 21

I called Jack Wheeler. The lodge he was restoring across the lake from my place had a large screened-in porch area that would be private and quiet. He said we were welcome to it. A short caravan pulled a tactical exit—Liz with me and Tony in his K-9 unit. Dr. Pederson Kouper was advised and said he would meet us there. Dr. Chali was also on his way.

The lodge was a thing of beauty. Built by old-world craftsmen from hand-hewn logs and set right on the shore with a stunning view of Spider Lake. Building that close to the water was no longer allowed, but Jack's place was over one hundred years old and grandfathered in. Some of the timbers supporting the large screened-in deck that overlooked the lake had to be replaced, and he had hired Bud to do the project. Over the winter, when the ice was thick enough, select local log timbers were delivered. Bud rented a tractor with a loader bucket and a PTO implement on the back that would help each pole up. Once they were close to plumb, Julie, Jack, and I—the cheap labor team—used hand winches and ropes at Bud's direction for minor correction. Bud had planned perfectly, and each post dropped into place. The timbers would last at least another one hundred years.

We now sat on that restored porch resting upon those timbers and watched as Tony threw a ball for Ty. The dog leaped to the task with a cannonball splash, brought the ball back, sat in front of Tony, and held it in his mouth until his partner gently pulled it out. After all that was going on, we all needed a little break.

Everyone came back together, and with Jack's pre-approval, I requisitioned soft drinks and lemonade from his refrigerator.

The discussion was professional and to the point. Drs. Kouper and Masters gave their opinions on a potential search area and laid it out on a map for all of us to see. The hypothesis put forth was simple: The cougar had been injured, and the injury would have been extremely painful. That pain would have been limiting even though he covered some ground. More importantly, his ability to hunt was also compromised, with one of his most important weapons out of commission, suggesting that once it made a kill, it would stay close to it until there was nothing left to eat, then move on.

We examined the map and where areas of different cover were located. Some parts of the proposed search area consisted of barely covered rock. Three other areas had heavy cover with a stream running down the middle. It was the kind of area that would be tough for human searchers to walk through but no challenge for a cougar or dog. Dr. Kouper showed us several high-resolution photos of cougar kills from sites he had observed in the past. They were covered with brush, leaves, grass, and dirt. The kills were so well disguised it was difficult to see the bodies, even when Kouper pointed them out to us.

"Tony, I would guess this is what you and Ty will encounter. The heavily vegetated area should probably be searched first, but that is your call."

"So let me explain what I would like to do and why. Our first priority will be to search the area closest to where the evidence was recovered, but not an area that has been searched on foot. Areas already searched will be marked as a secondary search area. Ty and I are going to work alone. I think Dr. Kouper and Liz have made some very reasonable and probably accurate assumptions about where we might find a body. They have arrived at these conclusions based on experience, personal knowledge, and preconceived notions. Ty is not burdened with preconceived notions. He has some experience that he undoubtedly retains, but mostly he's just a dog that has millions of scent receptors. His brain is wired to process these scents and act on them in the appropriate way.

"For example, Ty's brother is an exceptional bird dog. His owner uses him to find pheasants. A dog running back and forth across a field is bombarded with scents. When he gets the one he's looking for, namely a pheasant in this case, his scenting ability and training come together. He knows there are things he has been taught to do that coincide with locating that scent. Both the dog and handler recognize signals from one another, subtle cues that others might not notice. It sets off a chain of events, hopefully going well for the hunter and his dog. The Lab flushes the bird, the bird launches itself in the air, and the hunter shoots the bird. The bird falls to the ground, and the dog marks the spot where it fell. Then using scent along with his visual observation, the dog runs out to pick the bird up and bring it back to the shooter. In this case, the dog doesn't just bring the bird to the hunter; he carries the bird back, sits in front of the shooter, and holds it until the shooter takes it. Then the dog takes off to do it all again. He does what comes naturally to him, in conjunction with what he has been trained to do and what millions of receptors tell him to do.

"Ty is just like every other dog. His nose is his guide to the world, and cadaverine and putrescine are the scents he's looking for. He will search bare rock and tall timber with equal enthusiasm. In this case, if he finds what he is looking for, he will lie down and wait for me. He will find what's there for him to find. I have worked hard to allow him a fair amount of freedom in how he chooses to search. In areas like this, with no traffic or other hazards, it's pretty safe. We will start at the trailhead tomorrow morning and take a leisurely walk. He will know that he's working and will search for scent. I will have my long line and my short leash, but I intend to let him check this out for himself. As far as how long the search will take, all I can say is it will take as long as it takes. Dr. Kouper, is there any chance we might encounter another cougar?"

"It is possible, but I think highly unlikely. We did find some smaller tracks but didn't see another animal. We've had no additional problems with predation at this point. If there was something, I am sure I would have heard. People around here are hypersensitive to anything involving cougars. The only cat seen by the drone or searchers was the one shot," Kouper reassured him.

"Do you want someone to back you up with a rifle, Tony?" I asked.

"I don't know; we'll see in the morning. This is not a challenge Ty and I usually face."

We agreed to meet at the trailhead tomorrow morning at seven. Tony had spent a fair amount of his vacation time hunting, fishing, and hiking in the Northwoods and was well acquainted with the weather idiosyncrasies. Early in the day, the air would be cooler, usually accompanied by higher relative humidity and calmer winds, resulting in good scenting conditions. Cool weather was easier on a working dog.

While the others headed to their respective sleeping quarters, I drove back to the trailhead to meet with my deputies.

Much to my happy surprise, I was greeted by Chief Delzell.

"Hi, John. I brought you your favorite dark roast blend," she said as she handed me a cup of coffee.

"Thanks, Mary."

"I appreciate you keeping me informed. Town is a madhouse. How are you guys keeping up?"

"I'm trying to keep track of things, but this is getting more complicated by the minute."

"How is Julie taking it?"

"She absolutely, positively believes Anna is alive. She won't hear anything else. I asked Becky Chali to stop by and see her."

"John, you and I have dealt with death our whole careers. Everybody deals with it differently, that includes Julie. Let her have her space. She is as smart and levelheaded as they come. She'll find her way through this. What's up with the wedding?" she inquired.

"I am kind of afraid to ask. There is no way that we are going through with it under these circumstances. She just told me that Anna wouldn't dare miss it. Mary, I'm whipped. If one more thing happens, I do believe my head will explode. I need to be with Julie right now, but the job just can't seem to let that happen."

"I think I can take one thing off your plate. The media is anxious and looking for the next breaking news headline. Instead of having them wander around, we will ask them to stay set up at the parking area furthest from the trailhead. If they get organized, there is plenty of room, and they will be able to see what we have going on. Most importantly, they will be out of everyone's way. That's where all contacts with the press will be made and only by Jack Wheeler. Most of the press has settled down some and is pretty well-behaved. I don't know if you've noticed, but a lot of the media folks are interested in helping out. They have contributed to and helped serve food when it shows up. Four or five of them have volunteered to be on the search teams. While you could suspect ulterior motives, that doesn't seem to be the case. I think everyone really wants Anna to be found safe and sound. I will leave one of my officers here to work with Deputy Pave and get everyone situated."

It was clear the reporters got the news. They started rolling up their temporary sidewalks and jockeying things around to get everyone going in the right direction.

I headed home, to what I didn't know. I would do absolutely anything I could to heal Julie's heart.

I walked in and found Bud sitting on the couch by Julie. I was relieved. When Julie looked up at me, I could see her pretty face was tired and drawn, her eyes rimmed red. She had a cup of untouched tea on the table. Bud was trying to take up as little room as he could on the couch. He and Julie were cousins but closer than any brother and sister.

I sat in a chair nearby. I was searching for something to say, the right words—any words. Julie again came to my rescue.

She popped up from the couch, wiped her eyes, and said, "Oh my gosh, I almost forgot I thawed our last package of those big bluegills you caught through the ice, Bud. I have got a pan of cornbread ready to go in. I bet you're hungry; I know I sure am. Why don't you guys find something to do, and I'll call when everything is ready."

Bud and I walked out of the house to the dock.

"John, do you think Julie's going to be okay?"

"I don't know what to say, Bud. This is just a bad situation. We'll get through it together, but it will take some time. Sadness has its own way of healing, but we will heal. What about you, Bud? How are you doing? I know how close you all were."

Bud Treetall, a mountain of a man, tall and broad-shouldered with a heart of gold, crumbled.

"John, I never told anyone this before," he began with a huge sob. "I'm in love with Anna and have always been, ever since we were kids. I knew she never looked at me like a guy she might want to go out on a date with, but it didn't stop me from loving her. When everything happened with her husband, and she came back home, I prayed every night she might choose me. I never, ever told her I loved her; I was too afraid. Now I might never get the chance."

Seeing the unflappable, perpetually good-natured Bud so deeply hurt broke my heart.

"I'm sorry, Bud," was the best I could come up with.

"Tell me the honest truth, John. Anna's dead, isn't she? She was killed by the mountain lion, wasn't she? That's the truth about what happened."

"Bud, the truth is I don't know. It does not look good, but I don't know. That's why I requested the canine handler. He and his dog are specialists. They are trained to look for bodies."

"Shouldn't we keep searching with people first? I know I can get some more people to help out," Bud said.

"Bud, human remains were found in the cougar's stomach. We have not found Anna, but we did find some evidence that she may have been dragged off by someone or something. We need to understand that there is little we can do to help Anna anymore, but everyone who cared for her needs closure. The sooner we find her, the sooner the healing can start. It is my job to find her. I love you and Julie. We are a family, a good family, a strong family. We will survive this, but right now, I have a job to do."

Bud spent the night in our small guest cabin. At four-thirty, Julie was awake and downstairs reviewing applications from students who wanted to attend her school in the fall. I made some coffee and joined her, watching her read each word.

She lifted her head and looked at me. "John, I am sorry that I have acted so foolishly. My emotions got the best of me; I was overwhelmed. I needed to be here to support you and what you must do. I let you down, and I let Bud down. You know Bud has been in love with Anna forever, right?"

"Sorry, honey, sworn to secrecy on that one." That got me a little smile. "You know now that this may turn out badly, right Julie?"

"Do you want to know what I think, no matter how crazy it sounds? Anna is alive, John. I will not allow myself to believe anything different. I understand you have a job to do, but nothing you can say will convince me that Anna is no longer with us."

I needed to go, early in the morning or not. I put on my gear and kissed Julie goodbye. I got in my squad, and instead of turning left out of my driveway, I turned right, taking the long way to Musky Run. It was a cool morning, but I put my window down anyway. I poked along, and the sweet smells of the Northwoods and meadows drifted into my truck. A calm settled over me, and that was exactly what I needed to meet the day. Today we officially switched from rescue to recovery, and while hope remained, it was in the distance. I needed to be solid and at my official best to coordinate the day's activities. The sun began to rise, and since I was near a local boat landing and had some time, I pulled in to check it out.

Not much to my surprise, at this early hour, a truck and trailer with a boat were backed up to the ramp. I pulled up, shut off my engine, got out, and approached the two anglers.

It was an older gent with a much younger gent in tow.

"Hi, there," said the older fellow. "You're Sheriff Cabrelli, aren't you?"

"I am," I replied.

"I'm Sam Davis. This is my grandson, also Sam Davis. I don't believe we have met before, but I have sure heard a lot about you, good stuff. We are going out to fish for the day. The early morning seems to be the best on this water."

I shook hands with the two Sams. The youngster looked about eight and was grinning from ear to ear.

"Sheriff, my grandpa and I found a secret spot. Boy, did we clobber them over there. You know what we're going to do after we catch a bunch of fish?"

"No, what are you going to do, Sam?"

"We're going over to Big Rock Island. Then we'll clean the fish, make a campfire, and cook 'em in our old fryin' pan. After we get done eatin' fish, we're going to whittle the bark off some sticks, melt marshmallows over the fire, and smash the whole works between graham crackers with chocolate."

"Then, what are you going to do?" I asked.

The little boy looked at me like I had missed the ship.

"We're gonna eat 'em, of course, and they are really good. You want to come fishin' with us, Sheriff? Plenty of room for three people in the boat."

"I wish I could, Sam. I really wish I could. Unfortunately, there's some sheriff work that needs to get done. You two have a wonderful day. I need to get going. Need any help with the boat?"

"Nope, we're fine," said Sam, the senior.

I wished them good luck as I drove out. I couldn't help hoping there were enough people like the two Sams to take us into the future. Kids of all ages up with the sun, looking forward to an adventure, connecting with the only thing that sustains us—the land.

The traffic the rest of the way to the Musky Run trailhead was light to nonexistent. I pulled off at Scott and Muffy's Café and picked up four cups of coffee to go. They loaded them in a cardboard tray for me.

The waitress said, "If you come back again, Sheriff, and bring this cupholder, the fourth cup is free."

The driveway at the trailhead was blocked by a sheriff's car and a Musky Falls squad. The officer and the deputy finishing the night shift were sitting at one table reading what looked like a copy of the *Outdoor News* and a fishing magazine.

A marked county sheriff's Explorer was parked closer to the beginning of the trail. Tony Eagen was sitting at an old picnic table, off by himself, drinking a large cup of coffee with one hand and petting his dog with the other. He had the area maps spread out on the table.

I gave the night crew their coffees and walked over to join Tony. "Mind if I sit?"

"Nope. Have a seat," he said.

"I brought you a cup, but I see you already have one."

"I stopped at a cool little café on the way. Good breakfast and good coffee, a little fuel for the fire."

"How are things looking?"

"Good conditions, John. About as good as it can get. I wanted to get here early to let Ty sniff up some Northwoods ambiance before we get started. We are going to begin with this unsearched area," he pointed at the map. "It will help Ty get acclimated to the site without encountering ground disturbance and other scents. I thought about it, and you'd better go with me to be on the safe side. If we run into another cougar, I want to make sure Ty is protected."

"I think that's a good plan. When do you want to head out?"

"I am going to finish my coffee, get my gear together, and we'll go."

Tony fitted a special collar on his dog. As soon as he did, Ty was all business, ready to go to work. I grabbed my rifle and told the others we were heading out. I stayed behind Tony and Ty, keeping some distance between us to avoid Ty being distracted by my scent.

Ty was off leash and free to go wherever his nose would take him. He was in his element. He played the wind and followed his olfactory hunches. Tony never pushed him, and he talked to the dog in reassuring and encouraging tones. They were truly a team, partners in the truest sense of the word. K-9 officers often joked about how their dog was the smartest partner they ever had.

Tony directed Ty toward the area that had not been searched. With a wagging tail, he got to work. He was not hectic in his search, moving this way and that, following anything of interest. We covered a fair bit of ground before Tony called Ty to him.

"Ty has been working for forty-five minutes. He needs a break."

Tony took the search collar off, and Ty became visibly more relaxed. Tony gave him fresh water from a collapsible bowl and let the dog wind down for about fifteen minutes. Then the search collar was back on, and Ty was back on the job. After several area searches and breaks, we made our way to where Dr. Kouper thought the cougar might have holed up.

Tony stopped. "John, Ty is starting to pant. We need to give him a break. He can't smell as well with his mouth open. I don't want to cut this short today, but a lot of the ground Ty has been going through is heavy cover, and he's pretty tired. I don't want to wear him out, so we'll sit around here for a while and see whether we need to begin again in the morning."

Tony and I sat and talked about my new life in Namekagon County. He had been thinking about getting a place around Musky Falls when he retired. After a snack, Ty sacked out on the grass, half asleep.

The light wind changed direction. What had been blowing away from us was now blowing in our faces. It was such a slight change that it didn't register with anyone, except Ty. He rose to his feet and stared off in the direction of the incoming breeze. Tony put on Ty's working collar, and they walked off together. The Lab began to work with intensity, searching a more confined area. It was evident that he was homing in on something. He wormed his way in through the thickest cover while Tony and I had to bull our way through to follow.

The dog stopped on the steep edge of the stream bank, smelled the air, and then jumped into the water, half swimming, half walking his way across. We scrambled down the bank and followed. Just before we got into the stream, Ty stopped on the other side and walked back and forth on the opposite shore. He was meticulous in his search, slow and methodical. He recrossed the stream and started down the bank we were on.

"John, he's got something, something real. We need to stick with him but not push him."

Ty continued down the shore. He came to a high bank with an eroded area at the toe of the slope. There Ty laid down.

My heart sank. ∎

CHAPTER 22

Tony leashed and praised his partner. I took the small flashlight I had on my belt and shined the light into a well-hidden, shallow excavation. The first thing I saw was what looked like a piece of red cloth. I moved in closer, doing everything I could to protect the scene. It was evident that leaves and branches had been pushed into the bank undercut. I would not be able to tell what was in there until I removed some of the debris.

"Tony, I think we have a body. I can't tell for sure, but I think we do. There isn't much odor, but there is definitely some," I said.

"Ty thinks we do too, and he is almost always right," Tony said proudly.

"Let's just take a breath here," I said. "I will get the ME and Liz Masters on the phone and ask them to come over here as casually as possible. I don't want to get the press riled up. We can begin to process what we have out of sight. That will give us some time."

"Good plan, Sheriff."

It was a long forty-five minutes before Liz, her team, and Dr. Chali arrived. Once we came to the bank, I knew that I had to be the one to begin examining the site. I would treat Anna with all the respect I could muster. One of Liz's people would take still photographs, Liz would bag any evidence, and Dr. Chali would video. Tony and Ty would head back up to the trail, play catch, and take a break.

I took off my equipment belt and vest to skinny me up as much as possible. The ME gave me a set of disposable coveralls, a mask, gloves, and bootees. I got on my hands and knees and slowly removed the branches, leaves, and brush. The camouflage made it almost impossible to see the entrance. The cave appeared to be both earthen and rock. Without the K-9 unit, we would have been looking for a long time.

I slowly, carefully pulled away the larger sticks. I noted what were clearly cougar tracks in the mud. The tracks were photographed with a scale before I moved on. I cleared away piles of debris, eventually exposing the mouth of the cave. The odor was much stronger. I crawled in a short distance and shined my light around, switching to low power so it would illuminate but not negatively impact my vision in the dark space. I saw several bones that had been chewed clean. I asked Liz how she wanted to handle them and other pieces of evidence.

"We'll pass you a camera. First photograph them in situ, then hand them out, and we'll bag them," she directed.

"Can you see a corpse yet?" asked Dr. Chali.

"I think so, but it's deeper in the cave. It's close quarters in here, but I will try to wiggle in further to see what it is."

I crawled forward, and the space, thankfully, got a little larger. I was able to roll up on my side. When I did, I realized my head was at about waist level with a body partially covered with a red coat.

"Mike, Liz, I have a body. I am lying next to a body," I said.

"John, cougar kill or not, we need to treat this as a crime scene. Can I pass you some bags?" Liz said.

I could not answer.

"John, did you hear me? Can I pass you some bags?"

Again, I heard words but could not answer.

"John, are you alright?" Mike asked.

I had stepped off a cliff into my own personal hell. The world was closing in, squeezing the wind out of me. I could barely breathe. The cave was too narrow. My arms were unable to move to fight off the devil. Faces flashed before me. The smells and sights and sounds were all around me. I heard soft crying. I could not look at another face, another lost soul.

Someone grabbed my legs. "Stop! Stop pulling," I yelled.

"John, what is wrong with you? Are you alright?" called Liz.

"Just give me a minute," I responded sharply. "I need you to back off and give me a minute, please."

"No, John. You need to get out of there right now," said Chali.

"No, Doc. Please give me a minute."

I knew then that if I didn't go forward and finish this task, I would never wear a badge again after this day. I had come to a hidden place I had long thought existed, a brewing cauldron containing the darkness of life and reality, trying to crush my soul. I would crawl forward in the cave and gaze upon the face of America's sweetheart. I would provide a positive identity to the victim. I would do my job, for if not me, who else?

I crawled forward, inch by inch, with barely enough room to move between the cave's walls and the body. I held my small flashlight in my mouth and soon reached my goal. With my hands, I swept leaves and debris from the face and parted the long mud-covered, light-colored hair. Then I began to back out slowly. I just wanted to close my eyes and lay there for a while before answering the questions that were sure to come. But I continued to back out. I shined the light around the tunnel one more time and was stunned by what I saw. Once outside, many willing hands tried to attend to me, but I shook them off.

Dr. Chali was all over me. "John, what happened in there? Are you alright? What happened?"

"It was a tight squeeze. I found a body. It is no longer completely intact. It appears to be a female, based only on long hair."

"John, is it Anna?" asked Chali.

"I don't think so," I replied.

"How did you come to that conclusion?" Liz asked.

"When I was crawling out, I saw something. The person in the cave was wearing both shoes."

We began to process the scene, Dr. Chali and Liz leading the way. After we had recovered all available evidence, Dr. Chali and I removed the body from the shallow cave. It was a female, but it was not Anna MacDonald. The body showed early signs of decomposition and scavenging or predation. We carefully placed the body in a body bag and loaded it onto a stretcher. Liz's team continued to search the area. I alerted EMS to come to the scene for transport. The entire process was recorded, both audio and video. The ME would follow the EMS unit to the morgue, and Liz's team would continue processing the scene.

I looked across the parking area past the Winnebago ECC and saw Jack Wheeler coming my way. I walked toward him, and we met halfway.

"John, what's the status?"

"We recovered a body, but it's not Anna MacDonald. That means Anna is still missing, and at this moment, we aren't doing one stinking thing to find her. Besides not knowing where Anna is, I now have an unidentified corpse in the same area where Anna MacDonald went missing. That makes at least two potential victims that had to do with Musky Run. So I've got to ask myself if the disappearance and the body are related. Did they know each other and meet at Musky Run for some reason? Were they both out for a run and stumbled onto a crime in progress? Anna's Jeep is the only car in the lot. Did someone kill this other woman, and when they were dragging the body away, did Anna show up? But let's face it, the real question everyone wants an answer to is whether or not the cougar got them. Did the stupid sheriff fail to warn the public of a dangerous animal even though he knew it was true? I could list a couple of hundred more questions I need to answer. The big problem is the time I've wasted. I can't get that back, and it may have meant the difference between life and death for Anna. So, I don't want to say anything to the press right now because, frankly, I have no idea what I am going to do, but I need to do something."

"John, stop. You're being too hard on yourself."

"No, Counselor, I am not being hard enough on myself. I knew what this job was when I took it. I swore to protect and serve this community. Tell the press folks that Anna MacDonald is still missing, and we are going full speed ahead with the search."

I turned my back and walked toward the emergency command center. Once inside, I had Lois patch in Deputies Plums, Pave, Wichs, and Chief Delzell. Once they were all connected, I explained the situation and that we would begin the search again tomorrow morning. No one asked me anything. I am sure my surly tone and attitude curtailed that. Or maybe they saw me as a man who had screwed up.

I hung up and yelled from the doorway to Jack Wheeler. He turned around and cautiously approached me.

"What is it, John?"

"I'm coming down with you to meet with the press."

"I thought you didn't want to, and I'm not sure that was a bad choice."

"Please get them together, Counselor."

Twenty minutes later, I had a dozen cameras and recorders pointed at me.

"First, I want to thank you for being courteous and respectful. These past few days have been difficult for all of us. Today Dane County Deputy Tony Eagen and his dog Ty discovered the location of a deceased person. That person is being transported to a location for an autopsy and identification. In the meantime, the crime scene team is collecting evidence from the location where we found the deceased. The area around Musky Run is closed until further notice. I know what you are all waiting to hear regarding the identity of the deceased. At this point, I can't comment because we don't know. Now, if you want, I can take a few questions."

"Sheriff, you have a personal relationship with Anna MacDonald. Does it appear as though the body might be Anna's? Was it her? Did you find Anna's body?" a reporter pushed.

"I can't comment. We have not made a positive identification," I replied.

"What was the cause of death? Was it an animal attack?" another asked.

"The ME is working to determine the cause of death as we speak. At this point, we have no further information."

"Sheriff Cabrelli, have you suspended the search for Anna MacDonald?"

"We did temporarily to give the K-9 the best possible conditions. We have no plans to suspend the search until Anna MacDonald is found.

"Are you saying, Sheriff, that you did not find Anna MacDonald? That this is another body?"

"What I am saying is that I don't know."

"Can you describe the condition of the body?"

"Dead, the poor soul we recovered today is dead. We need to

treat the deceased with all the respect they deserve. Now you will need to excuse me, as I am sure you understand I have a great deal of work ahead of me. Musky Run will be patrolled 24/7, including closing off the parking area. We will make certain that all of you know ahead of time when a statement is forthcoming."

As I left, Jack Wheeler was again handing out his business cards that included his cell phone.

I had dispatch send a deputy to secure the area. Then I headed home. Everything else that I needed to do had to wait until tomorrow. I had nothing left. I was truly, completely exhausted.

All I wanted was to sit in my comfortable chair, put my feet up, and talk to Julie. I almost cried from happiness when I saw her car parked in front of the cabin. I dragged myself to the door, and it swung open. There she was, the smiling face of the love of my life. She walked over and hugged me like I'd never been hugged before. She told me to follow her. We walked outside and then to the end of our dock. We sat together and watched the water. A little breeze made the surface look like a tray of diamonds.

Our local osprey circled high, looking for dinner. I settled in for a moment and found peace.

"Julie, I have something important to tell you," I said.

"It can wait, John. Just sit back for a minute."

"It can't wait. We found a body, but it is definitely not Anna. It is not her."

"Oh my gosh, John. If it's not Anna, who is it? Where is Anna?"

"I don't know. I just don't know. I need some time to think."

We walked back to the cabin. I sat in my chair, leaned my head back, and soon fell asleep. Julie gently shook me awake and guided me upstairs to bed. As tired as I was, sleep came in fits and starts.

Unable to sleep, I got out of bed and went downstairs. I could not sort out the details; my brain was in a fog. I would need to ask Tony and Ty to stay and search more of the area, and maybe

Liz and her crew. We still had a missing person, and maybe we should go back to a ground search. There was no shortage of able volunteers.

I drove into town, and the early risers were out and about. I parked behind the building by the jail entrance. I knew there was no way of avoiding people today, and I wasn't necessarily trying to. Still, I couldn't tell anyone anything different than what we had already released to the media. I also had no solid plan of action.

It was early, but I called Liz anyway.

She answered right away. "So is the goal when I come here to keep me sleep deprived and send me back home ten pounds fatter? Because if that's what you're trying to do, you are well on the way to accomplishing it. I promised to take my crew out for breakfast this morning, and they picked a restaurant with the famous Northwoods special: two eggs, bacon, sausage, sourdough toast, hash browns with cheese and onion, a piece of homemade pie, and a bottomless cup of coffee. That sounds like a perfect example of overindulgence that I should avoid, but all I can think about is what kind of pie they have."

I couldn't help but start laughing. "It does sound good. I am hoping we could all meet up this morning, you and your people, Tony and Ty, as well as Professor Newlin and Dr. Kouper."

"The site is still sealed off, right?" she asked.

"I have people on each end. I checked on them on my way in. All's quiet," I said.

"Let's meet out there after breakfast. We are on our way to the restaurant now. I am guessing I should be done in an hour or so, depending on how much steam I've got left at the finish line. By the way, Tony and Ty are joining us, so I'll let him know."

"Thanks, Liz."

After breakfast, I met with the group, also joined by Dr. Kouper and Professor Newlin. Everyone was clear we were still on an active case. It was agreed that Ty and Tony, as well as Liz's crew, would stay. Dr. Kouper and the professor would trail along with Tony and Ty and look for any signs of cougar activity. The cat might have stashed food somewhere else close to the first cache.

Liz's crew would fly the drone and continue to search the grid they had started. We had a busload of searchers ready to begin. The Spider Lake fire chief organized people so the search would be as effective as possible. Chief Delzell sent three of her people, and three of my deputies came. Many of the group had already put in their time but showed up anyway. Bud and Dennis and Daryl Weaver were among the semi-permanent fixtures.

It didn't take anyone long to figure out that it was not Anna MacDonald's body we found if we were continuing the search.

Cougar experts were interviewed on the major networks. The history of the cougar in Wisconsin was peppered with speculation. The big cats got their own prime-time slot as previous mountain lion and human confrontations were revisited. Dewey Brewer was the man of the hour, appearing anywhere someone wanted him.

Later that morning, I got a call from a local residential drug treatment center.

"Sheriff, I think I may know who the dead person is. She may be one of our patients. When I heard you on the radio, and they gave out the phone number, I called you."

"I'm glad you did. We are in the process of trying to identify the deceased right now. What is your patient's name?"

"Lucy Lee Szabo."

Lucy was a chronic walkaway. She would take off for a few days, get high or drunk, then come back to the facility. They notified law enforcement each time she walked away to check her welfare. If they encountered her, they would usually bring her back. Staff hypothesized that she would go on her hiatus until she got cold or hungry, then "accidentally" bump into a city cop or sheriff's deputy to get a ride home. She wasn't a troublemaker, so people were relatively tolerant of her behavior. This time though, she had been gone longer than usual. One of the places she would often show up was at Musky Run Trail. She had been found there before in the company of a man having a "date" in his car late at night.

"I will pull her photo and see what we have. I will let you know. Again, thanks for calling me."

"Oh, one more thing, Sheriff. Summer, winter, spring, or fall, she always wore a red nylon jacket with 'Martins' Roost' embroidered across the back."

The red nylon coat on the deceased was identical to what Lucy Lee Szabo wore. Two of Lucy's long-term caretakers met with Dr. Chali at the morgue and were quick to make a positive identification. The deceased was Lucy. They told Dr. Chali what they knew.

Lucy Szabo had no family. During a previous incident at the center, she had taken off with a man thought to be dangerous. The sheriff's office, social services, and the staff at the center had turned over every leaf to find her. During that search, they learned she had no next of kin. She was a drug addict who struggled to stay clean all her adult life. She had a history of overdoses, some clearly what the case worker called "escape attempts." It was likely that this time she had been successful.

No evidence positively pointed to the cougar as her killer. However, it was apparent that the cougar had used her as a source of protein. The significant wounds from the cougar all appeared to have been inflicted postmortem. Two baggies that tested positive for heroin, one full, the other almost empty, along with a used syringe, were recovered from her coat pocket. Dr. Chali took tissue samples and, with Liz Masters' help, had them shipped to the lab.

Dr. Chali called Jack Wheeler and me. ∎

CHAPTER 23

Jack agreed to set up a press conference at the trailhead. The news folks had already figured out the search continued because we were looking for another person or likely another body.

Dr. Chali spoke first. "Thank you for your patience. I am Dr. Mike Chali, the medical examiner for Namekagon County. We have undertaken an exhaustive search of the area known as Musky Run Trail in our attempt to locate a missing person. Under a formal mutual aid request, we brought in a deputy from Dane County and his dog, specially trained to find missing persons that we have reason to believe may have died. The dog has done its job and located a deceased person in our search area. The deceased has been positively identified as Lucy Lee Szabo, age forty-four. She was a walkaway from Healing Pines Treatment Center. A preliminary examination has not given us a conclusive cause of death. We have taken several samples, which have been delivered to the crime lab for testing and examination. That's all we have at the moment."

"With all due respect, Dr. Chali, isn't it true that a mountain lion actually ate the deceased person?"

"We have nothing more to offer at this point. To comment without proof would be speculation," Chali answered.

"Sheriff Cabrelli, what are you going to do now?"

"We are going to continue our search and broaden the search area. Many volunteers are ready to go, most of whom have spent a lot of time hiking and hunting around here. The search effort will still be coordinated from the Musky Run trailhead. We plan to use every resource available to locate Anna MacDonald. That includes broad-scale media announcements, which I expect every one of you will help with," I answered. "Since Anna came up missing, you all have been very cooperative in broadcasting photos of her and her vehicle. Every lead has been followed up on. We are asking you, folks, for some extra help with our continued efforts. Besides broadcast and social media, we have reprinted our missing person flyers. Please pass them out to anyone who will take one. Volunteers will be making sure they are still on every pole and at every business. Someone had to have seen her. We need to find that person."

"Are you suggesting there is a person of interest in her disappearance?" shouted one of the reporters.

"I am not suggesting that at all, but we are looking in every direction. We are looking for anyone that may have seen her. Maybe another jogger or someone that used the trailhead parking lot at the same time. She is a celebrity and easily recognized. Maybe she stopped for gas or anything else."

"Are you still going to use the cadaver dog?" asked another reporter.

"Yes, we are. As I said, we will use everything at our disposal."

"Sheriff, in your opinion, has this become a recovery?"

"As far as I'm concerned, this is still a rescue. It will remain that way until we find something that changes what we know. We need to consider every possibility," I said, and then I just walked away through the crowd of reporters, searchers, and onlookers while questions were being shouted at me.

I didn't stop until I got to the beginning of Musky Run. I stood there and heard my own voice echo quietly around me. It was carried by the wind as it blew through the giant pines. It skipped across the water and called from the wilderness trail. It started as a whisper but quickly became louder, condemning me for my stupidity.

I had told the reporters, "We need to consider every possibility," yet that was just what I hadn't done. All our energy had been and continued to be spent on looking for Anna under the assumption that she had fallen victim to a hungry wild animal. It still seemed plausible, and we had evidence to support our theory. I had made a mistake, a grievous error. In my job, there is no excuse for not paying attention. The intensity of the disappearance, the cougar, the recovered body, organizing the search, and the race, among many other things, had left me with no room remaining in my brain for possibility. I was so sure we were going in the right direction that I never looked to the periphery. Everything out there blazed by while I chased what had seemed to be the obvious situation. A cougar killing someone in Wisconsin was certainly possible, but nothing like this had ever happened. Consider all the people who were lost or killed in the north country, and not one case was a cougar the suspect, maybe until now.

I needed to change my focus, go back, rewind, and take a second look at what I had ignored. It was Shakespeare again that came to my mind: "he who doth protest too much," a paraphrase of the famous line from Hamlet that spoke volumes in a criminal investigation.

I went to the ECC and asked Chief Delzell to come inside. I explained to her my thoughts and concerns.

"I need to follow up on this, Mary. We don't dare stop the search and wait for me. Can you handle things here while I see what I can come up with?"

The light went on and burned bright for the experienced sheriff's deputy turned Musky Falls chief of police, Mary Delzell, who realized our error and recognized the possibility that our mistake may have been fatal for Anna MacDonald.

"I can handle it here, Sheriff. Actually, Liz and the fire chief have got everything well in hand. Liz's tech team has got the social media posts going out far and wide. Do you want backup to go with you?"

"Not right now. I need to figure things out. You'll be the first to know if it looks like I need help. In the meantime, we need to continue the search. Ron Carver told me he had a whole new crew ready to go when needed," I said.

"That's good. Some folks here need a break and won't stop unless we make them, like Bud and the Weaver boys."

"Switch people out as you see fit," I said. "I'm heading out."

"Good luck, John. We have everything covered here."

Nothing more was said. I got in my squad and drove slowly away from the search scene to avoid attracting attention. When you shine the light on an ongoing criminal investigation, things will often appear that you didn't see before or maybe you should have seen. The key to success is second-guessing yourself and looking for your own mistakes, then having the energy and willingness to follow a new direction. I shined the light, and two things popped up, as bright as can be.

The majority of almost 20,000 annual homicides in the U.S. are committed by people known to each other. Husbands, wives, ex or not, were right up there at the top. On the other hand, only twenty-seven people have died from cougar attacks in North America in the past one hundred fifty years. It doesn't mean it doesn't happen.

There would be twenty-seven people that, if they were around, would attest to that. Our cougar had shown no real fear of people and predatory behavior toward a little girl on the trail. Still, the odds were against Anna falling victim to a mountain lion.

I needed to look hard at Cameron. His constant availability was not the usual behavior of a criminal, but something didn't sit right. The threats, the strange behavior, and Bear's prophetic words, "Where's the ex? Find him." Anna's ex-husband Stephen Cameron had not been the least difficult to find. In fact, he had been annoyingly visible. His TV interviews were heartbreaking. Sure, he had screwed up, but he still loved Anna and hoped and prayed they would get back together. He had played the role of a grieving ex-husband almost perfectly. I needed to find Cameron, and I needed to look at everything he had done since he got here, and I needed to do it fast.

My next move was to call Bear. "Bear, did you get a list of Cameron's credit card purchases, airline reservations, car rental, and such?"

"I did, Sheriff, and sent it to your email. By the way, just for the record, a judge might question the evidentiary value of the information due to lack of process," he replied.

"I get it, Bear, but right now, I don't have time to check my email, and I need something to go on. Do me a favor and bring me up to speed on what you found. I'm following up on Cameron right now."

"There are a couple of interesting things. Number one, his fancy rented SUV is about five days late. We talked to the rental company. They have been trying to reach him with no luck. The manager was really ticked off because he had someone else waiting for the car. They did give me a cell phone number. You can match it up with what you have."

"Does the rental company have a locator on the car?"

"Nope. Believe it or not, they didn't. They hoped I would take the complaint. Usually, seven days late is when the owner said they draw the line. I figured I would leave that up to you, Sheriff. If you need a bunch of eyes looking for the vehicle at some point, you could call the rental agency and put out a BOLO on Cameron and the car. Readymade, probable cause, just when you need it.

"Also, his flight back home was set for two days ago, and he was a no-show. Most of his credit card purchases were from restaurants, bars, and a local liquor store. The next was a little more interesting. He purchased $156 of unspecified items at Rolland and Andy's Tack and Surplus."

"Bear, you're on it—an investigative genius."

"Maybe so, Sheriff, maybe so. Let me give you a little advice. Find Cameron, and whatever you need to do, don't let him go until you have squeezed him good. Of course, always remember to respect his constitutional rights and treat him as you would any self-respecting potential criminal.

"Any more on the cougar? It is national news on just about every network. By the way, you're looking a little tired these days, although you do have some stage presence in front of the cameras."

"The search area has been increased, and we are putting as many people on the search as we can. The efforts are efficient and organized. We're just going to keep on keeping on," I replied.

I hung up with Bear and felt an emptiness in the pit of my stomach. I felt an urgency to find Stephen Cameron. I stopped at Rolland and Andy's store on the way to the sheriff's office. It was locked up tight. A crooked hand-written sign hanging from a nail on the door read, "gone to the fair." They wouldn't be open for two days.

I pulled into the sheriff's office back lot, hoping to avoid running into anyone. My mind was working overtime. I was convinced that

Cameron was on the run, that I had missed my chance to grab him.

I was halfway to the door when his fancy rental SUV squealed into the parking lot, and Stephen Cameron jumped out almost before the car came to a stop.

"Cabrelli, stop right there!" Cameron yelled at the top of his lungs. "Enough is enough. Who do you think you are? The body they found is not my wife, and you didn't have the common decency to let me know? What is wrong with you, Cabrelli? I heard about it on the news with a million other people. I am worried sick about my wife. Did you do this to torture me?"

Cameron got in my face as close as he could without making physical contact. A minute ago, I thought he'd taken off, but now I had him and had no idea what to do with him.

"You're right, Stephen; I should have handled this better. Every waking hour and half of my sleeping hours, I am thinking about Anna. I am sure you are too. Why don't you come to my office and sit down with me. I'll tell you everything I know. I am looking at other possibilities for her disappearance. Maybe you can help me with that. We can do it right now if you've got some time."

My phone rang again at the best possible moment, and the call was from the best possible person.

"John, it's Bear. I forgot to mention one thing."

"Commander Malone, thank you for getting back to me. I filed a mutual aid request yesterday. I hope that you will be able to help us."

"Cabrelli, you didn't file any request. What are you—? Oh, I get it. You're with him."

"I appreciate your support, Commander. Sending us an investigative team is really going to help. The truth is that with this case's search efforts and complications, we have fallen behind in pursuing other leads. Four of your people would do a lot to alleviate the issue."

I continued, pretending to have a two-way conversation. "In the morning sometime will work. As a matter of fact, I'm with Stephen Cameron right now. Hold on, I'll ask him."

I turned to Cameron, "Stephen, Commander Malone from the Department of Criminal Investigation is on the phone. We have requested extra help from them, and he is sending four investigators our way to help with your ex-wife's case. He's wondering if you could meet with them as soon as they arrive."

Cameron was clearly shocked and didn't immediately reply. He attempted to give me a disarming smile but didn't pull it off.

"Ah... ah... of course I will. I want to help in any way I can. Could they let me know when to expect them?" Cameron said.

"Commander, Stephen Cameron will be glad to meet with your people. He'd like to know when you might get here," I said. "Okay, I will. He's here now, so the timing is perfect. I'll see you guys tomorrow."

I disconnected. "Stephen, Commander Malone wants me to cover some general bases with you. They are getting geared up, but because of all the moving pieces, they will coordinate their arrival time with me. So, let's go into my office and see what we can figure out."

We went in the secure entrance, and as we walked in, Cameron turned to me, "You know, Sheriff, I sit here waiting and waiting for any news of my wife. I was sure hoping that Anna would bring me to your wedding. I was really looking forward to it. I hope we can work together to find her."

The strangeness of this comment was difficult to understand. He continued to talk about things that seemed totally inconsequential. There was almost a jovial tone to his voice. He sat across from me in a small interview room. Cameron had no idea that I had activated the camera and recording device.

246 | JEFF NANIA

"Tell me what you know, Sheriff. What do you think happened to my wife?"

"First off, Stephen, as I previously pointed out, she is your ex-wife, and that is one of the reasons we have not been compelled to share all the details of the case with you up until now. I'm sure you can understand that."

"Sure, Sheriff, I get it. So, what do you think happened to her?" he said.

"We still believe she was the victim of a wild animal attack. It is rare, but it does and has happened. We know that she was on Musky Run Trail at the same time as a large cougar. The cougar has since been killed. It was injured and unable to hunt as it normally would. Days before we killed it, the cat had stalked a little girl walking with her family, and the father chased the animal off with a dose of wasp and hornet spray. I'm sorry to say that as the days go on, the chances of finding her alive are reduced."

"How long will you continue to search for her?" Stephen asked.

"Until we find her, we will never stop looking for her," I replied.

"You'll have search parties out forever?"

"No, eventually, if the search remains unsuccessful, we'll have to stop. After that, we'll follow up on every tip or clue we get. As a matter of fact, that is what I'm doing today. A couple of tips have come in, and I am checking them out. They may be nothing, or they may be something. I'll chase them down regardless."

"Can you tell me what the tips involve?"

"I can't. Once Malone's investigators get here, they'll take over and run every tip down. If it turns out to be something, I will let you know. In the meantime, if you think of anyone who might want to do her harm, please let us know as soon as possible. Here is my card with my personal cell phone. Call me day or night, and I'll answer. Give me your cell number, and I will program it in so it comes up with your name. What's your number, Stephen?"

He hesitated, and I could tell he didn't want to share the number, so I put on a little pressure. "Stephen, I need your number in case we find Anna. You had better give it to me." He relented.

"Thank you, Sheriff, for talking to me. I really appreciate it. Maybe every once in a while, we could talk or even have a cup of coffee together and exchange information face-to-face."

"Maybe that will work out. I'm glad we understand we're on the same team. Oh, by the way, are you still staying at the Big Buck Lake Lodges?" I asked.

He almost seemed startled by the question but recovered quickly. "For now. One of my friends rented a couple of the lodges for the month and then went back to L.A., so I have the place to myself."

"What is the number of the lodge you're staying in?"

"Same as before, Sheriff, number fourteen," Stephen replied.

"Must have been a close friend to let you stay on for a while."

"To be honest, Sheriff, I was so despondent at the disappearance, he insisted I stay."

"Who rented the lodge?"

"A friend from the days before I got hurt. You know, Sheriff Cabrelli, Anna wasn't the only Olympic hero; I stood on that podium too. People still remember me, and they are always doing things for me. I never ask, but they offer, and sometimes I accept."

"I was just curious who rented the lodges," I asked again, giving him a question that he would think might be significant.

"I'm sorry, I've got to go. Thank you for your time, Sheriff Cabrelli. I really appreciate it. I'm sure you have a lot to do." The conversation was over, and Cameron was uncomfortable.

He left the room and went out the exit door. I didn't follow.

His cell phone number was different than what he had given me before. I called it prepared to tell Stephen that I was just confirming I had the right number. I got the voicemail for Marnie's

Cleaning Service. I called the Big Buck Lake Lodges office and got voicemail there as well. Not too hard to believe people take some time after a big event like the race. I called Malone back. "Bear, what was it that you forgot to tell me?"

"Stephen bought a box of 9mm ammunition on his credit card."

The bad cell number was something I could work with, and I drove out to Big Bucks Lake Lodges. Lodge fourteen was at the end of the drive. Cameron's SUV was parked in front. I walked up the stairs to the front door and knocked. No answer. I knocked again, this time with a little more authority. Still no answer. I tried the knob, and it was locked. The circumstances were changing, the case taking new twists. My heart was racing. The only thing I could think of was that Anna might be on the other side of the door. I would not leave until I knew. Good search exigent circumstances and success, bad search lack of cause. Let the lawyers fight it out.

A successful career in law enforcement includes paying attention and learning lessons. I set many of the lessons I had learned aside, drew my gun, then raised my foot and got ready to give the substantial-looking lock my best shot when the door opened. Stephen was standing in the doorway with wet hair and a towel around his waist. He stared at me and then the gun, then looked again at me with a smile, clearly amused by the situation.

"Sheriff, I think you can put the gun away. As you can see, I'm not armed. If you would like, I would be glad to remove the towel to make you feel more comfortable. Were you going to kick in my door?"

"I knocked, no answer."

"I was in the shower. As I stepped out, I heard you pounding and came to the door. Are you here to arrest me? It looks to me like that is what you intend to do."

In for an ounce, in for a pound.

"Stephen, I have backup coming, and we are going to search your lodge. We are looking for Anna."

"Cabrelli, doesn't that require a little something called a search warrant? Do you happen to have one of those I might take a look at? Don't you think I should call a lawyer? That would be the smartest thing to do, wouldn't it?"

"We believe that Anna may be in danger. We need to make sure she's not," I replied.

"Okay, Cabrelli, let me think about this for a minute. You are ready to kick in my door, gun drawn. No warrant, and since I haven't heard any sirens, probably no backup either. My wife is still missing, and you look like the fool you are. Anna's not here."

"Will you give me consent to search the lodge?" I asked.

"Call one of your other people. Once they get here, we will search the place together. You need to stop wasting your time with me and find Anna.'

Deputy Plums responded. Cameron, Plums, and I searched every inch of the lodge. A box of 9mm ammunition was in plain sight on the counter. Cameron claimed he was going to the local rod and gun club for some target practice. I asked him where the gun was.

"They rent them at the range," he replied. I knew that was true. On the same counter there was a large sheath knife.

"Mind if I look at the knife, Stephen?"

"Beautiful knife, isn't it, Sheriff? Handmade by a local bladesmith. It was really expensive, but the craftsmanship is worth every penny. I plan to give it to a friend of mine as a gift. You're welcome to look at it. I would assume you're checking for blood. You won't find anything—just don't cut your finger."

I pulled the knife from the sheath, and the blade appeared spotless, retaining most of a light oil coating. I sheathed the knife and put it back on the counter.

We also found a prescription bottle of oxycontin with his name on it in the bathroom. Nothing else. No Anna or evidence of her having been here.

"So, are you and your deputy satisfied?" he asked.

I didn't answer quickly enough for him, so he answered his own question.

"You found nothing. You definitely didn't find Anna. This is your chance. Make sure you have searched everything you want to search because when you leave, I am going to call my lawyer and turn this over to him. Do you need to do any further searching, Sheriff?"

Again, I didn't answer.

Plums and I had searched every nook and every cranny and found nothing. We struck out. More importantly, we had failed to make a case. As much as I didn't care for or believe Cameron, the truth was he had been completely cooperative. He was annoyingly present just when I thought he shouldn't be. The possibility loomed large that Stephen Cameron was just what he acted like, a bereaved ex-husband, traumatized by the disappearance of the woman he loves. No stone unturned. Follow everything to its natural end. I needed to find Anna.

As I drove out, my phone rang. No surprise, Stephen's lawyer was on the other end. ∎

CHAPTER 24

AMERICA'S SWEETHEART

Anna was dozing and woke with a start, and out of reflex, pulled against the steel handcuffs that held her. The pain that resulted brought her completely awake. She looked at her wrist, scabbed up with abrasions and dried blood. The handcuff was attached to a chain that was locked around a heavy, exposed pipe. The other wrist was similarly attached, chained so that her ability to move was limited. She was being held in a bathroom, with enough freedom of movement that she could use the toilet. The room had no windows, and she thought it must be in a basement. The cut on the back of her head had just begun to heal. Anna was certain that she had a concussion. Nausea had plagued her since she came to. During the first few hours of captivity, she threw up several times and was forced to lay in her vomit. She knew that she smelled. The first day when he left her alone, she screamed as loudly and as long as she could. When he came to see her, he noted the hoarse voice. He held a glass of water and let her drink, but the water was drugged, and soon she was asleep.

Her plate from last night's dinner was on the floor without a knife, fork, or spoon. She was only allowed to eat with her fingers. She thought it was probably canned dog food because of its cylindrical shape, circular ridges from a can, and smell. She ate it anyway. Anna knew she needed to keep her strength up if she ever hoped to escape.

Other than her head injury and the abrasions on her wrist, she remained relatively uninjured. Whether that would last was the big question. He would come to see her soon, like he did several times every day.

He was changing, and each day he seemed to become more dangerous. He would go from telling her he loved her to wanting her dead, often in the same sentence.

She sat quietly and thought, not in despair but trying to figure out how to escape. She was considering her chances when she heard him walk down the steps.

The bathroom door opened slowly, and Stephen Cameron peeked his head inside.

"Hello, darling. How are you this afternoon?"

Once he was convinced she was still restrained, he came in. He sat on the closed toilet, stared at her for a few moments, and then spoke again, "You know, Anna, you have caused this entire problem. If it weren't for you, none of this would have happened. When we sat at that picnic table, and I asked you to take me back, you should have said yes. If you had, your future would have been much different than it is now."

Stephen stroked her cheek softly, but she didn't move. "Did I ever tell you how pretty you are? I am sure that I did. Didn't I tell you how pretty you are? Didn't I tell you, Anna?" he shouted. "Maybe pretty is more fleeting than you ever knew."

He pulled a large hunting knife from his belt. Anna had seen it before; he loved to show it to her.

"I could take this razor-sharp knife and make you so ugly that no one would even look at you. Make a long cut on each one of your cheeks, deep enough that plastic surgery would never fix them, maybe another slice across your forehead. People would look at you then and say, 'Poor Anna. She is so ugly now.' You'd never be America's sweetheart again.

"I am sorry to say that lately, I have been thinking a lot about just taking this knife and stabbing you in the heart and looking into your eyes when I do it, watching the pain. Unfair, you would say, I'm sure, but I would argue no more unfair than you trashing me. You did almost destroy my life," he snarled.

"Anna, do you want to hear something funny? I mean really funny? Of course you do. I used to love watching you on those sparkling chewing gum commercials. I pretended I was sitting next to you and smashing your teeth out."

He changed again.

"I'm so sorry, but now you and I have a real problem. When I started all this, I just thought that given some time together alone, we could work things out. You know I didn't really plan it very well. I thought we could use this opportunity to reconnect and discuss reconciliation. But you have made it clear to me that you aren't interested. I think we would still make a beautiful couple. People have short memories. Soon they would forget, and we'd be the golden couple again. Now even if you told me you'd give it a chance, I wouldn't believe you. You'd run off at the soonest opportunity."

He changed again.

With an evil smile, he said, "I just thought of something. I have never been stabbed or cut, for that matter. I bet it hurts. Except, of course, the surgeon's scalpel, but I was under for that. You're a tough girl. Let's see how still you can stay. If you jerk or move, the chances are very good that the knife will go deeper than we really need for this experiment. Just a little cut, but where? Where should I cut? I can think of a lot of places—you know, special places."

Then Stephen grabbed Anna by the hair, bringing her face close. He rested the knife on her neck just under her chin.

"Now, don't move, my love. Don't move an inch."

Stephen stuck the point of the blade into Anna's skin. She felt pain and a warm trickle of blood run down her neck. Then he pulled the knife away.

"Did that hurt, sweetie? Did that hurt? It was just a little stick, that's all, a little blood. Now you tell me, did it hurt?"

Anna spat in his face. Stephen raised his fist to slug her and stopped. Then he started to laugh.

He changed again.

"That's okay, Anna. I know you are pretty upset by all of this. And we have a real problem. I have no idea what I am going to do with you. Let's just try and talk this over. Maybe you can help me figure things out. Just a little warning, I encourage you to be very, very nice to me. If you are, we may be able to work this out.

"The going theory is still that you were attacked and killed by a mountain lion while jogging on Musky Run Trail. Well, who would have thought they'd find a body and shoot a poor, defenseless cougar? They made a positive identification on the body, so they know it's not you.

"Earlier today, the sheriff asked me to come into his office and talk. John—I think I like John better than Sheriff—John and I had a nice talk. From now on, we're working together to find you. You know, John is a nice guy. I bet he and I could be really good friends, maybe fishing buddies. What do you think, Anna? Maybe Julie and John and you and I could go out on double dates. Wouldn't that be fun?

"I have made enough of a pain of myself and given enough interviews pleading for your safe return that no one suspects me.

You should have seen me on *Good Day America*! I was even able to work up some phony tears—the grieving husband standing in front of the Musky Run trailhead sign. You know, Anna, I could have been an actor, probably a great one at that. You have to laugh. Look at you sitting there in your own puke, eating dog food. If it makes you feel better, I had a great steak last night—a delicious rib eye with mushrooms and wild rice.

"Well, things were going pretty well until just a little while ago. Let me bring you up to date. After a nice conversation with Sheriff Cabrelli, I thought we were both on the same track. Something changed, and I just had an unpleasant visit from him. He pounded on my door and was ready to kick it down with a gun in his hand, when I finally answered. The nerve of that guy. He was certain that I had you imprisoned in my lodge. I made a fuss but, in the end, let him search wherever he wanted. Of course, that stupid sheriff didn't find anything because there was nothing to find. As soon as he and his deputy left, I called my lawyer. No doubt he has made plenty of trouble for Cabrelli by now. Things have changed, and someone from the State Department of Criminal Investigation is sending an investigative team. The pressure is on, and we are going to have to do something."

Anna spoke for the first time since he had arrived. "Let me go, Stephen. Take the chains off and let me go. You don't want to kill me. I know you still love me. Let me go."

"Oh, my dear Anna, that is what I really want to do. Really and truly, I do, but I'm afraid I just can't. The police would be after me, and when they caught me, they would put me in prison for a long time. The trial would be on the news, and I would be portrayed as a horrible villain. Of course, you would continue as America's sweetheart, a hero surviving against all odds.

"I do have an idea that might work out for both of us. What if I took you out in the middle of the national forest and just turned you loose? If I set things up right and called in some favors from a couple of my friends, it would give me enough time to get away. By the way, it may surprise you I do still have some friends. There's a place I think I can go where it will be very hard for anyone to find me. Now that I say my idea out loud, it sounds better and better. I think it's what we're going to do. I'll need to make some arrangements and pick up a few things. Then off we'll go into the great Northwoods. I'll drop you off and go on my merry way. I hope you agree that this is the best choice because if you don't.... Well, let's just say we are short on alternatives. I really don't want to have to kill you, but what happens depends on your choice. So, darling, what do you say? Do you agree with my plan?"

"Okay," Anna replied. She knew that once they got to where they were going, he would kill her and leave her body to rot in tens of thousands of acres of wilderness. Anna had no intention of going down without a fight.

"Now, Anna, I have plans in a little while with some friends who want to console me. They can't imagine what I must be going through, you know, with you missing and all. I hope I can struggle through dinner. If there are any leftovers, I could get a box to go. You know, they used to call it a 'doggie bag.' You could be a doggie and lick it off the floor! Now that would be entertaining. I'll see you soon."

Dennis and Daryl Weaver had been part of Anna's search team since the news first came out. They had been relentless in their search. This morning Chief Delzell told them, Bud Treetall, and a dozen others they needed to take a break. Twenty-four hours from now, they could come back. It was true; they were tired but would have kept going.

Dennis and Daryl also had work they needed to do. Their boss had let them off their regular work along with some others to search. They also worked side jobs as caretakers for a fancy group of cabins on the water. With all the part-time and seasonal residences around the area, the caretaker business was a booming sideline for anyone who was the least bit handy. The Weavers were conscientious and, like Bud, could fix about anything.

They were living off the wages from their regular job and putting away their caretaker wages, hoping to earn enough to buy a new fishing boat. The balance in the dresser drawer was growing, and they were close to their goal.

Then good fortune shined on them. The owner of Musky Falls Marine called Daryl and told him that a guy had just traded in a boat almost exactly like they wanted but two years older. Dennis and Daryl went down to look at it. It was in great shape and much less expensive than a brand-new boat. The marina owner said if they put ten percent down, he would hold it for a month. Then the lodge owner called them about some extra work, and they jumped at it.

All the rentals had a main floor which included a living area, kitchen, large full bath, and bedrooms. The lower level of each was finished with a reading and computer area and a half bath. They stopped at the rental office and found a list of needed repairs in the comment box outside the front door. The first one on the list was number fourteen. The guest had reported that the toilet on the lower level was not flushing right.

They pulled into the driveway and headed to the far end of the property, where lodge fourteen was located. Each building was marked with black hand-hammered numbers. They parked and got out of the truck. Dennis grabbed the plumbing toolbox and Daryl an industrial plunger. They unlocked the front door with a key furnished by the office. They walked in and were met by

Stephen Cameron.

"Who are you guys? What are you doing here? Hey, wait, I remember you. You're the two clowns who pitched me into the crowd the other night. Dufus and Rufus, right?" Stephen said with a laugh.

Dennis and Daryl did not think there was anything funny about Stephen Cameron.

"I asked you what you're doing here," Stephen repeated.

"We are the caretakers of this property, and the owner needs us to fix the downstairs toilet," Dennis said.

"Well, I am still staying here and don't want my privacy disturbed. So turn that truck around and go back the way you came."

"We can't do that unless we talk to the boss first," Daryl said. "If he says it can wait, it can wait."

"Fine, I'll call him and check this out. He's a good friend of mine. While I'm talking to him, I'll tell him he needs to get rid of you two. You stay outside while he and I talk."

Stephen closed the door. More trouble for him—or maybe not. *These two humiliated me in front of the crowd and, worst of all, my wife. Throwing an Olympic gold medalist into the crowd. What a laugh they must have had, a big moment for a couple of small-town losers.*

They wouldn't laugh now, would they? Sometimes you just had to seize the opportunity. They would never expect it. I would open the door and follow them downstairs, then just at the right moment when all they were thinking about was the toilet, I would drive my knife into their backs. One stab to the hilt for each. If they were still alive, I would make them look at me and then cut their throats. I would get blood on my hands and wipe it on Anna's face. It was not really a problem; it was an opportunity. People should realize how dangerous I can be.

Stephen returned and opened the front door. "I talked to the owner. You guys can come in and fix the toilet. It seems like a job you can probably handle."

Dennis began to talk back, and Daryl stopped him. "Ignore him, Dennis. We've got work to do."

They started down the steps to the basement, bathroom tools in hand, backs to Cameron.

How stupid could they be? They are no more than a minute or two from dying, and they're going to spend that precious time fixing a toilet.

Stephen slid the knife from the sheath he had hidden on his belt in the small of his back. He was excited; payback was so sweet. The idea of smearing their blood on Anna almost made him laugh.

Daryl bent down over the toilet and asked Dennis for a pair of Channellock pliers.

I'll stab Dennis first, right in the middle of his back. I'll pull out the knife and then drive it into Daryl. They won't die right away, but they will die. It will give me a little time to enjoy my handiwork.

Just when he was going to make his move, a voice yelled from upstairs.

"Dennis, Daryl, is one of you down there? I need you to move your truck so I can fill the propane tanks. You parked right in the way."

Stephen quickly sheathed the knife.

Dennis walked back up the stairs and went to move the truck while Daryl kept fixing the toilet. After about an hour, they had things working again and packed their tools. They assured Stephen that all the rest of the work needed to be done on the other end of the property.

On the way to the next job, Dennis and Daryl talked about their new boat. ∎

CHAPTER 25

AMERICA'S SWEETHEART

Dennis and Daryl's visit had unnerved Stephen. The pressure was closing in on him. He didn't know what he was going to do with Anna. He went back to the lodge next door and then to the basement. He was furious.

He burst into the room and struck Anna in the face with his fist. She was able to turn her head and avoid most of the impact, but the blow still dazed her.

"You have done nothing but cause me trouble ever since we met. Now your two boyfriends show up here and need to work on these places, so you and I have to leave. Not this minute, but soon. I am warning you—do not try anything! If you do, I will carve you into little pieces bit by bit. Do you hear me? Answer me!"

Anna didn't answer quickly enough, and Stephen swung the knife wildly, slashing her arm.

"See what you made me do, Anna. I should just finish this right now. I don't love you; I hate you. I hate you with every bone in my body. You ruined me, and now I am going to ruin you!"

The wound on her arm was bleeding profusely, and it was

painful. In spite of herself, Anna began to cry. He had worn her down to nothing. His constant threats, erratic behavior, and being chained like an animal were finally more than she could take. Anna knew he was going to kill her, and the end was near.

Stephen slapped her repeatedly across the face and then smashed his hand over her mouth to stop the sobbing. It didn't work, so he grabbed the chain on her wrist, brought it up, and wrapped it around her neck so tightly she couldn't breathe. Finally, Anna collapsed on the floor. Stephen sat on the toilet to think.

He really didn't want to miss his dinner date. Being seen with friends in public was not a move anyone would expect from a person of interest in his wife's disappearance. His friends would try to console him by talking about the film festival and race. He could barely endure the boring conversation. To top it off, the food was marginal, and the local beer was flat.

Once shed of his friends, he couldn't wait to get back to the lodge. He had made his decision. Killing Anna was his only choice. He had come too far, and there was no turning back. At this point, no one suspected him. He could continue in his role as the grieving husband. He'd take her deep into the forest and bury her where no one would ever find her. He had to do it now before the investigators got to town.

Anna was sitting on the floor of the bathroom. Blood had dripped off her arm and pooled next to her.

"Anna, I have decided to let you go. Like we talked about, I am going to take you far from here and let you out. You go your way, and I'll go mine. I promise I won't harm you as long as you cooperate. The important thing is that you do as I say. I picked up a few little items I hope I won't have to use, but that will be up to you."

Stephen pushed something against her and pulled the trigger on a stun gun, shooting 90,000 volts through her, and she crumpled on the floor.

It took quite a while for her to come around.

"Anna, we're going to get ready to leave, and you need to follow my instructions. If you don't, you'll be so very sorry. Do you understand, Anna? Answer me, Anna."

"I understand," she said almost inaudibly.

"I am going to give you the key to remove the handcuffs."

She took the key, unlocked the cuffs, and let them drop to the floor. Once removed, the pain in her wrists was like fire.

"Now, Anna, take off all of your clothes."

Anna could barely stand it anymore, and she began to sob.

"Take them off, Anna, or I will give you another dose of the stun gun and rip them off you."

She felt at that moment if she did what he wanted, it was over—her life would end. Stephen Cameron was a monster, a psychopath. He wanted to hurt her in every way he could. She needed to reach inside herself and find that inner strength that had served her so well before. Rise above the pain and what was about to happen and wait for her chance. It always came; she just needed to watch for it.

Anna removed her filthy clothes and threw them in the corner as Stephen told her to.

"Now get in the shower and wash the filth off. You smell like a pig."

The shower was wonderful. The hot water burned her wrists and the cut on her arm, but for a moment, he had let her go. She was free again.

After a few minutes, Stephen told her to turn off the water and step out of the shower stall.

On the floor was a small pile of new clothes: sweatpants, underwear, a sweatshirt, socks, and shoes.

"Put them on."

He leered at her as she dressed.

"So here's what's going to happen. I am going to let you go, I promise, but I can't risk you doing something foolish and me getting caught. I needed you to be cleaned up so you wouldn't attract unwanted attention. You look pretty good now—a little tired but much better.

"Tonight, we are going to get in my car, and you are going to drive. I am going to handcuff your left hand to the steering wheel. I will tell you where to go and what roads to take. Once we have reached our destination, I will let you go. Simple as that. Now, if you try anything, like crashing into another car or speeding past a police car, I will stick my knife as deep as it will go into your rib cage. Do you understand, Anna?"

"I understand," she said.

It was near dark when Stephen walked her out to the rented SUV. She got in the driver's seat, and he reached in to handcuff her to the wheel.

This was her chance. It was her coming from last to first and winning the race. What happened now would determine everything that would happen in the future. He would take her way back into the national forest to a place where no one could hear her. He would make her scream; just killing her would not be enough.

Anna would not die without a fight. Stephen ordered her to raise her left arm, their eyes met, and she took her shot. With all her strength, Anna slammed her elbow into his nose, which exploded in blood. Then she pivoted in the seat and put those Olympic legs to use, kicking him as hard as she had ever kicked anything in her life. The kick drove him into the door, and he slumped on the ground, stunned for a second. She started to run, but he grabbed her. Anna gave him another kick to his already battered face, and his head snapped back, slamming into the car door.

Anna took off into the coming darkness, hoping the night shadows would hide her from Stephen.

She hid under a deck, staring back in his direction. She couldn't see any movement or hear any noise. Anna needed to go, but in which direction she didn't know. She had hurt Stephen but not enough to keep him down for long.

Then she heard it, a crazed laugh, then a song. Stephen was singing the song they had played at their wedding. He coughed occasionally, and Anna hoped he was choking on his own blood.

Then his voice. "Anna, do you remember our wedding? The photographers and the tabloids couldn't get enough of us. We were the all-American couple. Then, of course, our wedding night, I'm sure you remember it. I sure do."

His voice was moving closer. He knew where she was. In a moment of panic, Anna crawled across the grass to what looked like a hiking trail. She stood up to run. The full length of the trail was immediately illuminated by motion-sensing lights, and so was Anna.

Stephen put the other item he had purchased to use. The crack of a gunshot shattered the night air. Another shattered a large window just above Anna's head. She ran.

A car engine started, and a door slammed. The bright headlights of Stephen's SUV began to search for her. He drove wildly across the grounds, down hiking paths and knocking over anything that got in his way. She broke into an open field, and the lights caught her. Stephen drove like the crazy man he was, intent on running her down. The field ended in a tall privacy fence blocking her way. Of course, the expensive lodges would be surrounded by a fence to keep out the prying eyes of non-guests. The only choice was to turn around and run back the way she had come.

Another gunshot broke the night air.

Suddenly, the dark road to Big Buck Lake Lodges was bathed in light. She could hear Stephen's car roaring up behind her and saw the headlights of another vehicle closing from the entrance. Yard lights came on, and she saw an old truck loaded with ladders and tools bearing down on her. She ran to it, and then both the truck and Anna stopped at the same moment. She was completely illuminated in the headlights. Two men jumped out.

Dennis yelled, "Oh my God, it's Anna. Anna, Anna! It's me, Dennis. Anna, you're here." The moment of recognition was short-lived. Another shot rang out, and Daryl Weaver fell hard to the ground.

"Run, Dennis, Run!" Daryl managed to call out.

Dennis grabbed Anna and, carrying her as if she weighed nothing, ran into the night. They got to the lake overlook and were silhouetted by the coming northern moon. Dennis threw Anna to the ground and covered her with his body. If Stephen's bullets found their mark, they would hit him, not Anna. They lay quietly listening, hearts pounding.

Dennis whispered, "Anna, I've got an idea."

He reached into the front pocket of his overalls and pulled out a cell phone. "Anna, take this and call the sheriff," Dennis said. "He'll know what to do. You gotta stay here, Anna, and don't move unless you have to. I need to go find Daryl. I think he's hurt bad."

Before Anna could say anything, Dennis left. She stared at the phone, almost afraid it would disappear if she tried to dial it.

With shaking hands, Anna dialed three numbers indelibly etched in our society—911.

The communicator answered, "911, what is your emergency?"

Anna tried to speak but couldn't get any words out.

The dispatcher said again, "911, what is your emergency?"

She took a deep breath. Then in a voice calmer than anyone would think possible, she said the words a country was waiting for.

"This is Anna MacDonald. I am outside at Big Buck Lake Lodges. We need police and an ambulance right away."

"Please let me confirm," said dispatch. "This is Anna MacDonald, our Anna MacDonald, the Olympian?"

"Yes, it's me," she replied.

"Thank the Lord! Anna, stay on the phone with me. We're getting help. Help is on the way. Are you injured?"

"Yes, I am, but Daryl Weaver has been shot."

"Anna, stay with me. Please, please stay with me."

The dispatcher needn't have worried; she was now Anna's lifeline, and that phone would have to be pried from her fingers. She could hear the communicator passing on critical information to officers. ■

CHAPTER 26

When the call came out, I was turning onto the road that led to Musky Run.

"All units stand by for a 10-33 situation. Any units in the area of Big Buck Lake Lodges, please advise."

At the same time my pager fired off. I responded, as did another unit, and we were directed to switch down to an emergency channel.

"Deputy Pave standing by," he said.

"Sheriff Cabrelli standing by," I said.

"Deputy Pave, Sheriff Cabrelli, we received a 911 call from a female subject who has identified herself as Anna MacDonald. She is requesting EMS and law enforcement. She claims to have been injured and that Daryl Weaver is on the scene and shot."

I talked to Deputy Pave on car-to-car radio. "I am on my way. When you get there, observe the situation. As much as I want you to run in and confirm the identity of the caller, we need to stand by and approach the scene in a manner that will allow us to secure things. Dispatch, who else is close?"

"State Patrol Sergeant Kruger is also en route but is ten miles out."

"Have you sent EMS?"

"EMS has been paged," answered dispatch.

"Advise Kruger to meet Pave and me at the lodges' entrance. Have EMS stage near the entrance. No lights, no siren—run dark when they get close to the lodges if they can," I directed.

"This is Sergeant Kruger. I copied that."

"Dispatch, page out Chief Delzell. Get her on the line and advise her of the situation."

All the while this was going on, the communicator was on the phone with Anna comforting her at the same time while continuing to try and get as much information as possible.

The dire situation was spelled out when the dispatcher said, "All units responding. According to the complainant, the shooter is active and still on the scene. The caller has identified the shooter as Stephen Cameron."

"Dispatch, please ask Anna to describe her location as exactly as she can," I requested.

"Stand by, Sheriff. Sheriff, we lost cell phone connection. We will try to reconnect. Stand by."

As I flew to Big Buck Lake Lodges, I struggled to put together an image from my memory of the layout of the property. The only entrance that I was aware of was the front gate. We would set up there, put together a plan, and get to it. The execution didn't have to be perfect as long as we achieved our goal— neutralize the shooter.

Dispatch advised that EMS was en route.

"Have you reconnected with Anna?" I asked the dispatcher.

"Negative, Sheriff. We will continue to try."

I pulled up to the front gate. Trooper Kruger and Deputy Pave were there and ready.

The entrance driveway was flanked on each side by a slight rise planted with white pine and spruce trees. It formed a corridor that led into the complex. Pave, Kruger, and I put together a plan of action. Each of them would walk as quietly as possible into the trees on each side of the driveway. They would establish a vantage point with the best chance of giving them the opportunity they needed. They were both expert rifle shots, but darkness and other factors would put those skills to the test. Besides the shooter, there were at least three others. In the dark, target identification is challenging. Once they were where they needed to be, I would approach up the driveway in my squad, headlights on bright. This would help my rifleman with visibility, and Cameron would be paying attention to me.

Just as Pave and Kruger started off, my cell phone buzzed. I looked at the caller ID—Stephen Cameron. We were being as quiet as possible, but an errant sound, maybe as simple as the closing of a squad door, must have reached Stephen's ears.

"It's Cameron on the phone. You guys move out." Pave and Kruger quickly disappeared into the dark.

I answered. "Hello, Stephen."

"Hello, Sheriff. Are you out there somewhere in the dark? Or are you cuddled up with Julie? I think maybe you are out there in the bushes waiting to ambush me. If that's true, you should be very careful. I have a gun, and based on tonight, I am a pretty able shot. Honestly, I have always had great hand-eye coordination, so I'm not surprised. Are you here, Sheriff, or not? Just tell me. It won't make any real difference. It has been a very complicated night; things have not gone as I'd hoped," Cameron said.

"I'm here," I replied.

"So, what do you think we should do, Sheriff? Let's face it; we do have a situation, don't we? You and I don't have many options. You have got to try to catch or kill me, and I have got to try to get away. Killing you would be okay, but it would just cause every badge carrier in the state to come after me. Anyway, let me tell you the reason for my call. As much as I would like to chit chat, I just don't have the time. I don't suppose you are much of a chit chatter anyway. So, Sheriff Cabrelli, tonight I am going to pay her back. She took so much from me; she ruined my life. I just can't let her get away with it, and tonight I am going to kill her. I will take everything she ever cared about, everything she ever loved. Sheriff Cabrelli, she is just a few minutes from being dead, unless—"

"Unless what, Stephen?" I asked.

"Well, maybe we could work something out. Anna and I had come up with a plan. I was going to drive her to a special place, drop her off, and we would go our separate ways. I promised to leave her unharmed. It probably sounds a little farfetched to you, but that's the truth. We decided together that was the best idea."

I heard Deputy Pave come through my earbud. "Sheriff, I am in position. I have a good view of the driveway and where it ends at one group of lodges. There is an older pickup truck parked there with its lights on. It looks like it could be the one belonging to the Weaver boys. I don't see anything or anyone else."

The abrupt break into Anna's cell phone conversation had new meaning. Stephen may have already killed her.

"Stephen, I need to know a couple of things before we do anything."

"Ask away, Sheriff. I don't see any harm in that."

"Do you have Anna with you?"

"Yes, I do, Sheriff, and she is just a few minutes from being dead. Actually, I am so tired of all this that I can't wait to kill her."

"Stephen, slow down here. We need to slow down."

"Too late for that, way too late."

"Has someone been shot?" I asked.

"No one of any consequence," he replied.

"We need to talk, Stephen. Just wait until we can talk. It won't hurt anything."

"Can't do it, John, I just can't do it. I am sorry that we never got to go fishing together. I think we would have been good friends. Now I have to go. I hope your wedding goes well."

"Stephen, don't hang up, stay on the line—" but he was gone.

Kruger spoke to me. "Sheriff, I have a good view of the opposite side of the pickup truck from Deputy Pave. Someone is sitting on the ground using a front tire as a backrest. It looks like it might be one of the Weavers. The truck bed is shadowing the face."

One located.

I advised dispatch to send all available units. "Tell them to be quiet and set up around the perimeter of the Big Buck Lake Lodges compound. We don't want to lose this guy if he jumps the fence. Make sure everyone knows this guy is armed and dangerous."

Then I changed my mind. Pave and Kruger were in position. Cameron knew we were there, so let's make it a police party.

"Pave, Denny, the cars are going to start to come fast and furious. We are going to try and flush Cameron out. I am going to move up the entrance driveway. Be ready."

"Pave, ready and in position."

"Kruger, ready and in position."

"Dispatch, I want all responding units to approach the area with lights and sirens, making as much noise as they can. I want the strobes to paint the grounds here," I directed.

"Ten-four, Sheriff. You advise all responders to run full emergency warning devices."

"Ten-four."

The quiet northern moonlit night was soon a chorus of wailing, yipping, and yelping sirens. The sky was bathed in red and blue lights. They seemed to be coming from every direction, some near, some far. I felt a certain comfort in all the noise, knowing that these were my people, every one of them courageous.

I began to move up the driveway. He had every advantage. It is always the searchers at the greatest risk. The one they are looking for needs only to hide and not move, waiting to take out the searcher.

I stayed behind cover as much as possible but couldn't help but think Stephen was watching me. I visualized him with his arm around Anna's neck and a gun to her head.

Squad cars pulled onto the grounds. Headlights and take-down lights illuminated the area.

Trooper Kruger said into my earpiece, "I have movement by the subject resting against the truck wheel. It appears to be a male that is crouching down. Sheriff, the subject kneeling behind the one I think is Weaver appears to be Cameron. No, stand by, Sheriff. It is Cameron—positive. I am going to take the shot."

I waited for the fatal bang, but it didn't come.

"Sheriff, I don't have the shot. Cameron is crouched down behind Weaver. Weaver is shielding him."

Then there was a voice, loud and clear, close to us.

"Anna, do you hear me, Anna? I know you do."

Available police and rescue units had arrived, and sirens were shut down again. The sounds of another northern night returned.

"Anna, where are you, Anna? Answer me, or you will be very sorry. I have company with me. One of your heroes from the other night at the opening ceremonies is with me. I shot him once, but he is very much alive. My gun is pointed at the back of his neck. His death will be on your hands if you don't show yourself. I will kill him and then take my chances. I am listening, sweetheart, my love. I don't hear anything. Okay, your choice—" Stephen's voice trailed off.

"Stephen, stop. Please don't. I'm here. Don't hurt him," Anna responded.

MUSKY RUN | 273

"I knew you couldn't resist, Anna MacDonald, America's sweetheart. It will be a simple trade—his life for yours. As soon as you are with me, I will leave him. Time is wasting. Come on, Anna."

"Anna, stop. Do not show yourself. We have him covered," I called. "Cameron, it's over. No one is dead yet. You kill someone, and all that changes. You will be in a cage forever. Now things can be worked out, but it has to stop."

"Sheriff Cabrelli, has anyone ever told you what a nuisance you are?"

"I suppose someone may have mentioned it. Now I'm here to help you. You need to clear your head and listen. What you decide to do in the next couple of minutes will define the rest of your life. You have accomplished some great things, and once you get yourself straightened out, you can again, but not if you're doing life without parole."

"Sheriff, Pave. Someone is belly crawling out from under the pickup truck, slow but making their way out. They appear to have something in their hand." I couldn't respond. Pave continued, "I have got the subject. He's crawling toward the front of the truck."

It dawned on me at that point who our unknown crawler might be. Complications increased again.

"Sheriff, I only want to talk to Anna one last time. Then I will give up. One last talk, Anna, then this is over."

"I am coming out, Stephen. Let Daryl go."

"Step out into the light. Let me see my beautiful wife," he said.

"Anna, don't do it!" I shouted. "He will kill you. Please stay where you are. Please."

Then behind Stephen, Anna came out from under the stairway that led to a wooden deck. She was still in the shadows, but it was her.

"Stephen, I'm here. Let him go."

Cameron leaped up using Daryl Weaver as a shield, with his gun still pointed at the back of Daryl's neck. He moved with his human shield toward the rear of the old pickup. Pave, Kruger, and I were waiting for any opportunity.

"Get over here right now. If you don't, you will be responsible for me blowing doofus' brains all over the driveway."

"No, Anna, don't do it. Please, don't do it. He will kill you," I said.

Then I checked in with Pave and Kruger, "Do you guys have a shot? Any shot at all?"

Pave responded, "Negative."

Kruger said, "I am going to try to crawl closer. I may have a better angle on a small rise in front of me."

I started to move forward, trying to get close enough to take a shot without hitting Daryl or Anna. Then Anna stepped out of the darkness and walked toward Stephen and Daryl.

"Let him go, Stephen. It's me you want, not him. Let me trade places with him."

"He is bleeding quite a bit. He's alive, but I don't think he can move. So, just keep coming toward us. I will make a space for you to slide in between us when you get here. Then you and I are going to back away from the truck out of the light.

"Sheriff, my wife and I have reached an agreement. I am trading doofus for her. It is really important that you don't make a mess of things again. One stupid move on your part, and she and doofus are dead."

Anna switched places with Daryl, and Stephen put his arm around her throat. The gun was tucked in his waistband, and he now had a knife in his right hand and held it against Anna's neck. He dragged her back toward the shadows.

Kruger called me. "Sheriff, if he keeps backing up, he will silhouette himself, and I'll have a shot. I am no more than seventy-five yards away."

"Okay, Denny. Take the shot when you can. Pave and I will rush him."

Cameron was now laughing, the mixed cackle of a maniac and a crow.

Then he stopped near the back of the old truck.

"Well, Sheriff John Cabrelli, here we are. Let me tell you what is going to happen from here. I'm sure you have snipers ready to kill me. They may get their chance; I don't care. You screwed up again, Sheriff, and now you will pay the price. Here, in front of everyone, I am going to cut the throat of America's sweetheart."

"Denny, do you have the shot?" I pleaded.

"Almost, but not yet."

Then the miracle happened. A large figure stepped up from behind the truck and shouted, "Hey," from behind Stephen. Cameron momentarily turned and swung the knife in that direction.

Dennis Weaver took his shot and swung for the fence with a number two shovel connecting solidly with Stephen Cameron's head. Cameron went down like a bag of wet cement.

Dennis just smiled and said, "Hi, Anna. Are you and Daryl okay?"

She just looked at Dennis and fell against him like she was going to collapse. He helped her sit down next to Daryl.

Pave, Kruger, and I charged forward and descended on Cameron. Stephen was either dead or unconscious on the ground, bleeding profusely from his head. I cuffed him immediately and searched him for weapons, recovering a knife, a stun gun, and a semi-auto pistol.

When we gave the all-clear, the EMTs rushed to treat the wounded. They bound Daryl's wound and, as quickly as possible, got him loaded and on the way to the hospital, where Dr. James was waiting.

Anna physically looked a lot worse than she was. When the EMTs wanted her to get on the stretcher for transport, she said, "No. I will go to the hospital when the sheriff can take me."

They were very concerned about any number of issues, but Anna was unwilling to change her mind. So, the EMTs stayed with her.

Another crew of EMTs grudgingly evaluated Stephen Cameron. He was unconscious but alive. Dennis' shovel had definitely left a mark. They handcuffed him to the stretcher and loaded him in the ambulance. Pave and Kruger rode along.

I called Julie to tell her we had Anna. ▪

CHAPTER 27

Liz Masters and her exhausted crew quickly descended on the scene and began the process of examining Anna's prison.

Julie was waiting for us when we got to the hospital. Anna got out of the squad, and they came face-to-face but stopped a few feet from each other, their eyes locked. Neither could close that short distance. Neither could understand that it was over. Julie had known all along that Anna was alive, that Anna would never miss her wedding. Then without hesitation, they ran to each other. The two best friends, who talked of their lives and how it would be, held each other, and then Anna MacDonald, Olympic gold medalist, and America's sweetheart broke down and wept. A nurse gently took Anna's arm and led her into the emergency room. She was joined shortly by Herb and Dorothy MacDonald, who had tears of joy streaming down their faces.

The Northwoods telegraph was, as Ron Carver put it, "hotter than a two-dollar pistol." People, mostly locals, descended on the hospital, all sitting quietly together. They did not know if Anna was alive, and rumor was that either Anna or one of the Weavers had been shot. They waited patiently for news. Reporters who had camped out since Anna's disappearance joined them.

The doors leading to the emergency room slid open a few minutes after midnight. There, in front of the crowd, stood Anna with Dennis Weaver. The crowd was silent. It seemed too much to hope for. A woman in the front who led the choir at Spider Lake Church burst out in song, and the crowd joined her in singing an old hymn known to nearly all, a song of hope, happiness, and joy.

When the singing stopped, Anna called out to the crowd.

"I am so grateful to have been born and raised in a community so full of love and caring that you put everything else aside to search for me when I was lost. Saying thanks will never be enough. But that's what we do in Namekagon County—we search for those who are lost, help those who need help, and pray for those who need prayer. The doctors were pretty sure that I shouldn't come out here tonight, but I couldn't wait to see you all again. I am a little banged up, but I am going to be just fine. Daryl Weaver was shot and is in surgery, but the prognosis is very good. I want you to know that if it were not for Dennis Weaver, my hero, I do not believe that Daryl or I would have survived. He risked his own life to save ours."

Dennis sheepishly stepped forward, and the crowd cheered. The dam that held back the emotions of the last few days burst. After several minutes of cheering and clapping stopped, Dennis stood in front of the crowd.

"Do you want to say something, Dennis?" Anna asked.

"Well, I don't know what to say. I guess I would say one thing for sure. It pays to buy a good shovel."

The story of Anna MacDonald and Stephen Cameron again became international news. Reporters who had camped out in

Namekagon County since her disappearance were well rewarded for their patience. Every network led with the story, most breaking into regular programming. Interestingly, the news crews who had been on the scene since the beginning found themselves part of the story. They reported the event differently, showing respect and integrity.

A preliminary hearing was held in front of Judge Kritzer. Cameron's lawyer, Attorney Verme, argued that Cameron should be given bail. He was not a flight risk, and other than what could, at worst, be a domestic dispute, he had no serious criminal record. He further stated that Cameron needed to seek additional medical treatment.

His request was denied.

A few days later, Attorney Verme was again in front of Judge Kritzer, this time with an order that Stephen Cameron be transported to a maximum security private psychiatric hospital for a thorough mental examination. District Attorney Hablitch did not raise issue with the request, partly because there was evidence to support that Cameron was, in fact, suffering from mental illness and because Cameron's presence cast a dark cloud on Namekagon County. Commander Malone coordinated the transport with the U.S. Marshall's Service, and in the dark of night, Cameron was removed from Namekagon County.

Anna wanted to stay in her house behind the bakery, but it was not private enough. Julie and I offered her our guest cabin, and while grateful, it wasn't what she needed. She went to stay with her parents at their lake home. It was a quiet and loving place to be. Dorothy fed her all her favorite meals to the point that Anna suggested that if she continued to eat this way, she would blow up like a balloon. Her mom thought she was too skinny and kept the food coming. So did the community members. It was expected that when someone had trouble, bringing food was always welcome. Her dad told Anna not to complain; he hadn't eaten this good in a long time. Anna went for long walks along the shore and swam almost every day, but she didn't run. Nobody asked why. They just let her heal. Julie, Bud, and I visited often while giving her the space she needed. Becky Chali came out to see her twice a week, and they talked for as long as she wanted.

Her external wounds healed quickly, but there was a sadness about her that no one had ever seen before. Becky expressed concern that if Cameron's goal was to break her, he might have been temporarily successful. It would take as long as it took for her to start to feel better.

We postponed the wedding. A celebration was not in order at this point.

After a month, Anna started to show signs of her old self. Then one day, Bud's big pickup truck pulled into the driveway. There was a canoe on the roof rack. Bud undid the rachet straps and slid it off. Then he carried it to the lake shore, set it down, and returned to his truck to get fishing gear.

He knocked on the door. "Hey, Anna. Are you home?" he said.

She came to the door. "Hi, Bud. What are you doing?"

"I heard that the crappies have been biting off Jones Point. I wanted to catch some, but I couldn't find anyone to go with me. Normally that would be okay in a regular boat, but you've got to balance things out in a canoe. Ya know, I'm kinda on the big side, and since I couldn't get anyone else, I thought maybe you'd go with me and balance out the boat so I don't roll."

The idea that Anna would balance out Bud was comical, but she agreed.

With the boat loaded, Anna put her hands on the gunnels and

looked up at the sun. Bud paddled the canoe with strong, even strokes. The water was calm, and because it was a "quiet lake," there was no boat noise. They paddled the canoe into an area of fish sticks created by felling shoreline trees to create a fish habitat. A narrow but deep stream entered the lake at this point, between twenty and thirty feet deep. It was a secret place for summer crappies. Bud hooked a minnow on Anna's rod, and she plunked it in the water. Before he baited his own hook, Anna had one. She was using a lightweight rod, and the fish was giving her quite a battle. Soon the ten-inch gold and black crappie came to the surface, and Anna was so excited she wildly swung it into the boat. This occurred at the same time Bud was moving forward to keep the canoe in balance. Everything was in control until the swinging crappie slapped Bud right across the face, taking him completely by surprise. A little shift in position by a man of Bud's size would easily tip a rowboat; the canoe was no contest. In a second, Anna and Bud found themselves wide-eyed in the water, clinging to the top branches of a fish stick.

Then it happened. From somewhere deep inside, Anna began to laugh for the first time in a long time. She laughed and laughed, and Bud laughed too. They were laughing so hard they didn't even notice the boat that quietly made its way to them.

"Hey there, Bud, Anna. I saw you flip over and thought you might need a hand," said Sheamus Ruwall, rowing one of his restored wooden boats.

Bud and Anna swam the canoe the short distance to shore. Sheamus grabbed their paddles, PFDs, and Bud's floating tackle box. The rods were not to be found.

Once Sheamus helped them get organized, he started rowing away from them with one final comment: "You know if you wear those life jackets, they'll keep you from drowning," he said.

Bud and Anna made their way back to her folks' place. They

loaded the canoe and gear in his truck.

Before he got in his truck, Bud asked, "Are you sure you're okay?"

She gave him a big hug and said, "Better than I have been in a long time. Thank you, Bud."

The determination, love, and fortitude that had taken Anna so far in her life rose to the surface. The high school senior who ran like the wind and came from behind to win the race took over, and she again became Anna MacDonald, the Musky Queen.

Anna called Julie the next morning.

"Julie, don't we have wedding plans to make?"

Julie was quiet. "Are you sure you are ready for this?"

"Julie, the real question is, are you ready?" she said.

"Anna, I have been waiting for this all my life. I am absolutely ready."

"How about John?"

"I suppose we should mention it to him."

Julie and Anna picked up right where they had left off. This was not going to be just a wedding; it was going to be a celebration. Namekagon County needed to have a good party.

Martha Bork and the church ladies enlisted the help of Julie's students and any residents who were available. Amber and Stella Lockridge were coordinating the setting up of the cafeteria. There was no guest list; everyone was invited. No gifts but everybody that could was asked to bring a dish to pass.

The lights over Ron Carver's workbench were seen burning into the wee hours.

Big Top Music offered a huge tent to be erected on school grounds. The YoHo Band would play during the reception.

The night before the wedding, Anna, her mom, Martha Bork, Liz Masters, Mary Delzell, Bear's wife Tanya, Reverend Redberg's wife, and Stella Lockridge took Julie to the local winery where they ate a lavish dinner and had the best wine available. No wild partying for these girls, although husband jokes started by Liz were allowed. To everyone's surprise, even Martha came up with a couple of good ones.

Bud built a campfire and put chairs around it. Pearce's Pudgie Pies filled the table. The group was small—me, Jack Wheeler, Ron Carver, Bear, Len Bork, Doc O'Malley, and Professor Newlin. Bear entertained the group with what he thought were humorous John Cabrelli stories.

Then while embers crackled, popped, and rose with the heat from the fire, distinctly in contrast to the night sky, the conversation took on a thoughtful tone. We were, for better or worse, men who had been there and seen the elephant. Each of us had come to certain realizations, mostly by our own happenstances. Some of those happenstances left marks on our bodies, and some left marks on our souls. Our choices had been, and would continue to be, judged by perfect people, craning their necks from the sidelines for a better view. We'll continue to choose the road less traveled and only vaguely suspect why. So many lessons learned, so many lost. Len told me we were all responsible for our own happiness. When that happiness involves sharing your life with someone you love, you are truly a lucky man.

Tomorrow I would marry Julie Carlson and become the luckiest man on earth.

Our wedding was to be a small, simple ceremony on the top of a rock outcropping overlooking Spider Lake, a spot we had come to treasure, followed by a community party at the school cafeteria.

The bridal limousine, a four-wheel drive crew cab pickup decorated with streamers and balloons, arrived and parked in the large northern meadow that adjoined the rock formation. Cars and trucks loaded with people followed. The crowd gathered in numbers significant enough to surround the rock and spill into the meadow.

I turned to Reverend Redberg. "I'm sorry, Reverend, I thought the wedding was going to be a few close friends and family."

The reverend patted me on the shoulder and replied, "No problem, John. It just looks like you have more close friends and family than you thought."

The crowd hushed as Bud got out of the driver's side of the big truck. He opened the rear passenger's door, and Anna got out and walked up to join me where I stood with Bear. I watched as Bud proudly offered his arm to Julie. She was stunning in a simple dress with flowers woven around the neck...and running shoes. Neither Julie nor Anna wanted to chance a slip.

The crowd was silent as the reverend began to speak. "I hope you can all hear me. Had we expected such a wonderful crowd, we would have brought a microphone. As part of my job as a pastor, I have performed many weddings. When people request an outdoor ceremony, I usually try to discourage them. Not to ruin their wedding but just for practical reasons. Rain, or weather of any kind, can quickly put a damper on things. That changed for me today.

"Today, it is my privilege and honor to join John Cabrelli and Julie Carlson in the holy union of marriage. We have gathered on this rock overlooking the beauty of God's creation to bear witness to a love of the ages. This rock provides us with solid ground on which to stand. And much like this rock, faith, love, and the community gathered here today provide a strong foundation for these two people to go forward together in life, not just as husband and wife, but as servants—Julie teaching God's children and John protecting us from harm."

After the reverend finished his message, Eva Zachery, accompanied by her brother, Jake, playing guitar and the reverend's wife on the zither, sang a song written and performed by Henry Deutschendorf, Jr. in 1974. By the beginning of the second verse, the crowd joined in.

> Come let me love you,
> Let me give my life to you,
> Let me drown in your laughter,
> Let me die in your arms,
> Let me lay down beside you,
> Let me always be with you,
> Come let me love you,
> Come love me again.

The reverend stepped up at the conclusion of the song, and Ron Carver approached the couple with a smile on his lips and a glint in his eye, an unlikely looking ring bearer. He carried in front of him a satin pillow covered with a satin cloth. He removed the cloth, and there were two rings, beautiful in their simplicity, an example of a master's craftsmanship.

"Congratulations, John and Julie. These are the best I've ever made," Ron said.

The Lake Superior agate was masterfully set in each ring with elegant but durable bands that would withstand their lives outdoors. It felt like an eternity before I slipped the ring on Julie's finger and Reverend Redberg pronounced us husband and wife.

The crowd cheered and shared hugs all around. It was a wonderful day in Namekagon County. The reception was a celebration of John and Julie, and Anna's return, safe and sound.

We drove home after the reception holding hands. We pulled up to the front of our cabin, and I lifted Julie from the truck and turned to carry her over the threshold.

We stopped, and my blood ran cold. The front door was standing open. I whispered to Julie and told her to get behind the truck. I drew my 9mm Smith and Wesson Shield from a concealment holster. My heart pounded.

I slowly approached the doorway and entered the cabin. Instead of danger, I was greeted by balloons and streamers decorating the kitchen table. In the middle of the table was a large basket containing a bottle of champagne, a new six-point Hudson Bay blanket, and two beautiful, handcrafted cups. Next to the basket was a note from Bud that said, "I am so happy we are a family."

I returned to the truck, smiling, scooped Julie up, and through the door we went, never stumbling. No ancient angry spirits allowed in our home. ■

EPILOGUE

Pederson Kouper went to great pains to make sure he wasn't followed or noticed on his daily visits. On most days, he parked a mile or more away from his destination and hiked in. He needed to climb up the east side of a low hill and get into position before full dawn. Once situated, he had a clear view of a short grass meadow with a gradual southern slope.

He knew she was here and guarded the secret carefully. He had searched day after day, trying to find any tiny sign showing him where she lived. Then one day his persistence paid off as he climbed this very hill to scout the area and caught some motion out of the corner of his eye. He laid down and began to sweep the area with his field glasses.

As the sky lightened, she walked out into the warm morning sun. Sleek and muscular, she appeared to be about three years old, a perfect example of *puma concolor*. Three spotted cubs trailed after her.

They were on the edge of Namekagon County, not far from Dannas' sheep operation. He could sit and watch from sunup to sundown. His location was perfect, and she had not yet detected him.

Her cubs, just ten or twelve weeks, would not be weaned until they were four to six months. But even at this age, the young mother would bring them her kills, and they would eat some of the fresh meat. One day he was thrilled to see the mother carrying a whitetail deer fawn and drop it in front of the cubs.

Two of them were on the small side, and one was much bigger than the others and was often the initiator of rough-and-tumble play. Was that one a big strong male like their father? The other two sleek and smaller, like their mother? Too early to tell. He wished he could watch every moment of their lives. It was not to be. Soon they would move on, exploring their own range.

Life always finds a way. ▪

I was never very good at identifying constellations,
but I can always find Orion.

—Warden John Holmes • 1939–2017

Award-winning Series

FIGURE EIGHT
BOOK ONE

After a career-ending event, John Cabrelli retreats to his late uncle's lake cabin where danger awaits—along with the truth behind his uncle's death in this award-winning first in series.

SPIDER LAKE
BOOK TWO

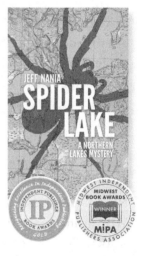

A missing federal agent, suitcases full of cash, a secluded cabin in the woods... Spider Lake, the award-winning second book in the Northern Lakes Mystery series, is an unputdownable crime thriller.

BOUGH CUTTER
BOOK THREE

Just as Namekagon County sheriff John Cabrelli adjusts to his new job, a body is discovered in the woods—and he must race against time to unravel the case when the lives of even more victims are claimed within the wilderness...

ABOUT THE AUTHOR

Jeff Nania is a former law enforcement officer, writer, conservationist, and biofuel creator. He is the award-winning author of four fiction books, *Figure Eight* (2019), *Spider Lake* (2020), *Bough Cutter* (2021), and *Musky Run* (2023) in his Northern Lakes Mystery series. His narrative non-fiction writing has appeared in *Wisconsin Outdoor News, Double Gun Journal, The Outlook,* and other publications.

Jeff was born and raised in Wisconsin. His family settled in Madison's storied Greenbush neighborhood. His father often loaded Jeff, his brothers, and a couple of dogs into an old jeep station wagon and set out for outdoor adventures. These experiences were foundational for developing a sense of community, a passion for outdoor traditions, and a love of our natural resources.

Jeff has been recognized locally, statewide, and nationally. *Outdoor Life Magazine* named him as one of the nation's 25 most influential conservationists, and he received the National Wetlands Award for his wetland restoration work. The Wisconsin Senate commended Jeff with a joint resolution for his work with wetlands, education, and as a non-partisan advisor on natural resource issues.

Now a full-time novelist, Jeff spends as much time as possible exploring outdoor Wisconsin with his friends and family.

Visit www.feetwetwriting.com to sign-up for email updates and read more from Jeff Nania.

 @jeffnaniaauthor   @jeffnania

Made in the USA
Columbia, SC
03 December 2023

27636682R00161